THE
HUSTLE

KAREN WOODS

Harper North

HarperNorth
Windmill Green
24 Mount Street
Manchester M2 3NX

A division of
HarperCollins*Publishers*
1 London Bridge Street
London SE1 9GF

www.harpercollins.co.uk

HarperCollins*Publishers*
Macken House,
39/40 Mayor Street Upper,
Dublin 1, D01 C9W8, Ireland

Published by HarperCollins*Publishers* Ltd 2026

Copyright © Karen Woods 2026

Karen Woods asserts the moral right to
be identified as the author of this work.

A catalogue record for this book is available from the British Library.

PB ISBN: 978-0-00-872362-0

This novel is entirely a work of fiction. The names, characters and incidents portrayed in it are the work of the author's imagination. Any resemblance to actual persons, living or dead, events or localities is entirely coincidental.

Set in Palatino by Amnet

Printed and bound in the UK using 100% Renewable Electricity by CPI Group (UK) Ltd

All rights reserved. No part of this publication may be reproduced, stored in a retrieval system, or transmitted, in any form or by any means, electronic, mechanical, photocopying, recording or otherwise, without the prior permission of the publishers.

Without limiting the exclusive rights of any author, contributor or the publisher of this publication, any unauthorised use of this publication to train generative artificial intelligence (AI) technologies is expressly prohibited. HarperCollins also exercise their rights under Article 4(3) of the Digital Single Market Directive 2019/790 and expressly reserve this publication from the text and data mining exception.

In memory of my mother Margaret and my brother Darren. My son in heaven, Dale.

Also by Karen Woods
Tracks
Tease
Vice
The Deal
The Con
The Truth
The Watch
The Trade
The Escape

Prologue

In that moment, the rest of the world slipped away. There was nothing but her and the tiny point her eyes were locked on. Everything depended on her next move.

Some things you never forgot – first love, true fear, real skill – and, in an instant, she knew what she had to do. The sharp silver tip caught the light and glinted. She let the weight of the metal in her hand feel part of her.

Life or death. It only took a moment to change it all.

Chapter One

Danni Cox looked out of the steamy windows and sighed as the rain hammered against them, loud enough to sound like small hands knocking to be let in. Her hands fidgeted – no outlet for the nervous energy that kept her on edge. She was on the move again, she never liked staying in one place for too long. How could she when he could find her any time she let her guard down? But this time felt different. Was she getting too bold? Would he find out, send his men to bring her back under his control? But being his prisoner once more was not the worst fate she faced. There was a price on her head, she knew that much. Maybe it was time to face up to it. Would she ever really be free if she was still living in fear?

A lot of so-called tough guys were all talk, Danni realised that. Big on threats and light on action. But Marco Reece meant what he said. She looked down at her hand and her expression changed as she stroked a single finger along it right up to where it ended abruptly. Half of her right thumb was missing, a thick scar curling around the top where the wound had healed badly. A chill crept through her at the unwanted flashback to the silver blade striking at her, his face as he sliced into her, warm red blood rolling down her hand. Danni rubbed at her arms, and she was back in the present moment wiping the vision from her mind.

She glared at Steve, frustrated. 'How long now, it seems like we've been travelling for ages?'

Danni and Steve had been an item for the last five years. He was all right, as blokes went, Danni reckoned. A bit too much sometimes, more of a talker than a listener, but then that suited her. Most of all, he looked after her, made sure she was safe. It might not have been a fairytale, but she realised he was pretty much the only one in her corner anymore when it came to keeping safe and away from Marco and his cronies. Steve had been there when she needed somebody, when she'd hidden away from the world and knew not one soul she could turn to. He was her angel sent from heaven, he'd said: in the right place at the right time to save her. They'd been together ever since, and as she'd built up some confidence and got back out in the world, he said they were the dream team. But Danni knew dreams weren't real. Life had taught her that the hard way.

So she'd kept on moving ever since she was an adult. But this move? This was Steve's dream, not hers. All she really dreamed of now was a quiet life, maybe some friends she could trust. She'd not been allowed any friends when she'd been with Marco. He'd called any women 'slags' if she tried to talk to them, told her she'd be labelled the same if she carried on. Claimed she didn't need anyone except him. But the pattern went back further than Marco. The only real friends she had from being young she'd had to leave behind when she'd been taken into care. Josie Taylor had been her wingwoman back then, the girls had been always together – until social services placed her miles from the part of Manchester where she'd grown up. The friends she'd made after that had been short-term things – people she met but never let herself get close to. She'd never dream of contacting any of them now, had not let any of them know what she was doing, nor where she had landed. That would put them in danger if they knew anything about her, putting their own lives and families at risk. No, she let no one get close, told nobody anything. And if you kept that habit up long enough – there was nobody left to tell.

So Danni had learned to be a lone soldier from an early age. She'd left Manchester when she got out of care when she was just seventeen. She'd run away to Leeds and started afresh, alone. She'd been so desperate for a clean start she'd even started using her middle name. Danni was the lost child, Leigh was the woman who she decided to be. Her own mother, Julie, probably hadn't even noticed she'd gone. Off her head somewhere she would be, or searching for her next fix. Because Danni knew she was never sober, a fact she'd learned too young, when Julie hadn't been shy of slapping her around when she couldn't find the money she needed to get more beer. Danni had spent a lot of time looking after herself back then: she was still at junior school when her mam started leaving her on her own, would go out god knew where, and so Danni had hunkered down, playing darts in her bedroom, listening to music, anything to fill the long, lonely hours before her bedtime. And then she had to endure the loud noises from downstairs after closing time. Her mother singing and dancing with random guys she'd brought back from the boozer, the laughing and the joking usually turning sour quickly, before the shouting started. Danni used to creep onto the landing sometimes, not sure of what she was seeing, but soon learned to stay in her room.

No, Danni never had a childhood, not one she wanted to remember anyway, just bad memories. She'd thought it was normal when she was small, but slowly had realised other kids had clean clothes and proper meals and started to try and hide what was going on. But the neighbours must have reported her to the authorities, or perhaps the teachers, from the occasions she did make it to school, skinny and scruffy, and it was only a matter of time before social workers came knocking at her door.

It had been easy to hide from them at first. Danni often ran away, and did it more and more as she grew up and could pass for older. If she knew her social worker was due round, she didn't come home for days; no one missed her or even cared that she was vulnerable and out on the streets of Manchester at the midnight hour. She looked back now and could see she'd just been a young, scared girl who was looking for someone to love her. Josie had done her best to help her, but they were both young and fighting a losing battle. Being taken into care had been inevitable.

The placements she had weren't terrible – she'd had to face much worse at home – but it was easy to fall through the cracks. It hadn't been difficult to slip out of the system when she wanted to disappear. Maybe she should learn that lesson again, she thought. What was she doing, stepping back close to a world she thought she'd left for good?

Steve reached over and patted the top of Danni's leg; he could see she was stressed out, the finger tapping, leg jiggling. 'About half an hour to Manchester, babes. I've got a few lads meeting us at the pub to help unload the van so it shouldn't take long for us to get settled. I take over the pub officially tomorrow, but the old landlord will be there today to make sure he goes through everything with us. He seems alright, you know.'

Danni looked out of the car window, the parade of landmarks they were driving past reminded her she was heading closer and closer to home. It would have been happy for most people – childhood haunts and sights revisited. But as she got nearer, a sense of dread was wrapping itself around her insides. It had been many long years since she'd been over this neck of the woods, and she wondered if her mother was still living in the same house. As she'd grown, she'd tried to reach out in a safe way – hoping she could let her mum know she was OK without putting her in any danger. So she'd dropped her a few phone calls over the years to see if she was alright, but on the few times she answered, all she got was either gibberish, drunken words she couldn't understand, or abuse – angry curses yelled down the line. The phone number had been cut off in the end, letters and birthday cards went unanswered and she was left with no other way to keep in touch. She should have taken the hint and kept well clear, she thought now.

'I don't know why we didn't stick with what we knew, Steve. That pub in Huddersfield was a good little gaff. Edge of the Pennines, a nice, quaint set-up, unlikely to bring us any mither.'

'Danni, the pub where we were was dead. We weren't earning a carrot. A few old-timers and the odd hiker aren't enough to keep a place going. This pub is going to be the business, love. It has great takings and a good crowd in each night. I'm thinking we can really make it here. We can have a DJ on at the weekends, karaoke, and you can even start serving food. John said there is a kitchen downstairs, so there you go, the world is your oyster. You need to think big. We could have a chain of places if we get this one right.'

She had to stop herself from snarling at him. Why did he assume she'd want to spend her life cooking? 'Stop telling me what I can and can't do,' she snapped. 'I'm not a cook and I'm not slaving away, sweating in a kitchen all day.'

'What do you want then, love? You could run a pub quiz – be the hostess with the mostest…'

Danni realised she'd been a fool. Maybe working away out of sight in the kitchen was for the best. It wasn't like she'd ever be able to relax behind the bar. It had been OK in Huddersfield – a quiet little place right on the edge of town, no bother. But back in Manchester? Sure, it was far enough away from Marco's patch in Leeds, but still, it felt risky. Her face might be recognised, even though she'd gone back to calling herself Danni. She'd killed off Leigh when she ran away from Marco. The thought of people seeing her was already sending panic through her body. 'I don't know why I even let you talk me into moving back around here. We were settled where we were. I'm going to be a sitting duck. I've got bad memories of being a kid and coming back here doesn't sit right with me. Manchester is my past and it should have stayed like that.'

Steve sighed. 'We agreed. We can't keep hiding away from the world, I need a life too you know. When we hooked up you were a nervous wreck. You said you could never go back to Leeds and I get it, but come on, how many other cities are you ruling out? When you were on your arse it was me who moved mountains to help you, are you forgetting that? If Marco had found you back then before he got nicked, he wouldn't have thought twice about offing me too. I took a chance on you, took you in, gave you a home and a job in the pub, helped you stop hiding, and now you should take a chance on me and stop pulling that sour face. Be bloody positive for once. Life has given us an opportunity – we'd be idiots not to take it. Manchester is a big place, anyway – your past is water under the bridge, you were a kid. The way I see it, we've already wasted half of Marco's sentence, hiding from a man who can't hurt you anymore. Anyway, his goons will be looking for a Leigh, not Danni. Let's grab our chance – look forward, not back.'

Danni dropped her head and stared out of the window at the grey skies above. Steve was right, but even a prison wall didn't feel like enough to protect her from Marco sometimes. 'Sorry, Steve, you know I hate change. It just worries me, that's all, seeing this place again. I know you think we are safe, but I tell you people like Marco don't ever let anyone get away with anything when they have been had over. I was made up when he got slammed, but he'll be freed one day and you can bet your last quid that I will be on the top of his list to find when he's on the outside.'

She'd never say it to Steve, but a part of her wondered if she deserved it. How could she live a normal life after what she'd done? She'd taken Marco's money. No bones about it. Fifty grand was a small fortune and people didn't just let things like that go. No matter that she had earned that cash for Marco – he wouldn't see it like that. Danni rested her head against the car doorframe and closed her eyes; she was right back to that night that changed her life forever. A young woman, vulnerable, sick of people taking advantage of her. A chance to change her life, to get her hands on more money than she could ever have imagined. She could still see Marco's face, his eyes wide open as he screamed her name at the top of his voice when he realised what she had done, the vein pumping with rage at the side of his neck, then him falling, eerily calm and controlled. The sensation of his meaty hand pulling her by the wrist, a moment where she realised there was no escaping, and then silence as he swung the silver blade of the machete at her. There had – she remembered clearly – been no pain, not at first. The gush of warm blood felt like it had come from someone else for a few seconds. Then a white-hot wash of pain as her senses kicked in again. She was never sure if it was the pain or the sight of the piece of her severed thumb that had made the nausea clutch at her. But even in the heat of the moment she knew she was getting off lightly. He wanted more than to maim her, he wanted to end her. And – she felt it in her bones – he probably still wanted that.

She opened her eyes and let out a long-laboured breath, blinking the fear from her mind. She needed something to take the edge off her own thoughts. 'Where are the fags, Steve?'

He rummaged about on the dashboard and gripped the pack of Benson and Hedges silver and passed them over to her. 'Spark me one up too, I'm gasping for one. I've not stopped all morning, packing this and packing that while you were sat on your arse moaning about the world and his wife.'

'Oi, I helped you, so don't make out that I didn't. I spent all last night folding clothes and putting them in the suitcases.'

'Well thank you, Jeeves the Butler. I've done the lion's share. All you've done all morning is bloody moan about getting back to Manny. It's doing my head in. Danni, this is a new start for us. I know you want to keep a low profile, but come on, I have to live too, and nobody will know we are in Manchester if we keep our noses clean. I'm sick of hiding away, I've done it for too long now. Work with me on this, aye?'

Danni knew it was too late to turn back, they'd come this far and maybe Steve was right. Marco was doing time, everyone else would have moved on, and there was probably a whole new generation of grafters running the crime scene round here. It would probably all be kids on bikes robbing phones and selling laughing gas. If they stayed away from anything dodgy, then maybe no one would come looking. It would be Steve's name above the door as landlord. She apologised and spoke in a softer voice.

'OK, love. I'm probably exaggerating things – getting it out of proportion being back in this place. Any luck, Marco will get himself in more trouble in the slammer and earn extra time. If I don't see that guy's face until hell freezes over, it'll be too soon.'

Steve rolled his eyes, sick to death of this man still being in their life. 'Exactly. As far as everyone will know, we are just normal people who have moved from the sticks to come and manage a pub. Just give it a try, who knows, we could be happy here.'

Her voice was soft. 'I will try, Steve. But I'm not going to relax overnight. I need to see the place, see the punters before I can stop looking over my shoulder. What if someone recognises me from back in the day? It only takes one phone call and I could be history.'

Chapter Two

Danni looked around The Fox and studied the pub's décor. It was old fashioned and looked like it needed a refurb. It smelt like it too. A stale stink of booze and sweat seemed to be soaked into everything – the threadbare carpets, the sticky woodwork. The tables were old, and the chairs were faded and worn, everything about it was cheap and stained with an air of desperation. Was this really meant to be their big break?

The Fox was set in the middle of a council estate in Harpurhey, not far from a small row of shops. The ex-landlord had told them the only reason he was retiring was due to ill health. He was telling porkies, Danni decided. Maybe they should ask about the two boarded-up windows they spotted on the way in, ask him what had happened there.

Danni had lived in Collyhurst as a young girl, only about ten minutes from The Fox. She knew Harpurhey was notorious for its crime rate, and that when you turned on the local news, you could bet that if something dodgy had happened in Manchester, it was Harpurhey that would be coming up on the map. All the same, it didn't bother her that the place had a reputation. She knew that plenty of good people lived in tough neighbourhoods – often people with more sense of community than the kind of folk who could afford to live in fancy gated homes and never bothered getting to know their neighbours. She remembered the people she grew up around – people willing to help each other out. Until she started hiding from the people on her road – ashamed of her dirty clothes, or if they'd seen her mum stumbling in with different men each night.

Maybe she would go and see her mum after all, face her demons and take a walk down the streets where she used to play. Plenty of years had passed – she looked different enough and, anyway, who would be looking out for her? She hated to admit it, but maybe Steve had done her a favour and made her realise she could do this. As soon as she'd crossed the threshold, she'd felt good. Over the years, she'd developed a knack for running these kinds of places. Forget being the kitchen skivvy here, she liked the feeling of being the landlady of The Fox – that little scared girl she used to be would be amazed to know she'd grow up to run a place in Harpurhey.

Danni stood tall behind the bar as Steve took a tour from John the former landlord. She put her hand on the cold lager pump and shot a look around the boozer, digesting her surroundings. Bleeding hell, she thought, it might have good bones but it looked like a casting call for an episode of *The Undateables*. She looked closer at the man at the end of the bar. She couldn't guess his age, his face sagging around yellow tobacco-stained teeth, and his clothes were dirty and creased. Oh god, he'd caught her looking.

'Alright, love, are you the new management?'

Danni nodded in hope he would not take offence. She didn't want to upset the regulars. She knew what it was to find refuge in a bar rather than judgement. All the same, she wasn't in the mood to start chatting now and she silently hoped he'd get back to drinking his pint. No such luck, he moved down the bar and pushed his pint along with him. His grubby hand reached across the bar. 'Pleased to meet you. The name's Jamo. You'll always see me in here. I'm part of the fixtures and fittings. I'm usually the first in and the last out of this place.' He sniggered.

She didn't flinch as she shook his hand, even if she couldn't wait to wash it. She remembered all the times she'd been short of a place to get clean. 'Nice to meet you.'

Jamo held nothing back and launched into full conversation with her like he'd known her for years. She had no escape. 'So, what's your name, have you managed a pub before or is this the first time? Because you'll need eyes in the back of your head in this place. Thieving bastards some of these lot are.'

Danni was puzzled. The few old guys in each corner and a nana nursing a sherry didn't exactly look like gangland thugs. 'Why's that then?' she asked.

Jamo checked around the pub and kept his voice low, speaking in a throaty whisper. 'Because the lads from the estate come in here and do all their dirty dealing. John got a crack from one only last week and they plugged the windows because he wouldn't let them stay after time. Ruthless they are, think they are a law to themselves,' his voice was even quieter as he checked again that nobody could hear him. 'I'm sure John had to pay them money too, you know, to keep the place safe. There's a reason why some of the local shops seem to keep having trouble with fires…'

Danni's eyes widened. She'd seen a couple of burnt-out places nearby. She knew Steve could handle himself and normally he wouldn't take any shit from anyone, but had he bitten off more than he could chew with this lot? And even worse, would it serve her up to the kind of people she needed to keep clear of?

Steve was no angel. That had never bothered her. So many of the people Danni knew had had to bend the law to earn a crust. And she knew how easy it was, once you'd crossed that line, to keep going. But Steve had always been upfront with her – told her right off that he used to be involved in the criminal world before he met her. Some of the stories he told her curled her toes, but he'd cleaned his act up and turned his back on that life a long time ago. He might not be a match for Marco Reece and his thugs, but Danni knew she and him could probably handle most of the small-time guys Jamo was on about.

Jamo slurped on his pint and wiped the side of his mouth with his sleeve. 'I hope you do a bar tab too because Old Johnny Boy lets me run up my bill and pay him when my Universal Credit gets paid. It's once a week, so you don't have to wait that long.'

Danni hesitated. 'I don't think we can do that. You'll have to speak with Steve, he's the one who's in charge not me.'

Jamo started spluttering, a proper barking cough. It took a few minutes for him to regain his breath. His eyes were watering, and she looked away too late to miss seeing him wipe his hands on his trousers. She was glad of the distraction when another man walked into the bar. He clocked Danni straight away. Jamo kept his voice low and spoke through fanned fingers. 'Your customers are not all bad, though. You've picked the right pub if you're looking for a bargain. You'll probably get a nice few perks running this place. That guy over there, sells everything, meat, batteries, plug-ins, bedding, clothes, anything he can get his hands on, cheap too. I know he has a set-up with John so he might do the same with you. You let him sell knock-off stuff in here and he'll bung you a few things for free.'

Danni shook her head. So much for keeping their noses clean. In their last pub in Huddersfield it had been quiet, sure, but the regulars they had were a nice crowd; farmers, a few nice old couples, a few younger lads usually around the pool table. Nothing like this bleeding lot asking for everything on tick or flogging knock-off gear before she'd even officially opened the place.

Jamo studied her for a few seconds and scratched at his head. 'So, are you a carrot cruncher or what?'

Danni was confused, what was all this slang, she didn't understand it anymore. She'd been away from Manchester for too long and it was going to take some time to get back in the loop of how the people spoke.

Jamo carried on. 'I mean a yonner, did you live up in the hills? I heard John telling someone you was from out of town?'

'I have lived all over, I'm originally from Cornwall,' she lied, relieved he'd not immediately clocked her as a local. There was no way she was telling this deadbeat anything about her past. The less anyone knew about it the better. And Jamo didn't look like he'd know a Cornish accent if one came up and bit him.

Jamo pulled his shoulders back and used his telephone voice. 'Cornwall? Bet it's posh down there, isn't it, sunshine and all that. Rich fuckers, never short of a few bob,' he sniggered and shot a look out of the window. 'Anyway, it's always pissing down here in Manchester. Fuck all to smile about really on this side of town, doom and gloom every day. You see, people around here have nothing to get up for, skint most of the time, no work, no get up and go. Don't get me wrong, they want to work just like I do, but these bigwigs all want qualifications and your inside leg measurement for any job they advertise. Then it's all zero hours, no sick pay, no breaks, taxed to shit. It's bollocks really, because given the chance I could turn my hand to anything, just need someone to give me a go. I could do a few shifts here if you like?'

Danni looked about the pub for Steve. How long was he going to be, already she felt pressured by Jamo. Like she'd ever give him a job – she'd only met him ten minutes ago and already she knew he'd drink the profits faster than they could earn them. Danni looked at Jamo's pint and noticed it was empty. 'Do you want me to refill that?' At least that might shut him up.

'Yeah, put it on my tab too,' he sniggered.

Danni didn't like being taken for a fool, but she wasn't looking for a fight today. And although Jamo wasn't a big fella, he looked like he would jump over the bar and punch her lights out if she said no. She'd already noticed the long red scar on the side of his face and his nose looked like it had been broken more than once. Danni filled the pint pot and passed it over. 'You can sort it out with Steve when he comes down regarding your tab, like I said, I don't make any decisions.' She could play the little wife when she needed to. She wondered now if she should use a fake name – she could be Carol from Cornwall, she liked the sound of that.

Jamo looked at his pint. 'So, are you going to sort this place out then, give it a lick of paint or something?'

Danni turned her head and looked around the pub at the tobacco-stained walls. 'Maybe, it could do with it, couldn't it?'

'The last time this place was painted must have been over ten years ago. If you need a grafter, then I'm your man. That's my trade you know.'

'Oh, so you're a painter and decorator as well, are you?'

Jamo snorted, 'Cash only though, love, I don't want my benefits stopping.'

Danni licked her dry, cracked lips and turned to get a drink. She bent down and fetched a cold can of coke from the fridge and opened it as she returned to the bar. Jamo was still talking. A proper gasbag he was. 'Nobody really works around here, love, if I'm being honest. We're all on the Pat and Mick, or PIP. Everyone tries to find work but there is nothing about, like I said before. And let's be open and honest here, if selling a bit of weed can give you enough to live on, what's the point in working nine till five for peanuts when you can earn good dosh, licking shot.'

At last, Steve was back.

Jamo waited until Steve was behind the bar with the outgoing landlord. 'John, can you word these two up about how I pay. Don't be selling me out and leaving me to deal with this on my jacks. Tell them I'm sorted, pay on time and all that.'

John shrugged his shoulders. 'I let Jamo settle at the end of the week. He never lets me down and he's a good lad too. In return, he lets me know the crack when anything is going on around here. I say look after him and he'll look after you.'

Jamo seemed satisfied and winked at Steve before wandering off over to the fruit machines.

Steve kept his voice low and made sure Jamo could not hear him. 'He's a right grass, that one. He'd dob his mates in if he thought it meant a free pint. Still, he's cheaper than CCTV and he comes in handy considering some of the clientele. Some of them'd have your eyes out and be back for the sockets given the chance.'

Danni shot a look over at Steve.

'Yeah, bro, always good to have some intel in places like this.' Steve sounded like he'd come off the set of *Top Boy*.

Danni nearly burst out laughing. Since when had Steve ever spoken like this? Was this his attempt to fit in in Manchester? Maybe their whole plan to lie low wasn't so clever after all.

John looked over at Danni. 'The kitchen always did well with food. Simple stuff – pies, curries, that sort of thing. We have a good afternoon crowd in from the factory down the road and don't forget the Monday club, they always have a scran when they're on the piss. You can make that kitchen your own.'

This was all too much for Danni. That was the second time today a man had decided the little lady belonged in the kitchen. 'I'm going upstairs to unpack, Steve. Thanks, John, for showing us about.'

Jamo lifted his head and shouted over to her. 'You go and get settled, lovely, all ready for tomorrow. Get some shut eye too, you're going to need it,' he chuckled.

Chapter Three

Danni walked out of the bar and was about to head up the stairs to the flat that would be her home now, when she looked at the door to the vaulted games room. She hesitated then stepped through.

There was dust illuminated in the air, it felt like no one had set foot in this room for years. Peeling posters on the wall advertised gigs from years back. There was the ghost of some marks on the lino where a pool table must have once stood and there, at the end of the room, was the darts board. Danni couldn't help herself, she went up to it, ran her hand over it and automatically picked up one of the darts lying beside it. For so many years, she'd only felt peace and focus when she was in front of a board, stepping up to the oche cleared her mind of everything else.

It had been a distraction at first, a game to play while her mum was drinking at their local. Then it had become her escape – some guy had brought a board and some darts round to the house. The bloke hadn't lasted, but the board had and, as a teenager, Danni got good, fast. Then it became her lifeline. On her own, that first night in Leeds, she'd walked into a pub and started playing just to push the loneliness out of her mind. Some cocky geezer had bet her twenty quid she couldn't beat him and that evening she earned enough to pay for a room for the night.

She'd never looked back. She'd soon mastered the art of walking into a quiet pub, late afternoons were best – quiet enough to get on the board, but ready for the end of the working day drinkers to arrive. She'd stand there throwing a few rubbish darts. It never took long before some man or other offered some 'friendly advice'. Some were handsy, some were friendly – but all of them were sure they could beat this waif of an eighteen-year-old who looked for all the world like she'd never held a dart before, let alone thrown one. She'd play along, missing the board, getting the counts wrong, asking about the rules. All the while waiting until the blokes had drunk enough to feel invincible. Most of the time she didn't even have to suggest a bet. Some fella would always suggest they put a few quid on – or play 'winner stays on'. Then she'd have to get clever. If it was a pub she wanted to come back to, she'd go all coy as the darts started finding their target, claim it as beginner's luck. Or on the days she was in a bad mood she'd just drop the act and wipe the floor with them, take their money and go.

And just like that, she had a living. Sometimes she'd try a normal job, cleaning or waitressing, but she always went back to the hustle. She was travelling all over the north, picking new towns, new pubs. Doncaster, Bradford, Wakefield. She worked out how to win big and move fast. They were good years, she looked back now. No one to answer to, no one to catch her.

She'd have got away with it too, she realised too late, if it hadn't been for a man. Marco Reece. He'd watched her one night in a pub in Headingley when she was at the top of her game. Unlike so many of the other guys watching, he'd not swaggered about claiming he could beat her. Instead, he'd hung back, watching as she took on every old soak in the pub, buying her drinks between matches, telling her how good she was. And at the end of that night, just when she thought he was going to hit on her, he didn't. Instead, he made her a business proposition.

Marco explained a little bit about the nature of his business. That first night, he didn't call it gambling or betting. He didn't call it hustling. He'd said he was in 'risk and reward'. He almost made it sound like it was a public service – letting people have a flutter. It didn't sound any more dangerous than the arcade games that glowed and hummed in the corner of most of the bars where she usually went.

But the first match Marco arranged for her showed her he was in a different league. It was secretive; invitation-only, address texted to guests at the last minute. High-stakes, flashy stuff. The first time she watched someone place a £1000 bet on her she thought she'd made it. Marco's cut for her made her feel like she'd finally succeeded – ten percent of big money still felt like riches to her. And she was just one part of the night's entertainment. There were people dropping serious dough on poker matches, losing a week's wages on a toss of a coin, betting on anything and everything.

That world had been seductive. For the first time in her life she'd had money for clothes, getting her hair done, never paying for a drink or a meal. She'd barely even noticed that Marco had slowly got control of everything – she didn't have a bank account, he bought her a phone, let her use one of his cars, even moved her into a flat he owned in Alwoodley. It was like nowhere she'd ever lived before.

So it hadn't seemed such a leap when it became more than business. He was showering her with so many gifts she didn't stop to think it was the winnings she was earning him. But she couldn't seem to lose. Still, even with thousands of pounds at stake, she was at her happiest at the throw-line. It was like there was a string between her and Double Top. It was a man's game and she stood out, would take on all-comers.

Danni didn't know when it had first gone sour. The first time Marco belittled her? Or told her she wasn't getting her cut that month because she owed him everything? Or the first time he'd backhanded her and split her lip? Whenever she'd been in trouble before – with her mum, with social services or even landlords who finally noticed the quiet woman with the nervous eyes was actually a hustler – she'd run. But Marco had closed the net without her even realising. He was a master at giving with one hand, and taking with the other. Like the day he'd given her a ring. It was what girls were meant to dream of – a ring, a promise to always be together. But he'd given her that the same day he'd told her about his wife.

Danni looked at the dusty dartboard now and remembered how, that day, she'd told him it was over. She'd thought she was earning money with the arrows. She didn't want to be anyone's mistress. She wasn't a tart. Suddenly the money he gave her made her feel cheap rather than rich. What exactly did he think he was paying her for?

But before she could leave him, the dibble had started sniffing around. The police were suddenly showing up everywhere – tailing him at work, following him home, and when he turned up with a bag of cash at the flat and asked her to hide it, it had seemed simple. Then she'd unzipped it and actually looked at the stacks of cash and something had flipped. Why would she ever give Marco this stash back? She'd earned it. When he came to collect she said the one word that no one ever said to Marco Reece: No.

'You fucking whore, Leigh!' he'd yelled at her, breath hot in her face. 'I suppose you think we're done? No one ever leaves me. Unless I finish them.'

She could see the vein in his neck pulsing. He'd been wild with rage. Waving his machete in her face, but she didn't flinch. Until an idea had clearly struck him. Time had almost slowed down as she worked out what was going on in his devious mind. The cruel fucker might want to kill her – but he'd do it piece by piece if he could.

But before she could let the flashback play out again, Steve marched in – clearly having finally shaken Jamo.

'So you've found the games room then, babes?' Steve smiled. 'The landlord said they had a pool team here before Covid, but it's just an amateurs' darts team now. Maybe it's time you got back in the game – showed them all how it's done.'

Danni went bright red. She lifted her hand up and waved it in his face, showing him her deformed thumb. 'How many bleeding times have I told you that I don't play anymore. Won't play. Can't play. Marco knew what he was doing when he chopped my thumb off, he didn't just make sure I could never hustle anyone again, he took away the only thing I was ever any good at.' There was a catch in her voice, but the day she left Leeds with the hold-all of Marco's money, crying in the taxi out of fear he'd find her, she'd vowed whatever else she did, she'd never shed another tear over him.

But Steve wasn't backing down. 'I get it. But how many years ago was that? This is our new leaf. I'm sure the hospital can do something – prosthetics or whatever so you can use it a bit more again. You've never let anyone even look at it, they can work miracles these days.'

'I'll tell you something for nothing: I'm never going to any hospital about my thumb. Marco probably still has eyes and ears everywhere and I can't shake the feeling he's just waiting on me turning up on the system somewhere so his yobs can find me. Even when it happened, I never went to the hospital, Steve, I've told you. You should have seen all the blood that I lost too. I thought I was going to die. I had to bandage it up for months, never let anyone see it. So get that idea out of your mind. I value my life, you know.'

Steve swapped lanes. 'You're a stubborn cow, I tell you. But you've got to admit, you can still throw darts, you're just set in your ways and never bleeding give it a proper go.'

'I still have nightmares about that night, I can still see the look in his eyes as he swung the machete at me. I was lucky he didn't come back for the rest of my fingers.' Danni curled her hands into fists.

'More than lucky, babes. Somebody must have been looking over you that night because Marco Reece is one proper head-the-ball. I wonder if his wife ever knew he was sleeping with you?'

Danni went white, guilt gripping her. Steve had never asked her too much about her affair with Marco and it was an unwritten rule that they never really spoke about their past relationships. He knew she'd used her middle name back then, knew about the money and the machete attack – but not about the details, the emotions. Danni sucked hard on her lips and shook her head. 'I'm not sure if she knew or not. I was younger then and didn't know what I was getting into. He'd mentioned his wife and kid a few times, but we never really spoke about his homelife. Monica she was called and that's all I really knew about her. Anyway,' she snapped, 'What did he expect? He'd been taking money from me for months. I was the one hustling all these darts players and he just jumped on the bandwagon to fill his pockets. I should have taken a lot more money from him, he should count himself lucky that I never marched to his house and told his wife all about us too.'

Steve fidgeted, never giving her any eye contact. 'Men like Marco always want a piece of the action. I bet he's still running deals from the inside. A greedy bastard he is by the sounds of things – from what you've told me and all the shit that came out when he was on trial. He's not a man that I would ever like to bump into on a dark night.'

'You don't know the half of it, Steve. Maybe one day I'll sit down with you and tell you the full story about that twat. Yes, I took his money and I'm glad. It gave him a taste of his own medicine. But look at me and the person I've become because of him. I'm a prisoner too, at least his sentence will end soon, mine will go on forever, or at least until he finds me.'

Steve sucked hard on his gums. 'He'll be out of the slammer soon and you can bet your life he'll be back in the game from the moment he lands back home. A few arses will be twitching when he's back on the streets, let me tell you.'

Danni shook her head, the colour draining from her face. She spoke in a sarcastic voice, 'Cheers for that, Steve, that will make me sleep tonight, won't it?'

Steve rolled his eyes and hunched his shoulders. 'I don't mean you, babes. No offence, he'll have bigger fish to fry than you. He'll have all sorts that's muscled in on his territory; they'll be in the firing line first, I've never known anybody to have Marco Reece over and live to tell the tale.'

Danni tightened her coat around her body. Steve was right and she knew it. She knew the day would come when Marco got out of jail and the clock was ticking now for his release date. She was living on borrowed time.

Chapter Four

Above the pub, the flat needed plenty of TLC. Danni hadn't even got beyond the landing at the top of the stairs before she could feel her skin crawling. Bloody filthy the handrail was, greasy and dusty at the same time. She walked into the living room and shuddered. Yellow-stained walls, rubbish scattered everywhere she looked. A stench in the air that smelled like wet dog or worse. She pinched her nose and ran to the window to let some fresh air inside. John must have just existed in here, there was no sign of a woman's touch whatsoever, she thought, no personal flourishes. She turned around and clocked an old brown leather sofa in the centre of the room. John had mentioned earlier about the furniture and told them they could have it. Sack that, she would never sit on that flea-bitten thing, it was rotten. The moment Steve came upstairs he could order a van, or a skip to get rid of all this crap. Danni had spent years trying to escape her past and now she liked nice things, pretty décor, a nice-smelling house. All the things she never had as a kid. This place reminded her of her mother's house, and it sent a wave of sadness through her body. Her mother had been poor for sure, but even though when she'd first rented a bedsit of her own in Leeds Danni had nothing, she still always made sure it was clean. She examined all the other rooms and none of them were much better, a right shit-tip and that was being generous. Danni let out a laboured breath and rolled her sleeves up. This was going to take her all day. There was no way she would rest until this place was spick and span.

By sundown Danni was exhausted, all day she'd been cleaning and sorting. At least now it smelt nice, floral fragrances bursting out into the air from the plug-in fresheners she'd just bought. Steve walked into the living room and his eyes opened wide. 'Bloody hell, this doesn't look like the same flat, you've gone to town on it, haven't you?'

'You can say that again, I feel hanging, I need a bath. Look at my nails. Every inch of me feels dirty and grubby. How John lived up here is beyond me. I've found cig dimps everywhere and he hasn't hoovered in here since the twelfth of never.' She fanned herself with her hand. She could see Steve studying her thumb and lowered her hands. He cupped his arms around her, knowing she hated anyone looking at her hand.

'Oi, guess what night it is tonight, babes? That Jamo bloke has sat at the bar all afternoon and only now did he mention what day it is.'

Danni shrugged – she had thought her night would consist of watching a box-set and curling up in bed for an early night. She wasn't in the mood for meeting any more of the regulars at The Fox.

'It's the ladies' darts tonight. Apparently, they meet every other Monday night. I was hoping you might put some food on for the girls. John said he usually does a few sarnies for them.'

Danni looked appalled; she couldn't have thought about anything worse. Her voice was high-pitched as she choked out a response. 'Me! Making butties and chatting darts? Steve, I'm dead on my feet and I don't want to sit downstairs tonight making small-talk. You need to remember, this is your shout not mine. I would have stayed in Huddersfield, watching the sunset over the hills. If you really want to know, if I was on the fence before, but after our intro to this place, I'd be happy to turn back tonight and return to our old life. That Jamo told me some stuff before and I'm not sure if we will even fit in around here with all these misfits.'

Steve quizzed her. 'Stuff like what?'

'Lads coming in asking for protection money. Shoplifters selling all their swag in here. We're meant to be keeping things clean.'

'Take no notice of Jamo. John said he's got a screw loose, not playing with a full deck of cards.'

'Well he seemed to know what he was talking about when he was speaking to me.'

He ran his fingers through his hair and looked over at her. 'Danni, stop bloody stressing. Have I not always looked after you or what?'

She dipped her head low, remembered when they'd met. She'd fled Leeds and Marco, richer than she'd ever been, but more scared than she'd ever been, too. At first she'd used some of the money to pay upfront for the rent on a tiny flat on the edge of Huddersfield, paying cash and calling herself Danni again. She'd bought a new phone – not that she had anyone to call – and some supplies, then locked herself into the poky, drab rooms for what felt like months. She'd thought she was going crazy – the pain of her wounded hand, the isolation and, above all, the fear that this was what her life would be now.

Every night she'd gone to bed expecting to be woken by the sound of Marco's men slamming her door down. But the weeks went by and slowly she let herself believe she'd done it, she'd got away. She even started to imagine a life beyond his shadow, but if she wanted to get away properly – maybe Scotland or Cornwall, she needed to get back out in the world. So she'd forced herself out to the end of the road and back. The next day she worked up to going into the pub she'd seen. She reminded herself of all the other times she'd started over – running away from home, care, Marco – she knew she could do it again, she just had to learn to swallow down her anxiety and play it cool. She'd walked into the bar, ordered a coke and sat there trying to look like she hadn't a care in the world. She managed it too, until she looked up and saw the dartboard at the back of the pub. Her thumb had throbbed and her pulse raced. That life was over, she told herself.

She'd come back the next day, determined to be able to pass for just another punter and slowly she'd got chatting to the guy behind the bar. Steve. He didn't ask too many questions, she liked that, but he made her feel something she'd never felt before. Not love or lust or like she was special. Marco had made her feel all those things and look where that had got her. No, Steve made her feel something she wanted more than all those things. He made her feel normal.

On the day she saw on the news that police had arrested Marco Reece, she told Steve everything. It felt like going to confession. She'd expected him to run a mile but instead he took her in and let her hide away from the world. Under his wing, she'd rebuilt herself. They got together slowly – none of the gifts and flattery she'd had with Marco, but something that felt equal. Before long she'd let go of her notions of a new life by the sea somewhere, and started doing shifts at the pub. And while she always had one eye on the door, as the years passed, she let herself believe that part of her life was over.

The one thing she'd never let herself do, though, was play another game of darts. She'd tried picking one up, holding it between her hand and her ruined thumb and that had been enough. Steve had caught her, standing there like she was facing a judge and jury and she'd told him how good she used to be. He'd tried to tell her she could run a team if she didn't want to play again, but they had so few punters it was never more than a fantasy. Danni preferred it that way. The few times she'd let herself throw a dart after closing time she was reminded of everything she'd lost. The money lying in a bag under the bed wasn't enough to make up for the trap she'd found herself in. She'd barely used any of it since moving in with Steve. What they earned running the bar wasn't lots – but it had felt like clean money to her.

It was Steve who'd ground her down with his talk of a move in the end – he didn't like the quiet life, preferred his memories of city life. When the lease on The Fox came up, he'd finally convinced her.

'I've never asked you for anything, Danni – answers, money, marriage. But I want this one thing. Marco Reece has been inside for five long years. Why shouldn't we use a bit of that fucker's money to get us a foot on the ladder in Manchester. I reckon it would lay some of your demons to rest, too. Seeing Manchester again. Proving to yourself you can do it. We'll try it for a few years – and if you don't love it, then we can move again before Marco is up for release. Devon, maybe, or even Costa del bleeding Sol.'

And that was why she was back here. Harpurhey. A commitment. A pub with a darts team. She wasn't sure she was ready for any of it. Especially not coaching the ladies' squad on her first chuffing night. She walked through to the dingy bedroom, Steve following.

'I'm sure they're nice women, Steve. But you know me, I like to keep myself to myself. I don't like being in the limelight.'

'Maybe helping out with the darts could be good for you. Come on, you were the best around by miles. I know you'd have turned pro if Marco hadn't sunk his claws into you. You could coach the girls because John said they are crap, never won a thing. Apparently, the other pubs' teams hate even playing them because they are so shite.'

OK, she could see what he was doing here and in his own way he was only trying to help. She smiled over at him and backed down. 'I'll do a curry for the girls to help out and I will stay downstairs for a couple of hours, but that's it. I'm not coaching them. The less anyone knows about me, the better.'

He dragged her back towards him and kissed the top of her head. 'And that's why I love you. We're going to be happy here, just you watch.'

'I hope so, Steve. I can't take my eyes from the ball, one slip up, one mistake is all it takes.' The hairs on the back of her neck stood on end and her airways closed up slightly, restricting her breathing.

Steve was a tower of a man and his expression changed. 'Look, even if someone recognises you, and sends word to Marco on the inside, he can't get near you, babes. I've always told you this and you need to believe me. And once he's out, well, I would die before I let that prick get anywhere near you.'

Danni knew he meant every word he'd said. But he didn't know Marco like she did, didn't know how far he would go to get what he wanted.

Steve shook his head and headed back down to the bar. Danni plonked herself down on the side of the bed and stroked her hand along the fresh white bedding she'd brought with them. Steve was a good man and he loved her in his own way, but did she really love him? Maybe she cared about him because, after all, he did every thing for her, helped her cover her tracks, told lies to anyone who asked him questions about her, had helped her create an identity that was a million miles away from the truth of who she really was. Danni dipped her head low, shoved her hand under the bed and pulled out the brown suitcase.

Her expression changed as she hauled it up onto the bed. With a quick click of the lock she opened it and sat staring at the money. There was twenty thousand pounds left. Maybe she should go back to Marco's gang and get word to him she would pay the rest back, cut a deal to end her life on the run from him. Her fingers glided over the bundles of money as she sat thinking. If Manchester was a mistake, would Steve really be prepared to up sticks and try somewhere else? Or would she need to go it alone? Was there enough there to start again, go far, far away and never look back? Maybe she could go to Spain and get a bar job; somebody would employ her for sure. But did she have the balls to do it? It didn't look like it. The courage she'd once had, had gone a long time ago. She was afraid of her own shadow these days. Any sudden noises made her jump, panic was part of her everyday life now. Every day it crawled into her body and reminded her of her past. Danni stashed the money back under the bed. Steve paid for everything, and she didn't need to touch the money she'd stashed. This was her nest egg, and the security if she needed to get away quickly. She fell flat on the bed and stared at the ceiling. Yellow it was, like old school dinner custard. First thing in the morning she was getting some paint and freshening this place up. She liked painting, it calmed her down. There was no way she was asking Jamo to help her out. She didn't like owing anyone favours, letting anyone in. She knew all too well that only ever ended badly.

Chapter Five

Danni finally decided to get up to go food shopping and crack on with making the curry for the darts team. The local shops seemed nice enough, just a few youths hovering about outside. Jamo had told her they were ruthless when the dark fell and the square turned into some kind of meeting place, but she had no problems here today. Maybe Steve was right, it might do her some good to mix with other people. The more she thought about it, the more it made sense. What, was she going to hide away for the rest of her life? She could rebuild her life back here in her hometown of Manchester. Maybe even get in touch with a few old friends if they were still in the area. How nice would it be to sit down and talk about the old days before her mum got hooked on the drink; she could find her old school mates, perhaps go for lunch with them, even go shopping together. Yes, when she was settled, she was going to do her homework and see who was still about in the area. As long as she kept it to the girls, she'd be safe. They wouldn't have dodgy connections to the kind of gang-leaders that would know the main men from other cities.

Soon the curry was made and all that was left was to have a quick shower and get ready before she went downstairs to meet this bloody darts team. Danni walked over to the mirror that was hung on the wall in the bedroom and examined her skin. It was as dry as Steve's sense of humour. She lifted her chestnut-brown hair up in her hands and held it high before dropping it again, limp. It had been ages since she'd had a good haircut. In fact, it had been a long time since she'd done a lot of things. She used to love going out, buying clothes and pampering herself when she had the dough. A look of sadness filled her eyes as she looked at her reflection in the mirror. She wasn't living anymore; she was just existing. Her expression changed and her fists curled into two tight balls at the side of her legs as she clenched her teeth together tightly. 'You wanna come for me, Marco? Fine, because when you do, I'm ready for you this time. Life is to be enjoyed, I'm sick of being scared.'

Danni stared at her reflection and nodded her head slowly, a serious look settled in her eyes. She walked away from the mirror and into the bathroom. Tomorrow was a new day; she would book herself in at the hairdresser's and go shopping. You only get one life, she thought, and Danni was ready to start living it again.

Alice Worsley walked into The Fox at seven-fifteen exactly, the same time as she always did on a Monday night. Her hair was nicely blown, and she'd put a bit of slap on tonight; bright-red lipstick. Alice was the captain of the darts team, and the one who would greet the away team, be the spokesperson. She loved it even though she said she didn't, it made her feel important, gave her a little bit of status in life. After all, her life at home wasn't all that, and she needed something to take her mind from her everyday problems. Didn't everyone? Alice walked to the bar in her grey court shoes, a puzzled look on her face when she spotted Steve stood behind the bar. She looked one way then the other and coughed to get his attention. 'Excuse me, is John about? I need my darts and the light switching on in the back room.'

Steve turned to face Alice and smiled. He came over to where she was stood and smiled. 'Hello, you must be Alice, captain of the ship. John told me you would be in. I'm Steve, the new landlord. Nice to meet you.' He stretched his hairy hand over the bar towards hers.

Alice looked taken aback but shook his hand. 'New landlord, since when? John never mentioned that he was leaving.'

'Well, he's gone now and I'm afraid it's me and my ugly mush that you will have to deal with from now on.'

'Has something happened? Because I can't see John just scarpering without saying goodbye to us all. I usually do the early cleaning in this place too, did he say? But I've been away in Blackpool on my jollies for a few days. Never thought I'd come back and he'd have done a bunk.' Alice didn't know what else to say and stood sucking hard on her gums. She knew people thought she was a battleaxe

THE HUSTLE

and any excuse she'd give anyone a piece of her mind. She was in a strop now and quickly fired her words out. 'Well, I guess the show must go on. Can you pass me my darts please, they should be just there in that drawer over there, and if you can, will you turn the lights on in the back? It would be a great help if we can see.'

Steve burst out laughing. 'Well as far as John was concerned, light or dark wouldn't make any difference to the way you lot are throwing. You've never won a bloody game, is that right?'

Alice went bright red. How dare he mock her darts team? They did their damnedest and so what they hadn't won a game, it wasn't from the lack of trying. She tucked her dark-brown hair behind her ears and eyeballed him. This doughnut was getting told. 'As a matter of fact, I've won the highest score of the league, two or maybe three years ago. The girls just need some more practice, that's all. I mean, we all work and have families to look after so where do you think we get the time to nail it? We're not like the fellas, boozing every night and hogging the board. We have about half an hour every Monday before the game starts, that's all.'

'Practice makes perfect though, doesn't it? Aye, I'll let you in on a little secret, shall I? My Mrs is one of the best dart players I've ever met. Maybe if you ask her nicely, she might give you some tips.'

Alice looked like she was chewing on a wasp. She was the captain of the darts team and if her girls needed any tips then she was the one who would give them to the ladies, not no bloody newcomer. Who the hell did this idiot think he was talking to anyway. He'd been here two minutes, and already he was shouting the odds out to her. No, he was getting told. She eyeballed him, moved closer to the bar and licked her dry lips. 'Listen, Steve-o, it's obvious you don't know how things work around here, do you? You manage the pub and I'll manage the darts team, just like I've always done.'

Steve knew she was getting angry, backed off and started looking for the darts she'd requested. Once he'd found them, he moved along the bar to the back hatch which served the games room. He placed them on the bar and tried again to win Alice over. 'Our Danni has made a lovely curry for you all tonight. She's a cracking cook, you know.'

Alice had heard enough. She gave him a half-hearted smile, picked her darts up and walked over to where she would be playing. Alice stood at the side of the oche and started throwing her darts, Steve watching. She was mumbling under her breath, still fuming. 'Saying we need practice, who the hell does he think he's talking to? I got a nine-darter once, what does that prick know?' she snarled as she walked to the darts board to pull her darts out. Alice was making sure she got her practice in tonight. She had to set the bar high for her team, show them that they could win a game if they tried hard enough. Steve had hit a nerve even though she'd never say as much. It was true; the darts team were a laughing stock in the league, nobody ever took them seriously. Her dream was to win the league, to stand proud with her girls as they collected their trophy. But the way they were all playing, that dream was a lifetime away. Even winning a match would be a fine thing.

Alice turned her head as another woman entered. She looked stressed to high heaven. 'Where's John?' she muttered. 'The sitter let me down again so I've had to bring the kids with me. Do me a favour, Alice, get me a couple of cans of coke and two packets of crisps and I'll shove these two in the disabled lav while I play my darts.'

Alice shook her head as she looked down at the two boys. 'Bleeding hell, Frenchie. How many times have I told you that you can't bring them into the pub? The shit will hit the fan if you get caught and what then? I'm not backing you.'

Amanda French – although she'd been pretty much universally known as Frenchie since she started high school – rolled her eyes and brushed the comment off. Her life was hectic; this wasn't the first time she'd had to bring the kids to the pub with her and hide them away while she played the match. John had told her lots of times that she couldn't keep doing it but needs must, she figured. Darts were her escape from family life and she would not miss a match for love nor money. Frenchie was ducking and diving now as she dragged her two boys through the pub by their coats. Once they were in the toilets she rummaged in her bag for the out of order sign and stuck it on the toilet door. 'Right, lads, you know the crack. I'll bring you both drinks and crisps soon. All I ask is that you behave, remember, no noise. Just play on your phones and be bloody quiet. Do not open the toilet door until you hear my voice outside. Do you understand?' The two boys nodded. Already they had plonked themselves on the cold, tiled floor and started playing their games. She blew them a kiss and she was gone.

Frenchie peeled her bright-red waterproof jacket off and ran her fingers through her short copper-coloured hair before she sat down next to Alice. 'What's up with your mush,' she hissed over at Alice, already aware she was in a strop. Alice shot a look over at Steve who was pottering about behind the bar, not really paying them any attention.

'It's that dickhead over there. John has pissed off and he's the new landlord. First impressions are I don't think he will be somebody that we'll get along with. You should have heard him before telling me of all people, that we should practice more.'

Frenchie's jaw dropped, but before she could say anything, the door opened and in walked the rest of the team: Betty and Jasmine. Betty looked like she was pushing eighty and got sick of folk saying she was the spit of Hilda Ogden from *Coronation Street* back in the day. She had a cackling laugh and was halfway through a story as she made her way across to the other women. Jasmine was quieter than the rest of the group, nervous, not a lot to say for herself. Handbags down, darts out and lined up on the table where they always sat before practice, they all went to the bar to order their drinks. Frenchie stretched her neck long to get a better look at Steve. Whether she loved or loathed someone, she never thought it hurt to show them her best side. She licked her bright peachy lips. She'd not long had her filler done, there must have been at least two mils of filler in them, and although some folk took the piss and called her 'sausage lips,' it didn't stop her – she was a more-is-more person. She yanked her top down a little – no use having been to Turkey for new boobs if no one got a glimpse of them, she figured. But Steve didn't seem to notice. She turned back to the girls.

Betty shook her black umbrella at the side of the table and shoved it in her brown handbag. 'Norris dropped me off at the church and he was parked up for ages before he drove off. I've been stood in the church grounds for at least fifteen minutes waiting for him to piss off.'

'Betty, why don't you just tell him that you play darts? It's not a crime to have a bit of fun, is it?' Alice sat staring at her, waiting on an answer.

'He would have kittens if he knew I was in the pub. He's a funny old bleeder is my Norris, he likes what he likes. I just let him think I'm at church, cleaning. It keeps him off my back.'

Alice chuckled and patted Betty on the top of her shoulder. 'Your secret is safe with me.'

The away team started to enter the room. They all had matching bright-yellow silk shirts with their names on the back. Alice looked around at her girls and her heart sank low. They were always the poor relations – shabby and, yes, she could admit to herself – not the best talent in the world. Alice knew the comments the other teams made about them, but she hadn't shared them with the girls since Frenchie kicked off big time. Frenchie had skull-dragged a woman about the pub because she commented on how ropey their team was. They had nearly been banned from the league. It was only Alice and John that had saved them, put a sad story together, said Frenchie had been under a lot of stress.

Alice got her girls together and, as always, gave them the pep talk; the reason they should triumph tonight, the future and the trophies they could win. These talks never really worked, but Alice felt as the captain she should give them some positive vibes before every match started.

Just then a small, slight woman entered and started bustling about the long table down one side of the room. This must be the new landlady – the so-called darts legend Steve had told her about. She didn't look like she'd say boo to a goose, let alone manage to hit the board. Alice noticed her looking at the board like it was on fire, and after she'd put some napkins and cutlery down she was surprised to see the woman didn't retreat back to the kitchen or bar, but sat down in the corner, watching Alice and Frenchie warm up.

Danni had only gone in to get things straight before bringing the curry out after the match. But how could she walk out again now? Steve was right; these women could do with some help. Even the way they stood, they held their darts all wrong. Danni shook her head as a dart missed the board. Even for a warm-up it was hopeless. No focus, no aim, they were just flinging darts about. The room went quiet now and Alice pulled out the names of who everyone was playing. Danni clocked who was who.

The match began and Betty was up first. Danni knew from her own experience never to judge a book by its cover, so she hoped for The Fox's sake that this little old lady had some surprises up her sleeve. She pulled her glasses from her grey cardigan pocket and placed them on the end of her nose. Jeez, thought Danni. Was that a plaster holding the glasses together, she wasn't sure. Danni moved about in her seat to get a better look, hoping Betty was going to astonish them all.

Betty stood at the white line, squinting before she took her shot. She did a little jump and let go of the dart. Danni watched the dart in disbelief; right over the board it went, landing plumb in the wall. She could hear the snide comments from the away team and Frenchie and Alice eyeballed them, reminding them about respecting the players. Danni looked down at her thumb automatically, stroked her other finger over the end of it before she hid it away quickly. Betty's game didn't get much better and she was lucky to even get a dart in the board. The arrows were all over the show; one this way, one that way. Betty didn't lose her smile though; she was effing and jeffing and jumping up and down on the spot after each shot.

The two ladies shook hands after the game and Betty rolled her eyes as she went back to join her team. 'My arthritis is playing up tonight. I just couldn't grip the darts properly.'

Danni watched the captain sigh and looked over at the one she'd worked out was called Frenchie. She was up next, and at least it looked to Danni like her head was in the game. She could see she wanted to win. Her leopard-print leggings looked like they had been sprayed on and her short red crop top left little to the imagination. Danni sat biting her lip as Frenchie tottered up to the line. At least Frenchie looked the part; her stance was good and she had a decent hold on her darts.

The leg went quickly and Danni was relieved to see Frenchie's darts at least landing in the board – mostly 5s and 1s, she admitted, but at least she was aiming for the twenty. As Frenchie reluctantly accepted defeat at the end of her turn, Steve peered through at Danni and caught her eye. She stood up and walked to the bar to talk to him, her voice low.

'I hate to say it but you were right. That old lady over there can't even see properly, her glasses are falling apart, and she looks like she's having a fit before she takes each shot.'

Steve sniggered and looked over at Frenchie.

Danni continued. 'One wrong dart and someone will puncture the airbags on that one. She's got a bit of raw talent, but I can see why they're the joke of the league. Grab me a beer, please, babes. I might need something stronger watching these lot if I'm being honest.'

'I told you before what John said. They never win. This could be your project, put these girls on the map. Playing darts was your gift and just because you've had a setback don't keep saying that you can't do it anymore. There are people out there who're in a much worse position than you. They don't just give up. No, they make the most of what they have and crack on. You do my head in sometimes and I can't believe you have given up. Shit happens, Danni. Just get over it.'

Danni bit back the urge to remind Steve 'shit happens' was the kind of thing you said about a break-up or bumping your car. Not being on the run from a maniac who wanted to slice you up. The match was over and the girls stood around the table helping themselves to curry and rice. The away team were celebrating their win and the home team, as normal, were getting used to losing yet another game. Alice spotted Danni. She left the group and headed over to the new landlady. 'Hi, I'm Alice. The curry is fantastic. We usually only get a few stale butties from John, but this is really nice. Everyone has said so too, so thanks.'

Danni blushed. 'No worries, it was just something I rustled up. Steve only let me know a few hours ago so I had to rush about getting everything that I needed.'

Alice twisted her head back over at the girls and kept her voice low. 'Sorry we couldn't manage a win for your first time watching. But I won't lose faith. Your hubby mentioned you played darts before.'

Danni stuttered. 'Take no notice of Steve. He always tells everyone that. I've not played darts in years. I lost the end of my thumb in an accident and I can't grip the darts like I used to, anyway. I'm about as much use as a chocolate fireguard to you all.'

Alice dropped her eyes low and tried to get a look. Danni followed her eyes and tucked her thumb under her fingers.

Alice sat down next to Danni and smiled at her. Clearly she'd decided Danni wasn't a threat. 'Did John tell you that I'm the cleaner here too. I come each morning about seven, make sure the place is straight before opening. I have my own keys, so you don't have to bother letting me in.'

'No, he never mentioned it, but you just crack on. Any problems, just talk to Steve.'

'I will. Anyway, how are you settling in around here?'

'I've not really been out much yet, but that guy, Jamo, told me a few things to watch out for.'

Alice chuckled. 'I bet he never told you to watch out for himself. He's got light fingers, you know. A few folk have had their phones or purses half-inched. We could never prove it, but he was the number one suspect. Still, he's not the worst of the blokes round here.'

Danni tried not to look alarmed. 'Jamo told me there are a few lads who come in here and John used to pay them protection money?'

Alice whispered now, looking around her. 'Maybe, but I can tell you more about them tomorrow, not now. Anyone could walk in.'

Danni could see she was getting distressed and changed the subject. So, have you lived around here for long, Alice?'

'Yeah, all my life. I don't think I would ever leave Harpurhey. You see, I know everyone around here, know where to keep clear of and who's doing what. Sometimes it's easier that way, isn't it?'

Danni nodded her head, unsure how much she could share with this woman, but she didn't fancy that Cornish nonsense she'd told Jamo. Alice was too sharp for that. 'I used to know a few people around here. Are Mary Jones and Josie Taylor still around these parts?'

Alice tilted her head on one side, the names clearly familiar. 'Josie Taylor? She's often in here, lives on The Manning estate up the road. I think she's got a few kids, and her fella comes in here every now and then too. I'm not sure about a Mary Jones though, but I'll tell you who would, she knows everyone around here…' She waved her hand in the air to get Frenchie's attention. 'Come here a minute!' she shouted over.

Frenchie picked her pint glass up and walked over, swigging a mouthful of her lager. Alice looked up at her. 'This is Danni, the new landlady. She said she knew a few people here back in the day. I told her Josie Taylor lives on the Manning estate and often shows her face, but Mary Jones, I don't know her, do you?'

Frenchie burst out laughing and plonked down next to them both. 'Of course I know bloody Mary Jones. I used to chill with her sister when I was growing up. Mary used to live in Collyhurst, near the flats, but I've not seen her for time now, think she's moved on. But Josie Taylor? Fingers like lightning, that lass. Cracking little shoplifter – get you anything you want. Sometimes she comes in here selling stuff; she'll be chuffed if her old pal is landlady here, I bet. Where did you say you know her from?'

Danni swallowed hard and twiddled with a piece of hair hanging down near her face. 'I knew them both ages ago. I haven't seen them for donkey's years though.'

Frenchie smiled and gulped another mouthful from her pint. 'I know everyone, I do. I've done a bit of lifting in my time too but nothing like Josie, she's a professional. I just get batteries, occasional pieces of meat, bit of make-up.'

Danni looked at Frenchie and didn't know what to say. Frenchie could sense that she was shocked and explained further. 'You see around here, love, you have to make ends meet. Nobody has got anything to fall back on, and what we do have we share. I've got a rule – I sell everything I nick for just under half-price so I'm helping people, aren't I?'

Danni just nodded.

'If you need anything then just give me the word. I go "shopping" on Wednesdays and Saturdays so I will add it to my list.'

Alice looked uncomfortable. 'She's not a full-time shoplifter, she works as well, don't you, Frenchie?'

'Yep, I do a few hours in a taxi office. But keep that to yourself. I do it on the side. The last thing I need is the benefit agency getting on to me for fraud.'

Danni was searching for something to say when she saw Betty walking up. 'Hello, I'm Danni, I've met Alice and Frenchie already.'

Betty went straight in for a hug. 'I'm Betty, this is Jasmine, and we are the ladies darts team.' Betty raised her eyebrows high before she spoke. 'Not very good, are we?'

Danni hesitated before she replied, she wanted to give some positive feedback. 'Well, there were some good darts played. Frenchie, you had a few decent scores.'

Alice chirped in, reminding them all that she was the captain for a reason. 'I got a forty-two and a thirty. If that dart hadn't fallen out, I would have got the bull.'

Frenchie held a sour expression. 'You're full of bull, alright. Mine was the highest score tonight. I got sixty. I've been practising at home on the lads' dartboard that they got for Crimbo off their dad. Give me a few more weeks and it'll be "one hundred and eighty".'

Danni knew the feeling of scoring a full house and smiled, not letting on. 'Practice makes perfect, ladies. Keep at it. I better get going, I've left Steve behind the bar on his own all night long. Nice meeting you all and good luck on your next game.' Danni stood up and walked away.

Alice watched her leave and shot a look over at Frenchie. 'I bet she could help us improve, you know. That Steve bloke said she is the best darts player he's ever met. She said she had an accident and lost the end of her thumb but come on, that shouldn't stop her training us, should it?'

Frenchie sucked hard on her gums. 'Leave her to settle and let's see what happens. Anyway, keep me covered while I go and grab the kids. I'll catch up with you all in the week.' Frenchie swigged the last of her lager and headed towards the loos.

Danni had gone back to the bar but heard every word Alice had said. Maybe she could give the girls some advice. There was something about being back in Manchester that was bringing her back to life. After all, home is where the heart is, didn't they say? She went back to polishing glasses with a smile on her face, and the kinds of dreams in her head that she hadn't had for years.

Lost in thought, she didn't notice the figure outside at the window, the thick bobbled glass giving no clue as to his identity.

Chapter Six

Marco Reece walked down the landing on B-wing in Risley prison like he owned the joint. All eyes were on him, nobody taking a chance of turning their back on him for a split second. He was known as a snapper and could flip at the drop of a hat. The screws knew even though this was meant to be a good day he was still somebody to watch to the very last minute. The officers stood far enough back so Marco couldn't grip any of them as he walked past.

Marco showed no emotion as he strolled along the landing, head held back, chest expanded fully. A few inmates shouted over to him, wishing him luck on the out. He didn't reply, kept his eyes focused and carried on walking. Marco swung his bag over his shoulder as he reached the iron door at the end of the landing. The officers were stood there waiting for him, trying to make out if they could get a conversation out of him or what. 'Can you taste the freedom, Marco?' the screw asked him.

THE HUSTLE

He inhaled deeply and walked through the door, growling over at them. 'Just hurry the fuck up and get me out of this place. Cut the fucking small-talk.'

Marco had never made any friends in this place, associates he called them, people he could use to run about for him and make him some money. Every convict in Risley had wanted to know Marco, to tell their friends they'd had conversation with the main man, but he had kept himself to himself and got his head down, done his time – and now it had all come good. Early release, they'd told him. Something about prison overcrowding. He'd laughed, having made sure he'd put a bit of cash in the right pockets early in his sentence to get a cell to himself.

No, he had gone in with a plan and stuck to it. He made it clear he was on a hair trigger – had gone psycho a couple of times early on to ensure his reputation preceded him. But then he'd sat back, got his boys to do the nasty stuff for him. Most of the time Marco had spent in the gym training, lifting weights, getting his cardio up to scratch. Running enough lines to keep his clout and his cash flow from the contraband, but never getting his hands dirty to jeopardise his model prisoner record. And now, here he was – five years into his ten stretch and ready to walk.

The officer filled out the paperwork and handed Marco's personal property back to him. A watch, a necklace, and two gold rings. Marco studied one of the rings and twisted it around in his hand before he slid it on his finger. Leigh had bought him this ring and it was something he once treasured more than anything else he owned. The other ring the officer handed over was his wedding ring, the circle of trust his wife called it. An empty promise, more like. Monica had known his reputation when they got hitched; any hole he'd fill it. He loved the dollybirds, pretty girls, big tits, white teeth. He was far from faithful to his wife and, deep down, she must have known her man was a player. She'd been raised by a crim, knew what he did, and he figured she knew the kind of man she was marrying – just didn't want it flaunted in her face.

Marco's watch dangled around on his wrist as he tried to fasten it now. The weight he'd lost was there for everyone to see. He'd have to sort himself out fast. He needed a few sessions on the sunbed too as soon as he could. He'd looked at himself in the crappy plastic mirrors they had screwed to the wall in this place. A pale complexion, dark circles under his eyes, hollow cheeks. He'd been used to eating at the best restaurants around town, so it was expected that he would lose some timber in the nick, but he needed to get on the gains once he was free. Marco pushed his ring on his finger and clipped his thick gold chain around his neck. He stood up and rolled his shoulders back as he walked up to the desk to sign for his property. 'How long now?'

The officer lifted his head up and looked over at the large clock on the wall. 'About another fifteen mins, pal. I've got another five men to sort out too so just relax and sit back. I'll shout you when I'm ready.'

Marco screwed his face up, trying to supress his rage. He hated being told to wait and if this had been any other time, he would have snapped this prick's jaw and put him on his arse. He shook his head and backed off to his seat. Marco sat down and dropped his hands between his legs, watching the other inmates filling out their paperwork. Each of them looked like death warmed up, grey skin, no self-respect. Prison broke some men, he'd learned that being locked behind a door messed with their heads and by examining at this lot they looked like they'd been down the block for months if not years. A man sat down next to Marco, and he could smell him before he could see him, a stale stench that hit the back of his throat. Marco eyeballed the inmate and spoke through clenched teeth. 'Fuck off away from me. Stand over there. Scruffy twat.'

The convict gulped, didn't need telling twice; he knew who this man was and what he was capable of. He jumped to his feet and stood with his back against the wall. No eye contact, gaze held down at the floor. Marco smiled to himself. He hadn't lost it.

More than fifteen minutes had passed and Marco was fidgeting. A gate arrest was never far from his mind, and he knew quite a few guys it had happened to. The police were crafty bastards and there was no way they would want him back on the streets again. They'd try and stitch him up at any cost and he was more than aware of this. He'd told his Mrs to have the solicitor on standby in case they pounced on him the minute he was set free.

All the men finally stood up and carried their belonging with them as they went through another door. Freedom was minutes away, he could smell it. The officer gave his usual spiel: 'Good luck, lads, I hope I don't see you back in here again.'

A few of the inmates shook his hand as they walked past the screw but not Marco; he kept his gaze in front of him and carried on walking. He owed them fuck all. Wankers, the lot of them.

There was cheering and shouting from a small crowd of friends and family as the inmates stepped foot outside the jail. Men ran to their loved ones who'd been waiting for them, hugging, kissing, tears flowing. Marco didn't join the crowds. He stood on the same spot and looked about. A whistle could be heard from his left. Marco turned his head slowly and smirked as he watched Kes Brady waving his arm above his head at him in the distance. Marco picked his bag up and slung it over his shoulder as he jogged towards the silver car. He opened the door and threw his bag into the back of the car. He climbed into the passenger seat and only when the door was shut behind him could he accept that he was finally free.

He nodded his head over at Kes, who was grinning. 'Welcome home, pal. You've been missed, I can tell you. Five years is a fucking long time, mate.'

'Tell me about it. It's a fucking shithole in there. Whatever we do, I'm not going back in there.'

Kes reached over and hugged his pal. Kes had been friends with Marco since they were young, and he always had his back. Kes knew he was lucky he hadn't been slammed with Marco too and it was only by the skin of his teeth that he got the charges dropped, not enough evidence, and a walk out of court rather than down to the cells.

Kes flicked the engine over and pulled out of the car park. 'So, what's first, home for a shag or a haircut and a few scoops with the lads?'

Marco looked out of the window and closed his eyes for a few seconds, digesting everything around him. 'A haircut first so I look the part and then a few pints with the lads, show them I'm back and mean business. Get my face seen.'

'Monica has been on the blower all morning asking what time I'm picking you up and telling me to make sure I bring you straight home. I think she's worried I'll have you on the piss all night.'

'She's waited five years, she can wait for a bit longer. She knows what comes first and I have to check a few things out before I head home to the ball and chain.'

Kes turned the music up a bit and pulled out onto the main road. 'You know things have been hard outside here, Marco. I've not told you everything, but shit has been going down. Different families gunning for control. The Murphys are up and coming and we've kept them at bay for the time being, but they want a piece of the action too.'

Marco clenched his teeth. 'They're getting fuck all and I'll tell them that too.'

Kes swallowed hard and kept his eyes on the road. 'Mate, you need to see things clearly first. The Murphys are not a forced to be messed with. They've already taken Mel Boswell down, took everything he had, left him in a bad way. Nil by mouth.'

Marco's nostrils flared as he shot a look over at Kes. 'So you're telling me we can't take the fucking Murphys down now. Give your head a shake, lad, and smell the fucking coffee. I'm back now and once they see that they will think again.'

Kes rolled his eyes and let out a laboured breath. Marco needed a wake-up call for sure, five years was a long time and his name had faded in the area like a pair of curtains in the sunshine. Kes continued talking. 'Like I said, things have changed. Half the shit we used to cream money from has gone now. We still have a few clubs but the money coming in is nothing like it used to be.'

Marco gave Kes a shifty look and studied him further. Kes Brady seemed to have lost his fight, his mojo. There were a few seconds of silence as Marco sat twiddling his gold ring around his finger. 'If it's cash flow that you're shitting yourself about, I've got loans we can call in. Dirty Dev, he owes me serious money. And what about Ginger Nigel? Bet he still hasn't cashed out.' Then he paused. 'And what about Leigh, has she turned up yet anywhere?'

Kes shook his head. 'Nah, bruv, I've had bigger fish to fry than looking for some bird. I told you she was trouble when you first met her, said she couldn't be trusted, and turns out I was right. Nobody has seen sight or sound of her. She's probably gone abroad or something because she's been under the radar now for years.'

Marco snapped, spit spraying from his mouth as he spoke. 'Has she fuck, she'll be hidden away somewhere under our noses. I want my fucking money back and she owes interest. She can pay me back in money – or blood.'

Kes was treading on eggshells. Marco had never told the boys that he had real feelings for Leigh, but they all knew he'd fallen for her hook, line and sinker. Monica didn't have a clue this bit on the side was different to all the others. If she did, she never let on about it. Monica always played the part of a good wife and, no matter what, she always stood by her husband. Kes had helped her out while Marco was doing his time and she'd never showed fear or gone cap in hand to any of the other families. A good catholic girl she was, believed in the vows of marriage she'd told him.

Marco opened his window slightly and sparked a fag up. 'Put the word out that I'm looking for Leigh. I know I said five, but up it – put a ten grand price on her head, that should stir up some interest. No one hides forever.'

Marco walked into the boozer with his new trim and a smile on his face. He was a gladiator returning home victorious. His crew all stood up, clapping, couldn't wait to hug the main man. Once he sat down, they started to put money on the table.

'Get some new clothes, get a new watch, get a new car.'

These men had cash about them, and this was a rule they all shared. If one of them got sent down, when they came home they were sorted out by their friends as soon as they were out. Marco had a fair few quid on the table and he nodded his head as he looked over at it. 'Respect to you all,' he said.

One thing for sure was that now that he was back in the game, he was going to sort them out, make them bigger than they had ever been. If any of them weren't pulling their weight, then they could piss off. He'd get some new blood in too and take this firm back to the top, back where they belonged.

Kes passed Marco a glass. 'Double brandy, mate, so take your time, you'll be a lightweight after all that time off the sauce.'

Marco chuckled and lifted the glass up to his mouth. He necked it in one and banged the glass on the table. 'Fill me up!' he laughed. The boys were set to have a good session. Marco Reece was a free man, and he was ready to get his head back in the game and show these muppets who he really was.

Monica Reece stood at the front door as Kes and a few of the other men helped Marco down the garden path. He was pissed as a fart and couldn't even stand up. Kes looked over at Monica and he could see she wasn't happy.

'Fancy letting him get in this state, seeing his boys before his bleeding wife? You should have brought him straight home like I told you.'

'I was going to, Monica, but he wanted to come and see the lads. You know what he's like, he never listens to me anyway.'

'One job you had of bringing him home, and you couldn't even do that properly. Our Trisha has been waiting all bloody day for her dad. Says a lot when he put you lot before his family, doesn't it?'

Kes didn't reply, just manhandled his boss inside and beat a hasty retreat.

Marco lay flat on his back snoring on the sofa. Monica turned the main light off and flicked the lamp on. He'd probably stumble upstairs in the small hours when he'd sobered up. She sat down opposite her husband and studied him. He was thinner than he'd been for years, lines on his face now deeper. She got up out of her seat and went over to the sofa, sitting on the edge of it.

'Marco, are you awake?' She picked his hand up and stroked it across her cheek. Her eyes closed slowly; life was going to be different now her husband was out. Trisha tiptoed in too and shot a look at her father laid out on the sofa. A pretty girl, dark-brown hair, big brown eyes that gave her an innocent look.

'What the hell, Mam. I thought all this was behind us now. He told us he was turning over a new leaf, not going back on the bevvies, was it all lies or what?' Trisha was a ringer of her dad, had his temper complete with its short fuse.

Monica moved back into her chair and sat back with her legs crossed. 'He just got caught up in it all – it's his first day out. You know what he's like when he's with Kes and the boys. I bet the first thing in the morning he's full of it, telling us both how sorry he is.'

'Well, I'm not listening to him.' Trisha frowned. 'I've had his lies all my life and I made a promise to myself that

I won't be doing it again. My dad's face all over the newspapers, it's not fair, it's embarrassing.'

Monica tried to calm her daughter. 'I know, love, give him a chance, aye. He's just got out of jail and he'll need a few days to find his feet. He worships the ground you walk on; you know that, don't you?'

'I do, but, like I said, I'm not listening to his lies anymore. I'm not being funny or anything, but since my dad has not been here, we've lived a nice, quiet life without any drama. Go on, tell me you've not enjoyed it?'

Monica shifted in her seat, her cheeks going bright red. Her voice was low and she checked her husband was still asleep before she spoke. 'We've both had a quiet time. But the reality is that he's back home now and we know what kind of world he lives in. Don't think I've not asked him to give it all up and walk away because I have. But he always tells me there's a big one coming in. And I can't pretend I don't know the game. My hands are tied with him, love.'

'Well, mine aren't. I'm going to tell him as soon as he sobers up. Selfish he is, Mam. We should have been spending quality time together, but he chose to go and get off his head instead. Because don't tell me he's not been sniffing too. Kes is always coked up to his eyeballs and I bet he would have been shoving it up Dad's nose too.'

Monica dropped her head low; knew her daughter had hit the nail right on the head. Before Marco had been sent down, he'd been getting too into the life, always drinking, taking drugs, prescription stuff alongside it all. She'd never have said it to her husband, but jail was the best outcome for him back then. She knew he wouldn't touch the shitty prison drugs; spice and other crap cut with all kinds of junk, including rat poison. No, jail got him clean, detoxed him, she'd seen that on her visits. But Monica knew there was something her husband was not telling her, something that lay heavy on his mind. She'd asked him too, asked if he wanted to speak to her about anything, telling him she would help him get sorted once he was out, but never once did he open up to her, tell her what was really going on. Their visits hadn't exactly been private so she was hoping he was going to be straight with her now. When he'd been sent down, things had been at their worst between them – she had been sure he had another woman, but hopefully all his problems had left him now. Five years was a long time to get over things, wasn't it? But something gripped her tight like a hand around her throat when she thought about it. Whatever she hoped for, her husband wasn't the kind to forgive and forget.

Chapter Seven

Marco peeled his eyes open slowly, the morning light blinding him. He looked about the bedroom as he rubbed his knuckles into the corner of his eyes. He was used to grey walls, hardly any sunlight in the room, shouting and screaming, banging on the walls. It felt strange to wake on a soft bed, the scent of clean linen. He rolled onto his side and he could see the back of his wife's head. He lifted his head up slowly. The hangover from hell was kicking in. He reached his hand over and stroked the side of his wife's face, remembering her warm touch.

'I've missed you so much, babes. Honest, every day it was just you and Trisha that kept me going, the thought of coming home to see you both.'

Monica was awake now, eyes wide open, clearly still annoyed at her husband. 'You didn't miss us enough to come home first though, did you?'

'Aw, don't start all that. You know how it is. The lads all wanted to see me, and we only had a few beers together.'

She was on one now. 'Are you having a laugh or what. You couldn't bleeding walk when you got brought home. It's funny, isn't it, hardly any of them came to see you when you were in jail and now that you're out they are all up your arse, like flies around shit. Like I said, they are not your friends, they just earn money from you.'

Marco sat up straight, already sick of complaints. 'My head is banging and I don't need you chewing my ears off the moment I've opened my eyes. I said I'm sorry, for fuck's sake give it a rest, will you? The lads gave me a right few quid last night so you can go shopping, get a new bag or something. Anything to straighten that mush of yours.'

'I don't need a bloody new bag, Marco, I need my husband, that's all. You said things would change when you got home and look what's happened the moment you're a free man. Trisha is not happy with you too. You will be getting a mouthful from her, trust me.'

'Monica, we have lived this life since we've known each other. I'm calming down, like I told you, but you can't expect me to play Happy Families all day when there is money to be earned out there. It's what I've always done, the only thing I've known.' Marco stretched.

'Surely, we have enough money now to walk away from this life and start again somewhere else where nobody knows us?'

His tone changed, became snappy. 'What, run away? You know failure is not in my make-up. When I want to walk away you will be the first person to know. I have a few scores to settle and then and only then will I give this lot up. You're forgetting I come from nothing. I didn't have a penny when I started out. I hustled my way through the ranks and started my own thing, remember. And you loved it – I was the best bookie around here, taking thousands of pounds from all these wankers who thought they knew the game better than me. They bet on the boxing matches I set up, dart games, chicken fights, anything that they thought they could earn a few quid on. Men with more money than sense.'

'That was then, and this is now, Marco. People are gambling online now.'

'And that's why I need to start it up again, get them all excited to spend some money again properly. Who cares about some poxy online game. I give people proper stakes, proper thrills. Give me a year, Monica, and we can leave here together with enough money to set us up for life. People owe me money and I'll be collecting that now I'm back out. People who have taken the piss out of me and not paid up, they are all going to get a knock.'

Monica knew she may as well have been talking to a brick wall. Marco was right though; when he was on his A-game, he was the best bookie Leeds had ever seen. All the gangsters placed bets with him, all wanted the excitement of winning a few quid, getting the invites to his exclusive nights. But he played a dangerous game, set things up, knew the outcome before they did. She'd seen what had happened to her own father when he tried his hand at fixing a few bets. She knew the kind of men that staked fortunes didn't take kindly to being had. Forget that nonsense about revenge being best served cold – these kinds of men served revenge hot, fast and deadly.

Chapter Eight

Danni sat down in the bar drinking her cup of coffee, steam rising from the top of it, trying to stop herself from daydreaming about picking up a dart again. She inhaled deeply and told herself to forget it. Steve walked in behind her and smiled.

'It's not a bad boozer this, is it? The takings were mint last night too, we made twice as much as we did in the last pub we were at.'

Danni nodded her head, still not sure what to make of coming back to her hometown. 'I'll go to the supermarket later and do us a big shop. There's a giant freezer in the kitchen that I've spotted so I will get some stock.'

'Yes, get some pies and that, stuff we can use for the punters for dinner times. I'm thinking we will smash it if we can offer some reliable pub grub too. Doesn't have to be fancy – just hot and sticks in your ribs.'

Danni pulled her shoulders back. 'And who do you think will be cooking it? I hope you're not looking at me to do it?'

'Come on, Danni. We have to work as a team here. I'm doing everything else; we're talking a few pies and chips here, not a bloody roast dinner. Surely you can do that, can't you? It's money for us both, not just me.'

'I'll help out, but I'm not turning into a full-time chef, Steve. This pub was for you, not for me. Anyway, I've just said I will help out, wind your neck in, will you? Ask that Alice from the darts team if she fancies any extra hours; she does the cleaning so she may as well do some cooking too.'

He shook his head, wanted to say something but stopped at the last minute. He knew there was no way he wanted to deal with one of her strops so early in the morning. 'Just get some stuff from shopping.'

Steve walked away from her and she sat alone again, sipping on her coffee. Danni saw a movement out of the corner of her eye and looked out of the window but couldn't see anyone. Maybe she would go and see if she could find her old school mates or neighbours today, see if they remembered her. Danni sat running her finger over a broken nail, she felt bad now and wanted to make amends with Steve. The man only had her best interests at heart and she was always having a pop at him for no real reason. And, as she looked at it now, he'd only asked for some help. It wasn't that deep, was it?

Danni picked her mug up and walked behind the bar towards Steve. She hugged his large body from behind him. 'I'll do the cooking, so put your dummy back in.' The argument was over, and she was glad Steve held no grudges against her. He pulled her in front of him and planted a big, fat soppy kiss on the side of her face. 'Love you.'

She smiled back at him and made a love heart with her fingers. 'Love you more,' she whispered as she went upstairs to get ready.

She took one last glance out the window – she couldn't shake the feeling of being watched – but she knew she had to ditch this paranoia if she was going to make this life work.

Chapter Nine

It was just after noon and there were a few regulars in the pub already sat around the bar. Steve recognised most of the types: fellas who were unemployed and not looking for anything else, guys who wanted to get away from the Mrs to avoid having their ears chewed off about all the jobs they had not done in the house, and other blokes just looking for a few scoops with the lads.

Jamo was there as usual, too. He looked like he'd just got up out of the feather; ruffled hair, stains on his clothes, unshaven. He was already on his second pint, and he was full of positive vibes today. Steve bet he must have got his Universal Credit payment. He knew he was right when he clocked Jamo had the newspaper open and was studying the racing page.

'Get a tenner on that one there, Steve. I've been following the nag for weeks and it's due a win. It's dead cert.'

Steve was sceptical. Jamo looked like he couldn't pick his nose never mind a winning horse. He brushed him off.

'Nah, Jamo, it's a bleeding donkey. Here's your winner right here; Maggie's Delight. I watched her last race and she got beat by a nose. That's my winner for today, I'll put a few quid on it.'

Jamo picked up his pint and swigged a large mouthful. Steve could piss off if he didn't want his advice. He'd won big had Jamo, thousands of pounds on Yankees and round robins. But saying that, he'd lost a lot too. He knew the bookies were always the winners, it was just a shame it took him so long to work that out.

The cold air from outside rushed in and Jamo shivered. Then his eyes widened as two men walked past him. 'Alright, lads,' he stuttered.

The men just nodded their heads, no words spoken. Steve still had his head down in the newspaper. A flat palm banged on the bar in front of him. 'Two bottles of Bud, mate.'

Steve lifted his head up and eyeballed the two men. 'Please usually follows when you ask for something, lads. Manners cost nothing, do they, gents?'

Jamo was agitated, glaring at Steve then looking back down at the floor. But Steve pressed on. He'd been around long enough to know these two looked like people you would never mess with. He also knew that you didn't just roll over the first time you met them.

'Say that again?' the elder of the two men asked Steve.

'You calling us rude?' chimed in the other.

'Yeah, say that a-fucking-gain, mate,' the first one finished through gritted teeth, leaning over the bar, inches from Steve's face.

Jamo jumped in before this got heated. 'Yo, lads, turn it in, will you? Steve here has just become the new landlord, he doesn't know the script yet. Steve, meet Ben and Bert Royal. Everyone knows them round here, you just haven't had chance to get introduced.'

Ben, the elder of the two brothers, was fuming. 'I don't give a fuck if he's new or not. Who the fuck does he think he's speaking to? I'll snap the prick's jaw if he speaks to me like that again.'

Steve wasn't sure how to handle this and judging by Jamo's facial expressions he needed to think on his feet and diffuse this situation. Steve stretched his hand over the bar towards Ben. 'The name's Steve. Like Jamo said, I'm the new landlord.'

Ben looked at the hand and turned to his brother. 'Bert, I'm going for a piss. Word this prick up, will you, for when I come back. I can't be arsed with dealing with dickheads today.'

Bert watched his brother leave the room and eyeballed Steve. 'Here's how it is, Stevey. I don't give a flying fuck if you are new here or not, don't ever come at any of us with your bullshit.'

Steve was just about to reply when Jamo jumped up from his seat and came to Bert's side and patted the top of his shoulder. 'Come on, pal, no need for this. Like I just said, the guy's new to these ends. Give me five minutes with him to tell him the score and then I'm sure everything will be sorted. Steve, pass them two bottles of beer over, will you?'

Steve reached down and grabbed two bottles of Budweiser, not sure if they were peace offerings or weapons. He was no stranger to a few fights. He wasn't proud of the fact but he'd been a football hooligan in his younger days. Leeds fans were well known for the beef they had with the away teams and Steve had often been right at the front kicking and punching whoever got in his way. He wished he'd had warning, could have rung a few of his old pals for these clowns, showed them how the real men fought. Or he could ring the heavy mob from his working days, yes, no fucking about from them, they would down them and never blink an eyelid. Steve placed the two bottles on the bar, just about to tell this arsehole how much he owed him, when Bert picked them up and walked away without saying a word.

Jamo jumped in and stopped Steve from saying anything more, his voice was low, his face blood red. 'Mate, I would keep it quiet if I were you. I was telling your Mrs about these two the other day and, trust me, you don't want to get on the wrong side of them. Old John had an agreement with them, and might I suggest you get something in place too quick-smart because, trust me, you don't want to mess with any of them. Crazy they are, nutters.'

Steve was livid. 'I don't need to speak with anyone, fucking rude, jumped-up kids they are. Respect costs nothing, Jamo.'

'It'll cost you everything if you push this one, mate. Trust me on this one, take it on the chin and let sleeping dogs lie.'

Steve stared over at Bert who had sat in the corner of the pub and was now joined by his brother.

'So go on, fill me in, who the hell are they? Pair of clowns! Ben and Bert – they sound like something off a kids' TV show.'

Jamo was clearly not happy to be having this conversation in the boozer while the two brothers were still watching. Jamo walked back to the end of the bar and sat on his stool, his eyes flicking around. 'Ben and Bert run shit around these parts, they are usually team-handed and there are a few more of them who come in here with them. Ben is the one to watch, if you ask me. He will stab you up given half the chance. Bert is a muppet, but he's backed by his brother so it's a no-win situation, you fight one you fight them both, and their crew.'

Steve looked over to the corner of the room. He could see Bert passing another drinker a small bag of something. Money changed hands and the customer walked away from them. 'Come on, this is taking the piss,' he spluttered to Jamo. 'They're fucking dealing in my pub and they're not even hiding what they're doing.'

He stormed from behind the bar and marched straight up to the Royals like a man on a mission. He stood in front of them. Too angry to think or feel any fear. 'Lads, I'll be straight with you. I don't know what arrangement you had with John, but I won't allow drug-dealing in my boozer so take your business elsewhere because, like I said, it's not going down in here.'

Ben lifted his head up slowly and stood up. He sucked hard on his gums and went nose to nose with Steve once more. 'Who the fuck do you think you are talking to, bro. I'll tell you once to fuck off back behind that bar and mind your fucking business. If you're still stood here chatting shit in ten seconds, I'll show you how things work around here. Fucking do-gooder.'

Jamo cringed and dropped his head into his hands as he watched from a distance.

Steve backed off a couple of feet and made sure he wasn't a sitting duck for these two. 'I said this is my pub and my rules, not yours.'

But Ben was fast, Steve didn't stand a chance. One headbutt and he was dropped in seconds and Ben was stood over him. 'Prick, like I said, you don't tell me anything.'

Steve was trying to get back up from the floor, but Bert was there now, and he knew when he was beaten. Bert dragged Steve up by the throat so Ben could look deep in his eyes. 'I'll be back in tonight, and I want three ton. I want that every fucking week too. John should have told you about us. It's a shame you will need to find out the hard way, isn't it?' Ben picked his bottle up from the table and launched it at the wall, shards of glass spraying around the boozer. Like it was a routine, Bert flipped the table in front of him and threw a bar stool across the pub before he followed his brother. Bert turned to Jamo as they left, his eyes bulging as they spoke to him. 'Make sure that dickhead knows the score for when I come back.'

Jamo swallowed hard. He wanted no part of this. His words were stuck in his mouth. 'I'll sort it, don't worry, I'll tell him.'

Steve stood up, rubbing his head and looked about the pub. Why did nobody jump in and help him, did they not all see what had just happened? He moved over to the table and put it the right way up. Then he went back behind the bar and pulled his mobile phone out of his pocket. 'Let's see what happens when they are arrested. Won't be laughing then, will they?'

Jamo almost choked. 'Steve, put the bleeding phone away, will you? Snitches get stitches around these parts, mate, and trust me if you ring the dibble those two fucking pricks will send their worst guys through your door and you can kiss goodbye to this place. Listen, Steve, park your arse down there for a few minutes. I think I need to spell this out to you.'

Steve rubbed at his neck, sore where Bert had half-strangled him. 'Come on then, tell me the crack because the way I feel at this second I want to run after them with my baseball bat and knock ten tons of shit out of them.'

Jamo stood up and found a table where they could both sit down, still shaking. He waited for Steve to be seated and he rubbed his hands over his greasy hair. 'Mate, as hard as it is, these things happen around here. The rich get richer, and the poor get poorer, it's always worked like that. The old bill don't give a fuck about anyone in the middle. They just protect the posh twats and the top and try to round up the lowest of the low. They never come out for anything round here if they can help it – not burglaries, domestics, nicked cars. They steer clear. So that leaves a nice little space for toe-rags like the Royals to step in and run these ends. Their word is the fucking law round here. So just pay up and you'll have an easy life. So what, they are dealing in here but come on, it happens everywhere.

You scratch their backs, and they will scratch yours, simple. Winner winner, chicken dinner or so they say.'

Steve was still raging. 'So I pay them three hundred pounds a week for what?'

Jamo was getting frustrated. 'Duh… to protect you, to make sure your windows don't go in every night, because let me tell you something for nothing, if you don't cough up then them fuckers will plug your windows every night and that's not the half of it, they'll blow your car up, smash the place up. On my life, just cough up and you'll be sweet.'

Steve's eyes were wide open, his head shaking. 'They're getting fuck all from me. Do you think I will be held to ransom by those two muppets? It's not even pissing protection money if I'm only paying them to protect me from themselves. I'm not getting a name for being a pushover when I've barely been here a week. Those two cheeky bastards have met their match.'

Jamo tapped his fingers on the table nervously. 'It's not just those two, is it? We're talking twenty or even thirty of them if you count all the kids working for them who are desperate to shank someone and make a name for themselves. And you haven't even met the Farrows yet, have you?'

Steve puffed out his cheeks. 'Go on, tell me who they are then…'

Jamo continued. 'The Farrows and the Royals are at war. If you think Ben and Bert are bad, then you should meet Si and Tim, they make these two look like fucking kittens. Honest, mate, you don't want to piss them off if they come calling. It's up to you who you work with but you'd better pick a side. If you're determined not to pay your taxes to the Royals, then I'd word the Farrows up and go under their wing. Once Ben knows they are looking after you he might back the fuck off but then again, might decide your pub is the perfect fucking battleground. All's fair in love and war, isn't it?'

Steve could see this wasn't going to be as easy as he first thought. Manchester maybe wasn't the dream move he'd anticipated. It felt like there were gangsters living on every corner, people willing to stab you up for a quick earner. 'Jamo, you need to sort this out for me. I just thought I would scare them off, I didn't expect them to react the way they did. Danni will lose her shit if she knows what went on today, so do me a favour and keep this between us. So, who do I go with, the Farrows or the Royals?'

Jamo scratched his chin. 'Just pay the Royals until the Farrows get wind that they are running this gaff. Then just let them two sort it out. Obviously, you have bad blood with the Royals now so maybe Si and Tim are your best bet. If they come in here, I'll give you the heads up so you can have a quick word with them.'

Steve sighed. 'Thanks, pal, I appreciate it. I'll get you a pint, on the house of course.'

Jamo stood up and walked back to the bar and sat back on his stool. A free pint was a result, but it was going to take more than a pint to keep the Royals happy.

Chapter Ten

Danni walked around Harpurhey market and hummed to the music thumping out from one of the stalls, old tunes, the ones that got her toes tapping. The sun was out and everybody seemed in good spirits. Maybe she'd been too negative about Manchester. This place seemed nice, community spirit, customers chatting, stall owners all with something to say. It looked like the kind of market Danni remembered from childhood, the ones where all she wanted was ten pence to get some sweets in a pink and white stripy bag. It seemed like they sold everything. In between the stalls selling all the usual vapes and phone cases were the old fashioned stuff too, the stuff you actually wanted: cakes, pies, meat, clothes, shoes and handbags, tools.

Danni stood at a bedding stall and she could hear a commotion at the side of her. A market trader had a young lad in the death grip. 'You thieving twat, how many times do you need telling to keep away from my stall. I'll ring the police on you if you ever come back here again.'

The lad must have only been thirteen years of age but the mouth on him was terrible. 'Get the fuck off me. Go on, let go of me otherwise our kid and his boys will be here in no time and watch then when they snap your fucking jaw.'

The stall holder looked like he knew this was a fight he would never win. The lad was right, his family would likely be here in minutes if he so much as laid a finger on this kid. The man kicked the lad up the arse and flung him away from his stall, fuming. 'Go on, piss off and don't come back. Scum you are, nicking from your own. I'm here every morning at five o'clock to try and earn some money and I'm not having the likes of you trying to take the bit of money I earn. Tell your dad to get a bloody job and look after you like normal parents do.'

The youth ran off but not without shouting abuse behind him. Danni felt bad for the owner, buying some sheets she didn't need just to help him out. The man told her they were Egyptian cotton and he'd got them on the cheap, but she wasn't buying his story. Danni walked away from the stall and headed to the Asda only a few minutes away. It had been years since she'd last stepped into this area and although the years had passed, it still felt familiar to her. Danni filled her trolley, then stopped at her favourite place in the store, stood looking at the latest books that had been released. She liked reading, it kept her calm, took her to places that were a million miles away from her own problems. When she'd been too scared to face the world, she'd read for hours on end, wondering why her life hadn't turned out like one of the novels she read. Danni liked romantic stories, didn't want blood and guts on every page. She liked a happy ending and after finishing a novel it always made her feel warm inside. Of course she knew that in real life a happy ending was never going to happen, at least not for her, but still she smiled when love conquered all. Danni picked up a book now and was reading the back cover when a woman came and stood near her. Danni kept her eyes forward, but she could still see her from the corner of her eyes that the woman was shoving all sorts into her coat pocket. Bleeding hell, what was wrong with people around here, were they all up to no good or what? Danni picked another book and placed them in her shopping trolley and was about to walk away when the woman turned and stood in front of her.

'Danni? Danni Cox, is that you?'

Danni froze, her heartbeat doubled. She stared at the woman and tried to place her, she did look familiar. Danni was sure it must have been one of her friends' mums and was about to make her apologies and walk away when the woman spoke again.

'Oh my god, it's you, isn't it, Danni? Don't you remember me, it's Josie Taylor. I used to hang with you when we were at school.'

Danni looked closer at the woman and although she looked a lot older than her years, she was indeed her best friend from school. Danni burst into smiles and went in for a hug. 'Wow, I've not seen you for years, how are you? What are you up too these days?'

Josie looked a bit embarrassed and patted at her pocket. 'I'm still the same old, me, still earning money the only way I know how. Remember when I used to rob us a Twix to share from the corner shop? I've upgraded since then. But what happened to you anyway? One minute you were here and the next you were gone. A few of the kids said your dad come and took you to live with him but another kid said you got taken into care.'

Danni could feel long-supressed emotions rising. Was she really going to tell Josie Taylor her life story while they were stood in Asda? No, this needed to be a proper conversation when they were somewhere quiet. Danni swerved the question. 'You know what life is like, full of fucking surprises.'

Josie didn't seem to notice her old friend being evasive. 'I'll tell you what, if you're free in about ten minutes let's have a real catch-up – there's a little cafe just outside here. We can get a cuppa if you want to?'

Danni was on the spot, torn between wanting to keep that early chapter of her life closed and, at the same time, desperate to talk to someone who knew her back then. She remembered what Frenchie had said about knowing Josie. Perhaps it was only a matter of time before they'd found each other again. What harm could a chinwag do?

'Yeah, I'm only grabbing a few bits from here and then I'll meet you.'

Josie grinned and started to walk away. 'Mint! I'll just finish my shopping too, see you out there in a few minutes. Mine's a cappucino if you get in there first, Dazz.' She winked at Danni and headed down another aisle.

Danni stood frozen for a few seconds; her head had gone west. Josie would be asking questions about where she'd been all the years, she needed to think on her feet and get her story right before she sat down with her old friend.

Not quarter of an hour later, Danni carried her shopping out of the supermarket and looked around her, trying to find the cafe Josie had suggested. Bingo, it was just a few minutes away from her. She made her way inside. Josie was there already, sat in the corner with a gang of women around her. As she got closer, Danni could see Josie was handing them stuff from her bag. 'Cheap as chips them, my lovely. I'm here all the time. So, if you need anything, I'm your woman.'

Danni edged closer but held back until the women had all left. Josie, it seemed, was like a one-woman department store, selling all her knock-off stuff here in broad daylight. Josie rammed the money into her back pocket and clocked Danni. 'Dazz! Come and sit down, my old mucker, I've saved us a table. It's so good to see you again.'

Danni walked to the counter with her friend at her heels. 'Two coffees, Zena. Cappuccinos, and make sure mine has loads of that frothy stuff on the top and plenty of that chocolate powder you shove on. The last one you done was as flat as my chest,' she chuckled. One thing had not changed for sure, Danni realised, Josie was still a gobshite. She turned back to Danni. 'You drink coffee, right?'

Danni nodded her head and sat down at the table Josie had saved. Josie pulled her thick parka off and draped it on the back of her chair before she flopped down on her seat. 'I've had a nightmare day, let me tell you. The security guard in Farm Foods is all over me and he followed me all around the store. I had to tell him to piss off in the end. I had orders from there too. I've lost out on about thirty quid today because of that wanker.'

Danni couldn't help but smile as she sat facing her. Josie never wasted a second when she could be talking, she wanted to know the ins and outs of a cat's arsehole. 'So, talk to me then, where have you been hiding all these years?'

Danni panicked. May as well bite the bullet. That was the good thing about having had an eventful life, she figured. There was plenty to tell and still keep back the worst bits. 'What you heard was right, Josie. I was taken into care after I ran away one too many times.'

Josie's face dropped and she held a concerned look. 'Fuck off, are you joking with me?'

'No, straight up. Once the police went to my mam's house, they realised that she couldn't look after me.'

'My mam would have let you move in our house with us. I wish I would have known. Fucking hell getting slammed in care is no joke.'

'I think it was for the best if I'm being honest. I know I never said much about it, but I bet you saw what was going on. My mam was bad on the beer and whatever else she was on, and I was the last thing on her mind. Don't get me wrong, it was hard at first, but you get used to it, don't you? Sometimes it's easier to have no one than to keep being let down by the person that's meant to protect you.'

'Nah, you never get used to being neglected, Dazz. Did your mam not even come and see you, fight to get you back?'

Danni's eyes clouded over and hearing somebody asking her outright filled her whole body with sadness. She'd asked herself the same question over the years, and she could never understand why her mam had never tried to bring her back home. 'No, no Christmas presents, no birthday cards, it was like I never existed to her.'

Josie's eyes pooled with tears. 'That's so wrong. I wish I would have known because I would have spit in her eye when I seen her. She's a disgrace. I hope you have fucked her off out of your life?'

'Not deliberately, but I suppose I have. I don't even know where she is. I've not been around here for years, is she even still living around here?'

Josie reached over and stroked the top of Danni's hand. 'I've seen her a few times over the years – mostly in the pubs. I'm not going to lie to you, she's still a pisshead, always steaming drunk. But I think she's still in the house you lived in all those years ago.'

Danni swallowed hard, trying to digest what her friend had just told her. Anger fought with sadness. 'I don't even know what to say to you. I've always thought that she moved away with a man and sorted her head out, but to hear she's still boozing knocks me sick in the pit of my stomach. I used to send cards sometimes, you know at Christmas or Mother's Day – I never heard a word back.'

'She's not a mother, Danni, because mothers never give up on their kids, no matter what. I've got four of the little bastards and even though I tell them every day I'm going to sling them into care I never would. My kids are my life; you have good times and hard times with them, it's not all plain sailing, is it? What about you, do you have any kids?'

Danni shook her head. 'No, I can barely look after myself, never mind a kid.'

The women started laughing and Danni started to remember old times. Josie might have looked like life had been hard on her, but she was still the same inside – Danni felt the warmth of being around someone who didn't judge. 'My other half is running The Fox pub in down the road now, we've only just taken it on – you need to come in for a few drinks with me.'

Josie rubbed her hands together. 'The Fox? Nice one. I've done some decent business in that place. You don't mind if come and flog a few things, do you? Everyone loves a bargain around here, let me tell you.' Josie checked her watch, not giving Danni time to answer. 'I'll finish this brew then I better shoot. My boyfriend has got the kids and he'll be itching to go out with the lads for a few beers. You know what men are like, always bloody moaning. Are you married and that? I was going to marry my Sef but I would lose too much of my Universal Credit if I declared he had moved in with me. So, I just tell everyone I live on my own.'

Danni was about to speak but, just like old times, Josie was a right gasbag and barely let her get a word in edgeways. 'I've had a mare with guys if I'm being honest. All my kids have different dads and not one of them is worth a toss. They don't give me a penny towards bringing the kids up too. Sef isn't that bad, though, he just likes a few beers and a spliff every now and then. He's not like the others who manhandled me, lied to me, cheated – I've had them all.'

When Marco had slapped her about, Danni had had no one to tell. She'd not even left the flat until the bruises faded. How many other women lived like this in silence, she wondered. 'Bloody hell, Josie, you have been through the mill, haven't you?'

Josie sipped on her coffee. 'It messed with my head that did. I always thought it was my own fault that I got a slap but now I'm older I realise it was them with the problem, not me. I swear down, I was always at the hossy with fractured ribs and cuts and bruises. A full week I stayed in for, once. I nearly got the kids taken from me too once social services got involved. They were on Child Protection for over a year, and I had to bend over backwards for them to get them off my back. Prove I'd cut contact with their lowlife dad.'

Danni decided she could tell Josie a version of the truth. 'I'm with you there, Jose. There was one guy, I thought he was the one, but he turned on me and thought he could slap me about too.'

Josie shook her head slowly.

'I met Steve not long after the split and all I can say he helped fix me. He says it was fate that we met, because no sooner had I left my ex and Steve appeared from nowhere. Spooky, really.'

Josie took the last slurp of her coffee and looked out of the window. 'Honest to god, it's made my day seeing you again. I tell you I could have done with you around a few months ago when my mam died. It sent me to my knees you know, heartbroken. She suffered at the end you know, lost loads of weight, never awake much.'

Danni could see how much it hurt her friend to talk about it. 'It must have been hard seeing her like that, Josie. At least she is at peace now and out of any pain.'

'I know. I tell myself that all the time, but it still doesn't stop the hurt you feel in your heart, does it? You only ever get one mother, don't you?' There was a silence for a few seconds and Josie wiped her tears on the side of her red jumper. 'Bloody hell. Sorry, Dazz, that's insensitive of me when your mam is a piece of work.'

Danni necked the last mouthful of her coffee. 'Like I said, I had to say my own farewells to my mam years ago. Now you've said she's still round here it's making me think I should go and see her. I just think I might need to build up to it. But, Josie, whatever happens, let's not lose touch again. Call in and see me at the pub when you have the time. It's been great catching up with you. I wish I would have kept in touch with you, even wrote to you both.'

'Pointless that, love. I can barely bleeding read. I told myself that when the kids have grown up, I will go to college and really do something with my life, you know get a proper job so I don't have to go on the rob all the time. I've done OK with it, but I know it's only a matter of time before my luck runs out.'

Danni wanted to help her. 'We might have a few shifts going behind the bar if you fancy it. I'm not sure how many hours yet until I speak to Steve, but I can definitely keep you in mind.'

Josie burst out laughing and stood up, putting her coat on. 'Nah, babes. I earn too much doing what I'm doing to go back to potwashing and pints. Plus, Sef would shit a brick if I was working behind a bar. I know for a fact it would only be a matter of time before he accused me of shagging somebody.'

Danni stood up too now. 'Anyway, it's there if you have a change of mind. But still, drop in and come see me. Maybe you could even join the darts team on a Monday night, you used to be good, didn't you, when you used to come round mine to play?'

Josie tilted her head to the side, remembering the endless games she'd played with Danni in her bedroom. 'I did, didn't I? And if I launch a slipper over at the kids when they are pissing about, I always hit me target,' she giggled.

Danni was laughing her head off as they both walked out of the cafe together. It had been so nice catching up with Josie and reminiscing about the good old days. She'd never spoken to anybody like this in years and it reminded her about her roots. Her mam and then being in care had robbed her of her past and today had shown her maybe it was OK to remember things. Danni gave Josie a hug and they kissed each other on the side of the cheek as they parted ways. Josie shouted back at her before she disappeared, 'I'll come and see you soon.'

Danni stood alone for a few seconds, absorbing everything that they had spoken about. Her mother was still alive and living in the same house. This city was home – whether she liked it or not. You could take the girl out of Manchester, she thought, but you can't take Manchester out of the girl.

Chapter Eleven

Danni sat watching Steve behind the bar. He'd been quiet when she got home and packed the shopping away. And now he still didn't look himself tonight, he seemed mithered. She walked over to him and placed some empty glasses on the bar. 'Are you alright, babes, you seem distracted?'

Steve carried on loading glasses into the dishwasher. 'Nothing I can't handle, Danni. When it's quieter I'll fill you in on what's happened.'

Danni couldn't let this lie. There was no way she was waiting to hear what had upset his apple cart; she needed to know now, not later. 'Leave them glasses and come over to the end of the bar and tell me what's going on. You know I hate it when you don't tell me something straight away, my head goes into overdrive.'

Steve checked around the boozer, the afternoon crowd were drinking up and the evening lot hadn't yet arrived in full force and he knew he could take five minutes to speak to her. He slammed the door shut on the dishwasher and sighed as he walked to the end of the bar.

Danni was already there waiting for him, and she urged him to start talking. 'Oh my god, is it Marco, has he found me? Please tell me I'm not right!' She was panicking now, her mind exploding with the thought of it, jumping to the worst-case scenario.

Steve calmed her down, pulled her closer. 'No, bloody hell, the geezer is banged up – he can't get you. Just calm down, I can't get a word in edgeways with you when you're like this.' Steve dipped his head slightly and carried on. 'It's all been going on while you were out shopping today. Two clowns came in here thinking they can dome me, talking to me like a piece of shit.'

'Who, who's been here?'

Steve double-checked nobody could hear them again and started filling her in on today's events. 'Two fucking head-the-balls, name of Ben and Bert Royal. You should have heard the way they spoke to me. The prick launched a bottle behind the bar and flipped a few tables.'

Danni was hanging on his every word now. 'Steve, did they hurt you? What did they say, what are they kicking off for?'

'They said they want three hundred pounds a week from us. Protection money, I think. They said John used to pay them before he left and now it's our turn. Jamo was here with me and, I'll give him his due, he saved my neck because if he hadn't spoken to them to calm them down a bit, they would have gone to town on me and this place.'

Danni slammed a flat palm on the bar. 'Who the hell do they think they are? I hope you told them to piss off. Why would we ever pay for protection from anybody?'

'And that's what I said to Jamo. He said I should give some rival family, the Farrows, a backhander to sort them out, but that would be like jumping out of the frying pan into the fire, wouldn't it? They're both as bad as one another, or so I hear. Honest, Danni, that Ben had something about him that I didn't like one little bit. He's a bloody headcase. Jamo said they mean business too; they have a few boozers around here on their books, so fuck knows when they'll come back – but I know they won't leave it.' Steve pointed over to the corner of the pub. 'He was sat over there like he owned the bloody joint, dealing drugs right in front of my eyes, not a care in the world. I'll tell you something for nothing, Danni, no wonder John wanted gone from here. I bet he was living on pins all day and all night with this lot around here.'

Danni felt the colour drain from her face and she rubbed at her arms as a cold chill crept over her body. She was used to this life, thought she had left it behind a long time ago, but she still knew people got hurt if they didn't play ball. Marco had taught her a lot in the time she'd spent with him, taught her that people got badly hurt if they didn't pay their debts, it didn't take much for people to go missing. She closed her eyes for a few seconds. Marco stood over some man he'd just one-bombed for not paying up. She shook the image from her mind and spoke through clenched teeth. 'So, we stand tall and see what happens. If him and his brother can come in here again demanding money, tell them they can fuck right off, they're not getting a carrot from us.'

Steve wiped the beads of sweat that had formed on his forehead. 'I want to do that, Danni, but he's going to come back here team-handed and then what?'

'We can cross that bridge when we come to it. If he sees we are weak he will walk all over us. We need to stand our ground and tell him he's getting nothing from us without a fight.' Danni talked a good game.

Steve looked over at the other end of the bar and spotted a customer stood there waiting to get served. 'We'll talk later on. Tell nobody nothing, let's keep this to ourselves. I'm thinking to give the old crew a call, even the numbers out at least.'

'Just hang fire until we know more. We need to be tactical, only fools rush in.' Danni had just repeated what she'd heard Marco say to her over the years. He'd plan every attack carefully, taking his victim down when they least expected it. The element of surprise, he called it. Steve walked away from her, the worries of the world on his shoulders.

Upstairs, Danni closed every single door behind her, checking behind each one, finally standing against the bedroom door until she could convince herself no one else was up here with her. Slowly she moved to the edge of the bed and bent over, dragging an old suitcase out. She knew if she'd asked Steve what was the most valuable thing in this room he'd have said the bag with Marco's money in it. But this other case was far more important to her. With shaking hands, she clicked the silver lock and dragged it up onto the bed. It took a few seconds to open, rusty locks that kept jamming. She blew out a large breath to help calm her nerves. She opened the suitcase and looked inside. It had been years since she'd even let herself look, the pain too bad, her life, her memories all stored away here. Her long, slender fingers touched a photograph of her mother. This was one of the few things she took from her house before she was taken away. The social workers gave her an hour to grab anything that she needed, but there was barely anything worth taking. A few clothes, a couple of posters and pictures and her darts. That had been it, really. She held the photograph up closer to her and ran her finger across her mother's face. This snap was taken when her mother was well, when they were in Blackpool for the day. She remembered that day vividly, the sunshine, the beach, the fun fair, so much uncomplicated happiness. There were lots of other things in this case. Her hands rummaged through things from her past: a Take That poster, a keyring with Robbie Williams' photo on it. Danni smiled as she remembered her crush on the pop star. She was mad for him and even wrote him a few letters and sent them to his agent. Robbie would have saved her if he'd been around, she'd been sure. Danni sat on the bed; she felt like she was right back in her childhood bedroom. The noise from her mother shouting and fighting with her latest boyfriend always scared her. Some guy throttling her mother downstairs once. Then there had been that one time when she met a nice man, Wilf, and her mother sorted herself out for a while, stopped drinking, started to look after herself. Wilf was the one who had bought her her first set of darts too. But, as per usual, the relationship went tits-up and he didn't stick around for long. Julie had hit the bottle once again and she just fell into a deeper darker hole than ever before. Danni took on the mother role for months after that. She cooked and cleaned the house, made her mother get washed and changed, but Julie was too far gone to care; she only went out of the house to get more beer and fags. Danni could see now that she had been heartbroken and dealt with it the only way she knew how. Each night she sat downstairs and played love songs, crying and singing her head off as she got drunker and drunker. Danni used to dread her coming into her bedroom, slurring her words, sobbing. But then she'd switch, become angry and start slapping and punching her daughter in her bed. The wine always made her mum weepy, but beer made her aggressive. Danni folded the white piece of paper back up and wiped the single tear that had rolled down her cheek. She reached over and opened another small box, a much more recent addition to the suitcase.

A diamond ring stared back at her. She swallowed hard and picked the ring up. It was a promise ring Marco had told her, a ring that meant one day he would marry her, make her his wife. Bullshit it was, pure bullshit. It was just another one of his sweeteners to keep her quiet and make sure she was going nowhere anytime soon even though he was going back home to Monica. The diamond looked dull now, not like it used to look when it was new and on her finger. She placed the ring back carefully in the box and slammed it shut, the memory of the night he gave it to her flooding her mind. 'Bastard,' she mumbled under her breath.

Danni lifted up another compartment in the case and pulled something out wrapped in a yellow tea towel. Her breathing was fast and her hands were hot and sweaty as she loosened the fabric. Danni lifted the silver pistol up in her hands, fearful just to hold it. With caution she slid her two fingers along the cold metal barrel. She'd nicked this from Marco when he'd left it unattended. He'd had the house up looking for it, but he never found it. This wasn't just for her protection. It was protection from him. Danni held the gun out in front of her now with two hands, looking at her reflection in the mirror facing her. 'I'm ready, Marco, ready for anyone who thinks they can hurt me again.'

Then she heard noises outside, footsteps, coughing. She quickly wrapped the gun back up and flung it back into the suitcase with all her other belongings. Just as Steve walked into the bedroom, she'd secured the suitcase back under the bed. Steve looked down at her and raised his eyebrows high. 'What are you doing down there on the floor? Not counting Marco's money, are you?'

She stretched her hand under the bed and pretended she was looking for something. 'Nah, I've lost the back from my earring. I was sure it rolled under the bed.' She held the side of the bed to stand to her feet and flicked her hair back over her shoulder. She felt clammy. 'I must have lost it in the shower. Never mind, they were only cheap.'

Steve walked over to the wardrobe and pulled out a clean shirt. 'I've been sweating all day working that bar. I need to freshen up before we get busy. Are you coming downstairs tonight to give me a hand?'

Danni smiled over at him. 'Yeah, but just give me a bit to do my hair and put a bit of slap on.'

He was by her side now and he wrapped his arms around her. 'You don't need make-up, babes, you're gorgeous just the way you are.'

They shared a kiss and Steve looked deep into her eyes. 'I don't want you worrying about all this crap with the Royals either. I've shat bigger than those two muppets. As far as I'm concerned, it's game on. I spoke with my boy Roddy before and him and a few of the old lads are going to come down and see what the craic is.'

Danni hated being involved in this shit but knew they shouldn't face things alone. 'I just hope they can help. I'm not disrespecting Roddy and the boys, but this lot seem like they don't care who they hurt to get what they want. Rodders is older now, not how he was even five years ago. Things change, Steve, the stakes are a lot higher than what your lot have had to deal with. I've always said I don't want to know everything you did back then – I believe you when you say it's in the past, but from what you have said, it was scraps at the footie, robbing a few flash homes for fancy motors. Not fucking protection rackets and extortion.'

Steve gulped. 'Like you said, let's play it by ear. I'm going to see what the boys think when they get here. If it's not something they can help with then we'll have to come up with another plan, won't we?' He stood thinking for a few seconds and scratched at his head. 'Oh, Alice and Frenchie are downstairs, they've come in for a practice they said. Apparently Frenchie's mam has got the kids and she is young, free and single tonight. Well, that's what she said to me anyway.'

Danni chuckled to herself, it was strange having female friends again. It reminded her. 'You'll never guess what, love, I met an old friend today when I was out shopping. She said she will call in and see us.'

Steve smiled. 'See, how good is it that you have friends already. Maybe this will do you good instead of being hidden away every bloody night.' He turned and headed back downstairs.

Danni looked at the case where the gun was stashed. She hoped she never had to use it – against Marco or the Royals. But knowing it was there felt like insurance. She'd lived her whole life being overlooked. Now she realised that was her superpower. The next man to come for her? He would be the last to ever underestimate her.

Chapter Twelve

Danni watched Alice throwing her darts, frustrated. Her hand itched to pick up a dart. She sat forward in her seat and watched as a man came over to join them. Cocky, full of himself, exactly the kind of punter that would have made a great mark back in her hustling days.

'Here, give me a go and I'll show you how to play real darts.'

Alice snarled at him. 'We play real darts, love, we don't need your help. We're better than you anyway.'

The man laughed and shouted over at the other men who had just sat down at another table near them. 'Lads, have you heard her, she said she's better than me.'

A man shouted over at Alice and Frenchie. 'Put your money where your mouth is then, let's spice things up.'

Frenchie was game immediately, already digging deep in her purse for money. Her cage was rattled, and she was ready to prove a point. 'Go on, how much do you want to fork out on the bet, name your price. Because this will be the easiest money I've ever made.'

The man rubbed his two hands together and stood near Alice and Frenchie. He tried to dip his head into her purse to see how much she had. Frenchie shut her purse quickly and shot a look at him.

'Come on, pal, I've not got all day. Name your price.'

Danni looked down at her right hand and stared at her thumb. Maybe, just maybe, she could hold a dart again and put this tosser in his place. She went to stand up and then sat back down again. What the hell was she thinking? This was not her fight, but she hated men like him thinking they could intimidate a woman.

The man pulled a wad of cash from his back pocket and smiled over at Alice. He flipped three twenty pound notes off and banged them on the small wooden table at the side of them. 'Sixty quid.'

Frenchie gulped, she only had fifty pounds in her purse to last her all week. She'd just got paid and she'd not even been food shopping yet. Alice could see Frenchie was struggling and she walked over to her and whispered something into her ear. Frenchie smiled over at the man. 'Game on then.'

Alice fetched her handbag and went inside her purse for the money. The man took his coat off and rubbed his hands down the front of his jeans. 'So, which one of you am I playing?'

Frenchie stepped in front of Alice and made the decision for them both. 'Me.'

Danni felt alive, moved closer to the game.

'So, five hundred and one, the best of three games?' The man was all smiles.

Frenchie nodded her head and rolled her darts around in her fingers. The men were all heckling now and trying to put Frenchie off her game. Danni stood up and shouted over to them, couldn't hold her tongue any longer. 'Lads, no need for the noise or the insults, keep it shut and let them play the game.' It was the least she could do.

Frenchie smiled over at Danni, glad of the support. Frenchie was throwing first.

Danni sat side on to her, ready for the game to start. Alice came and sat next to her, and whispered, 'Bleeding hell, what have we done? We should have just pissed him off and got on with our own game.'

Danni reached over and patted her hand on Alice's lap. 'Let's see what happens.'

'I can't even look, tell me when it's over.'

The game started and Frenchie got a decent score with her first three darts. She punched her clenched fist into the air. 'Get in there, you beauty!'

The man stood facing the board now. Danni watched him with eager eyes. Everything about him told her he'd played darts before, his stance, his focus. Danni held her breath for a few seconds as she watched him throw. She was right, every dart a double or treble. Frenchie looked deflated as he smiled over at her.

'It's going to be like taking candy from a baby this is.'

And he was right. Frenchie's game went from bad to worse. The man threw his last dart and shouted out in a loud voice, 'Show me the money, girls.' His mates cheered along with him as he told them the drinks were on him.

Frenchie and Alice slumped down on the chair next to Danni. 'What a wanker, look at him, the big head. I'd love someone to come along and wipe that smile from his face.'

That was it. Almost without thinking, Danni jumped up and grabbed the darts from the table. 'Oi, double or quits?'

The man turned around and scowled at her. 'Sit back down, love. I don't want to take your money. Especially not when…' He nodded at her hand. 'You're a cripple, darling.'

It was like rocket fuel to Danni. 'I'm not bothered if you aren't. Let's up the stakes to one hundred pounds then?'

Whispering over at his table, the men were nodding their heads. The man went inside his back pocket again and replied to her, 'Make it two hundred pounds and you have a game.'

Danni was in the moment now; she didn't care how much this game was for, she just wanted to whip his arse and put him back in his place. 'Three hundred pounds if you want?' She wasn't backing down, no way, she was eager now.

The man banged three hundred pounds on the table and looked at her. 'Go on, put the money in and it's game on.'

Danni rushed behind the bar and quickly whispered something into Steve's ear. He went into the till and counted out three hundred pounds. By now, all the regulars had figured out this was a show not to be missed and all crowded into the back room to watch the match. The noise was rising, everyone laughing, shouting over to their friends.

Behind the bar, Steve rang the bell to get their attention. He looked proud rather than fearful. 'Quiet please. Any talking from anyone while a player is at the oche and they will have to leave.'

Danni held the darts in her hand, the cold metal barrel rolling along her fingers. She positioned the dart down her thumb and squeezed at it, securing it. Sure she'd thrown a few darts after hours, and if she was honest, even her at her worst was better than most people at their best. But she hadn't done this – the lights, the onlookers, the pressure – not for years.

Alice was the referee now and she would be the one adding the scores up. Not that Danni ever got her maths wrong. It might have been years since she played but she could do every sum between zero and five hundred and one in her sleep.

Alice smiled over at Danni and nodded. 'Come on, love, do this for the girls.'

The man was first to throw. 140. Not bad at all.

But Danni was in a trance now, eyes focused, her breathing steady now. She threw her first dart and it shot off to the left of the board. She could hear sniggers behind her. 'Come on, girl, sort your head out, you can do this,' she told herself. At least the next dart hit the board, but she knew she wasn't throwing like she used too. Rusty, not used to the new style she had to play because of her injury.

The man stood and threw his darts, but this time his score was average. It was the boost Danni needed to get back in the game. She'd been here before and knew she could bring it back. She'd always loved pretending to play the underdog when she was hustling, loved judging when to start really showing what she could do. Her stance changed and her face was serious. Boom! Three double tops. 120. Not enough to properly scare the bloke – but anyone who knew their stuff would know that was no luck.

The man had seen his arse for sure now and the laughter seemed to have disappeared from him. The rest of his friends seemed quieter now too. 'It's a fluke, she'll never get anywhere near that again. Come on, put this to bed and let's have a beer.'

The game went on and Danni grew in confidence with each dart. She remembered all her old tricks. She avoided anything flashy – no 180s or going anywhere near the bull. Instead she let herself outplay him just enough each time to make it still – just – seem like chance.

By the last dart, the whole room was silent. A one-twenty checkout to win. Frenchie was as white as a ghost, the colour drained from her. Danni looked over at her before she threw her last dart and winked. Her eyes never moved, she never even blinked as she threw her last dart at the thin strip below the twenty. Everything seemed to move in slow motion, everybody was out of their seats trying to get a better look. Danni never had to do the maths, she always knew what she needed. But she also knew that anything fancy here would draw too much attention. Double, double, double would look cocky. Instead she threw a triple twenty and a single with her first two darts. Leaving just double top to win. She took aim.

As everyone heard the soft thud of the dart's tip bedding into the board, Alice jumped up in the air and grabbed Frenchie. 'She's done it, she's only gone and done it!'

Double top. No one else needed to know that Danni could have hit it with her eyes shut.

The man snarled and flung his darts onto the floor. Alice and Frenchie ran over to Danni and hugged her. 'Bloody hell, you were amazing, how on earth have you learned to play like that? You need to show us.'

Frenchie grabbed the money from the table and let out a laugh to the man before she spoke to him. 'Who's laughing now, smart arse?' She gripped the notes in her hand and went straight back to Danni. 'There you go, babes, well deserved.'

Danni peeled three twenty-pound notes off the money and passed it back to Alice. She shouted out so the man could hear her. 'The drinks are on me, girls.'

Frenchie and Alice started dancing around towards the bar and Alice rammed her two fingers up towards the men.

But Danni was shell-shocked now, reality kicking back in. Her breath wouldn't come easy and she dashed outside for some fresh air.

Danni sucked in mouthfuls of the cool night air and walked one way then the other. 'Breathe, girl, bloody breathe,' she muttered. Her mouth was dry, and her body was hot and clammy.

Alice was outside too now, and she rushed towards Danni. 'Are you OK, lovely? Come on, just breathe and take your time, there is no rush.'

'I'm fine, Alice, just a bit overwhelmed. I've not played for a long time and, to tell you the truth, I wasn't even sure if I could anymore.'

'You were amazing, you shut that dickhead right up, for sure.'

Danni was starting to relax, her heartbeat slowing down. 'I just couldn't stand that prick winning. I've met his type, many times before, a long time ago.'

'Yes, me too. I'm not a violent person, but I wanted to punch his lights out the smarmy bastard.'

Danni was back to normal now. It was just one match, she told herself. It was over with. The chance of anyone in that room getting word back to Leeds was tiny. Wasn't it?

'Come on, let's get back inside. I'm freezing my tits off outside here.' Alice shivered.

They both started laughing and went back inside. Danni went straight behind the bar and poured herself a vodka and coke. She wasn't a big drinker, but she needed something to take the edge off. Steve hugged her before he kissed the side of her neck. 'You were fantastic tonight, babes. I've never seen you look as happy as that. It's your gift and you shouldn't hide it away. Let the world see what you have.'

Danni blushed; she'd told him about her hustling days but this was the first time Steve had ever seen her play darts properly. But he was right though, the feeling of holding the darts back in her hand and playing made her feel good inside, alive.

'Forget about coaching – you need to join the darts team, help the girls win the league,' Steve said.

'One day at a time, Steve, one day at a time.'

The cat was out of the bag now and Danni knew she could never not play again. But she knew each dart she threw brought her one shot closer to Marco.

Chapter Thirteen

Marco sat down with his boys and riffled through his small leather notebook. It had lots of names inside it, ticks and crosses next to most of them. Some of these debts were years old, but he still wanted his money back. He needed capital to put more nights on. There was a big boxing match on tonight that he'd set up, and already his boys were out taking bets from anyone and everyone. But it cost money to make money, and Marco wanted every pound owed back in his pocket.

He sat rolling a silver pen around in his fingers. 'Any sign of Leigh?'

Kes shot a look at the others sat in the room and raised his highbrows high. 'Not yet, but the word's out and if she's anywhere nearby it won't be long before she's found. With a large price on her head someone will be eager to cash in.'

'They better make it soon. That slut owes me money and I want every penny paying back.'

Kes could see his temper was rising and came behind him and patted his shoulder. 'All comes to those who wait pal. Just put her on the backburner for now and let's get some new cash earned. There are some big bets on this fight tonight and if it goes to plan, we will be quids in. I've already spoken to the Farrow brothers from Manchester and their boy is going down in the fifth round just like we planned.'

Marco smashed his clenched fist into the desk. 'I want my fucking empire back, not just being a fucking bookie. I want it all back, I want to be the man people fear again. I'm not sure about these Manchester boys getting involved in the scene up here. Do you trust these Farrow fellas?'

Kes tried to keep the peace. 'They're sound. It doesn't hurt you to borrow a bit of clout from other cities. You can't just expect to walk back into this world and be on top of your game again. We've kept hold of most of what you had but times have changed and there are a few up and coming men who are fucking ruthless. I met the Farrow brothers when I was in Manchester a few months ago and we've been working with them for time now. I've got the Jones clan in Bolton too and few more heads here and there. It's all about manpower, who will back us if the shit hits the fan.'

Marco jumped up from his large black leather chair. 'I'm fucking ruthless. I'm the one they should be scared of. I need to make an example of someone, get them all talking.'

He plonked back down in his chair. 'Get Jerry and make an example out of him. That little shit owes me five grand from the bet he's never paid for. If he doesn't pay up in twenty-four hours, cut a finger off, or a hand, let everybody know that it was me who was responsible for it.'

Kes swallowed hard and looked at the other men in the room. He nodded his head over at them. 'You heard the man. Go call in every loan and bet, and anyone – not just Jerry – who doesn't cough up, cut the fucker's hand off.' Kes eyeballed each and every one of them until they moved.

The men stood up and left the room. They had their orders and now they had to do what was expected of them. Kes sat down next to Marco and pulled his fags out. He sparked two cigarettes up and passed one to Marco. 'Here, calm the fuck down, man. On my life, the sooner Leigh is found the better because I know she's playing heavy on your mind, and you can't think straight.'

Marco stared at him for a few seconds before he spoke. 'You know me so well, don't you. She had me over and I won't relax until she's found.'

Kes knew he was dicing with death but said what was on his mind anyway. 'It's more than that, Marco. You still care, don't you? I can see that, so don't try and pull the wool over my eyes. I see it in you. You've never got over her.'

Marco sighed, made sure nobody could hear him. 'Every day when I lay in my pad I thought about her, the love turning to hate then loving her again. What the fuck is up with me?'

'She got under your skin, mate, that's what happened. I've been there and done that myself, so I know where you're coming from. The difference is you have a wife and if Monica ever got wind of this, she'd go sick. Honest, I've seen Monica when she's angry and I for one wouldn't like to mess with her.'

Marco cringed and closed his eyes slightly as he stroked his fingers through his hair. 'As sad as it is to say it, Kes, I think my marriage is over. She's been a good wife, ticks all my boxes, but she's not Leigh. I should have told Monica it was over a long time ago. Even when we are having sex I'm still thinking about Leigh and that's not right, is it?'

Kes sucked in a large mouthful of air. 'No, it's not, but if we find her what then? What will you say – sorry I cut your fucking thumb off, and you robbed me blind – shall we give it another go?'

'I haven't thought that far ahead, Kes, I just want to see her again.'

Kes shook his head. 'So, is it that she took your money or that you still love her?'

Marco slammed his flat palm against the desk causing a pot of pens to fall off. 'Fuck knows. She hurt me bad, Kes.'

'And like I said, you nearly cut her fucking hand off. I'd say that was stalemate, wouldn't you?'

There was a noise outside the room and they both froze and looked at each other, neither moving a muscle for a moment. But when Kes jumped up and opened the door and looked both ways, the corridor was empty. 'I'll go check it out, boss.' He loped off down the hallway.

Marco expected Kes back in minutes but instead the door opened and in walked Trisha. 'Why are you here? Where is your mam? Everything OK?'

She walked in and sat at the table near her father. 'Everything's fine, Dad, chill. I was just passing and saw your car outside and thought I would come in and get a lift home from you?'

Marco smiled at her. She was still his little girl, despite having turned eighteen almost a year ago. Marco started to put his coat on and cleared some paperwork from the top of his desk and locked it away in the small drawer. He shoved the silver key in his inside pocket and came from behind his desk. 'Did you get a nice dress for tonight then?'

Trisha opened her bag and pulled out a black cocktail dress. 'Bloody one hundred and fifty pounds that was. Look at it, there is nothing to it. I could have made one myself for that price.'

'Nice things cost money, love. And you've been brought up with the best of everything. It's my own fault for spoiling you.'

'There is nothing wrong with spoiling your only daughter, is there? That's what fathers are for and plus you've been away for years, so you are playing catch-up.' Trisha smiled. 'And besides, when you step down and I take over this lot then I'll treat you the way you have always treated me.'

Marco chuckled as he looked at his daughter. She was the apple of his eye, and he could see his own traits in her. Trisha was clever, never missed a trick. Even when she was still a kid she was streetwise and knew the craic. Monica had tried to protect her, hide her away from the world her father lived in and never spoke about what her father did for a living. Even when he got sent down

Monica had never told her the real reason for the long sentence. But Trisha was on the ball and without her mother knowing she'd learned from her father and was earning her own money her own way – and she was smashing it. She'd got a job at a local casino and Marco was proud that she had an eye on big things.

Trisha looked over at her dad and twiddled with her hair. 'Dad,' she said in a gentle voice. '*Is* my mam alright? She just seems sad all the time, like she's pining for something.'

'She's said nothing to me. But we both know your mother. It will come out sooner or later what's up with her. She just likes to take her time to digest what's happened.'

'Maybe take her out, spoil her, show her that you care. Her world was turned upside down when you were in jail, she never stopped crying when you first went in.'

Marco sighed. He didn't really want to be having this conversation. 'You have to remember, Trisha, I've been away for a long time, and it must be strange for her now that I'm back home. There is such a thing as too close for comfort.'

Monica sat at her dressing table and finished applying her make-up. She was watching her husband in the mirror. 'It will be nice for us to go out together. I've not had a night out like this for a very long time. Don't get me wrong I've been out with the girls for lunch and the odd drink but it's not the same as going out with you by my side.'

Marco was sat on the edge of the bed putting his polished brown shoes on. 'I won't be with you all night. I'm working, remember, so don't be pulling a face when I'm here, there and everywhere.'

'Bleeding hell, Marco, can't you just have one night off and sit with me? You never used to leave my side when we were younger, what's changed?'

Marco stood up and tucked his white shirt into his black trousers. 'Nothing's changed. I'm just doing what I've always done. You have to take on board that I've been away for a long time and people think I'm a has-been. It's up to me to show them they're all wrong. Everybody will want to wear my crown, take what I have worked my balls off for and I have to make sure I'm bigger than I've ever been. Show these bastards that I'm untouchable.'

'You said when you come home we would leave that life behind, go away, spend loads of time together. Was that just jail talk?'

'I might have said that, but you know as well as I do that this is my world, where I belong. How the fuck do you think we have been able to buy this house, drive the cars that we do. Come on, you can't have the best of both worlds, can you?'

Monica sprayed perfume on her wrist and neck and twisted her head so she could see her husband fully. She was not backing down, no way. She had a voice and she was going to use it. 'Marco, I kept to my side of the bargain when you weren't here and it's the first night. We are going out together and you want to leave me sat on my own, don't you think I've been on my own for long enough? It's not asking for a lot, is it?'

Marco's nostrils flared as he walked over to where she was sat. He poked his thick finger into the side of her head. 'Are you not listening or what? Get it into your thick head that I have to work. These are powerful people putting money on the fight tonight. I want them having the time of their lives and walking out of there several gs lighter.'

She moved her head quickly, aware he could snap at any second. He had in the past. Monica stood up and swallowed hard, but she was still defending herself. 'You need to calm down, you do. I gave you the benefit of the doubt when you first come home but looking at you now, nothing will ever change will it. It will always be about you and your bloody big ego. Just remember who really has your back when it goes tits-up again, because it will you know, and do you think your boys will be running up to the prison visiting you? Because I'll tell you something for nothing, they bloody won't. It will be left to me just like always.'

Marco roared at the top of his voice, twisted his body and punched at the wardrobe door. 'Shut the fuck up. Do you hear me, shut up.'

The bedroom door flew open and Trisha was stood there. Her eyes wide open, she shot a look at her mother and then her father.

Marco rushed past her, needed out of here as soon as possible. He swerved past his daughter, mumbling under his breath. Trisha was frozen on the spot. 'Mam, are you alright? I heard the shouting, what's going on?'

Monica bit down hard on her bottom lip and flicked her hair over her shoulder as she looked at herself in the mirror. 'The same as always, just your father being a selfish bastard again.' Trisha walked to her mother's side and hugged her. 'Come on, Mam, my dad is a hothead, and you know what he's like when he's worrying about stuff.' Monica raised her voice. 'Worry! That man doesn't know what bloody worrying is. It's been on my head all the worry for five years. I'm the one who has been running about like a blue-arsed fly collecting money here, there and everywhere, not him. No, he's been lying on his back in his cell just giving his orders out as bloody normal.'

Trisha squeezed her arms around her mother for a few seconds and kissed the top of her head. 'Things are changing, Mam, trust me. It will all change soon. Come on, finish getting ready and let's go and have a good night out. Let's party like there's no tomorrow…'

Chapter Fourteen

Danni started every day the same way, reaching over to check her phone. She had alerts set up for Marco's name and couldn't get out of bed until she'd checked them. Ever since she'd been on the run she'd not risked any social media – living in fear that someone would tag her, but since getting here she'd felt safe enough to start up a few accounts for the pub. Danni opened her social media pages now and scrolled through the updates. There were two friend requests, one from Josie Taylor and another one from Mary Jones. Danni smiled and accepted them both, eager to look at their photographs on their profiles.

Steve was stirring and she could hear him moaning and groaning. She sent the message and placed her mobile phone back on the bedside cabinet. 'Morning, ugly mush, I thought you would have made a coffee by now, you must be slacking.' Steve gripped her in a bear hug and pulled her closer towards him. 'I think coming back to Manchester has been a good move not just for me but for you too. You look happier than I can remember and what about last night? You chucking a few darts and winning that money. You were amazing, babes.'

She blushed. 'It was a one-off, Steve. Alice thinks I'm signing up for the darts team, but she can think again.'

'Why not?'

'Why? If I help them win the league that's it – local news stories, pictures online, it only takes two clicks for Marco to know it's me.'

'Babes, this is the happiest you have been in years. You are safe here in Manchester and I will never let anything happen to you. These are your people around here, your friends, do you think they will let anything happen to you either?'

'Wow, I met one old friend and you think I can just go back to how I used to be. Steve, I was a hustler, I conned people out of money. I wasn't exactly Miss Popular?'

'You did what you had to do to survive back then and from what you've told me, that prick who you were with made a shit-load of money from you too. I'm not saying go back to hustling people, I'm saying get some normality back, do what you love, see the people you love.'

Danni knew he was right and rolled onto her back. 'Josie said my mam is still living around here too, still drinking.'

Steve was quiet for a few seconds before he spoke. 'Do you think you will go and see her?'

'I don't know. I've been thinking about it, but I can't see the point. She's still a pisshead and seeing me won't change anything. I was in care for years, Steve, and she didn't come and see me once. If she cared, she would have done everything in her power to get me back. I could be dead for all she knows.'

Steve could see she was struggling. 'Just think about it, babes, do what's best for you. I know I'm not in your shoes, but I think I would want answers from her.'

'And she won't give me any answers. Her answer is at the bottom of every bottle of beer that she drinks. It's always been like that.'

Steve kissed the side of her cheek and jumped up out of bed. 'I know you don't want to talk about your mam, so I'll leave it there. But I'll support you in any decision you make, you know that.'

Steve stood at the bar talking to a few of his customers. Jamo had just come in and he had a face like a smacked arse. Steve nodded at him. 'Bleeding hell, what's up with you?'

Jamo shook his head and settled on the bar stool. 'The evil sods have stopped my Universal Credit because I never went to the job centre last week. I rang and told them I was ill but they're having none of it. How the hell do they expect people to live with no income. No wonder I look for a bit of cash in hand.'

Steve pulled a pint and took it over to Jamo. 'Come on, lad, they will sort it out for you.'

'I know but not until next bloody week. I've got about a quid left on the electric and a few pence left on the gas. What the fuck am I supposed to do until then, I can't even get the bus to see them, peppered I am? This government is messed up, the rich get fucking richer and the poor get fucking poorer.'

Steve let him have his outburst and just listened to him moaning. He pulled twenty quid out of his pocket and pushed it into Jamo's hand. 'Here, that will help. I've had a win on the horses and sharing is caring, isn't it?'

Jamo looked at the cash in his hands and filled up, his words shaky. 'Mate, you don't have to do that. I was just angry and all that.'

Steve smiled. 'Well if you don't want it then hand it back over. I wouldn't like to offend you, would I?'

Jamo shoved the money straight in his pocket and a big grin filled his face. 'I'll remember this, Steve, I will. As soon as I get back on my feet, I'll give it you straight back. Top man you are, top man.'

Both men turned as the door swung open – neither wanting to admit they checked every new punter in case it was the Royals back for more. But it was Josie Taylor who marched in and smiled at Jamo.

''ey up, how's it all going? I've not seen your ugly mush for ages, you all good? And you must be Steve, Danni has told me all about you. Top guy she tells me you are.'

Steve reached his hand over the bar. 'Lovely to meet you. Danni will be down soon she's just getting ready. Let me get you a drink, what do you want?'

'Oh, I'm not really a drinker, but since it's free give us a double brandy and coke.'

Steve raised his eyebrows and turned his back to get the drink. Jamo nudged Josie and winked at her. 'He's a good lad is our Steve, helped me out he has.'

Josie looked around the pub and lifted her bag onto the bar. 'Steve, Danni said it would be alright to sell a few things in here if that's alright with you. You know, things that have fallen off a lorry, shall we say. Here, here's a packet of razors for free to say thanks.' Josie didn't wait for a reply, she was on her toes already approaching the customers with her swag.

Jamo sniggered over at Steve. 'Me and Josie had a bit of a thing years ago, you know. Decent bird she was in all fairness, but you know me I like a quiet life and her kids done my head in. Didn't knew she knew your Mrs – I thought she was from bleeding Cornwall?'

Steve watched Josie selling her knock-off stuff and wondered if she was the right kind of clientele. But Danni was here now, and heading his way. 'Josie is here, love. She's just walked in, she's over there, selling some stuff.' Steve was getting used to the people around here and how things moved, he just had to sort out the Royals now and he would be sweet.

Josie was soon back over, counting the money she'd just earned. She placed it neatly on the bar and started to separate it into piles. 'Twenty quid for shopping, a fiver for gas, a fiver for electric, and a ten bud for Sef. And, last but no means least, my savings pot, twenty quid for that.'

Danni was surprised. Josie didn't seem like the kind of woman who saved money, she looked like she lived from hand to mouth. Josie scraped the money together and stashed it in her back pocket. She lifted her eyes up to Danni and spoke, 'I've always been a saver. You never know what's around the corner, do you? My mam drummed that into me, you know, always save for a rainy day. And I have. I've got a right few quid saved too, but I'd never tell Sef that. No, that's my safety net in case I ever need it.'

Danni nodded her head. She'd learned the hard way that every woman should always have a nest egg of their own, and not rely on anyone to fund their lifestyle. She'd got her rainy day fund now of course – but twenty grand in used notes and a small silver revolver wasn't really the kind of safety net she could recommend.

Danni was just about to take Josie over to meet Alice and Frenchie when a draught hit her. She didn't recognise the figures silhouetted in the doorway but everyone else clearly did. It was like someone had turned the volume down in the bar. Ben and Bert Royal walked in and stood at the end of the bar as if they owned the place.

Josie elbowed Danni. 'Look lively, look what the cat has dragged in. See them two over there, the Royal brothers, nothing regal about them. Our kid had beef with them both last year and they stabbed him up. Twenty-odd stitches he had; the blade just missed his lungs, the docs said.'

Danni watched them both with keen eyes, ready to burst into action if she needed to. Josie was watching them too, just like everyone else in the pub. Bert nodded his head over at Steve and pulled him to one side. Danni couldn't hear what was said but she could tell by Bert's face that he wasn't happy. 'I'll be back,' he shouted as he dragged his brother out with him.

Steve wiped the sweat from his brow and let out a laboured breath before he made his way over to Danni and sat down next to her. 'I told him to piss off and that he wasn't getting a carrot from us. I lied and said the Farrows are looking after us and we didn't need their help.'

Danni swallowed hard. 'But we don't even know the other lot, do we?'

'I had to think on my feet, and I didn't know what else to say. At least it's bought us a bit of time, hasn't it?'

Josie sighed and tapped her fingers on the table. 'They'll be back, you know. Expect a call in the middle of the night from them lot, dirty low-lifes they are, scum of the earth after what they done to our kid, shanking him and leaving him for dead.'

'What did they stab him for?' Steve was hanging on her every word.

'They said he robbed a grow from them with his boys.'

Steve scratched at his head and held a blank expression; she knew she would have to explain further. 'The Royals have houses where they grow weed. Big bucks it is for them when they are ready.'

Danni asked the obvious question. 'So, was it your Kevin who took the weed then?'

Josie didn't hesitate. 'Fucking dead right it was. Our lad got about ten grand out of that hit, but the Royals don't know that so keep it to yourselves.'

'It's certainly dog-eat-dog around these parts, isn't it?' Steve still looked pale.

Josie nodded her head. 'It gives them a taste of their own medicine, because I know for sure they have nicked peoples' weed before, no honour amongst thieves is there?'

Alice and Frenchie had emerged out of the back room now, and sat next to Josie and Danni. Josie gave them both the onceover and sat back in her seat. 'I'm up for a couple of games of darts. I've got to be home in an hour or so but Danni here said there might be room on the team, and I would like to see if I'm any good.'

In the back room, Danni was glad of the practice session to take her mind off Ben and Bert's visit. Sure, a few practice rounds with the girls wasn't going to be a problem. But she hung back and let the others have their turns first. Josie wasn't bad, her friend admitted. All those hours as teenagers had stuck with her.

But when it was Danni's turn at the throw-line, she wasn't in the past anymore. She was alive, focused, in control. And with the vault to themselves, Danni didn't have to hold anything back.

Three darts, no hesitation, one hundred and eighty. Danni grinned. It felt good. More than good. She remembered now how powerful it had made her feel – a woman in a man's world. Taking on the world and winning.

Alice was cheering along with Frenchie. 'Go on, girl, I've never seen anybody get a full house in all my time playing darts.'

Even Josie who'd seen Danni do it hundreds of times before was clapping. 'Here, let me have another go, I'm just getting warmed up.'

Josie concentrated and threw her darts. A good score too. Alice was by her side now. 'Why don't you join the darts team, the pair of you. We need some new blood. Come on, girls, give the team a break and help us win the league.'

Danni was just about to say no, but Josie was by her side and draped her arm around her neck. 'You know what, we will. What about it, Danni, me and you playing darts together like the old days? These girls are right, we could help them win a few games.'

Danni knew now wasn't the time to admit why she couldn't join the team. She'd just have to play along for a while and find a reason to duck out later.

Alice hugged Danni. Steve clocked them all and Frenchie shouted over. 'Hey, Steve, two more recruits for the darts team. Get ready for us winning the league now. We can't lose with these two on the team with us. Betty and Jasmine will be over the moon.'

Alice covered her mouth with her hands, she'd not thought this through. 'Right, we will have to work out who's playing each week. I don't think Betty will be that bothered but Jasmine will see her arse. We can draw names and make it all fair, that should do the trick.'

Steve shouted back from behind the bar. 'I will order you lot some new shirts if you win your next game, nice ones, your names on the back of them. How fair is that?'

Steve and Danni were sound asleep in bed that night when the harsh clash of glass smashing woke them. Steve shot out of bed and went straight to the window. He could see three men swinging hammers about, looking up at him. No fear or concern at getting caught. Steve backed off from the window and started to look for his clothes on the floor. 'Danni, the bastards have plugged the windows.'

It took a few seconds before it registered with Danni what was going on.

'Danni, I said they have smashed the windows, are you awake?'

She was now and, like him, she reached down onto the floor to grab something to wear. Steve gripped his baseball bat from the top of the landing before he went downstairs. He held it ready to strike if anyone jumped out on him, then ran into the pub swinging the baseball about, screaming at the top of his voice. 'Come on, you cowards, let's have it, come on.' Steve flicked the lights on and shot a desperate look about the room, always standing with his back near a wall. No one. He ran to the window and stuck his head out between the remains of the broken glass. He could still see the men walking casually off through the night. He thought about running after them – but what good would that do? Danni was next to him now and she could see what he was thinking. 'Just stay inside, Steve, phone the police and tell them the windows have been broken, say nothing more, you seen nobody, you know nothing. If you chase after them you won't learn anything new – we already know these are the Royals' grunt workers doing this. Grab them and all you'll get is no more answers and them swinging the hammers at you instead.'

Danni knew these kind of men too well. First they broke your windows. Then your bones. They took your peace of mind. Then your life. This was only the start, she could feel it. The first thing her and Steve had to do was to secure the pub, after that they needed a plan, and fast.

Chapter Fifteen

Marco sat counting the take from the boxing match, stacks of cash all over the table. It was a good raise, and he was quids in and felt a bit of his old confidence returning. Kes was sat next to him, rubbing his hands together.

'What did I tell you about them Farrow boys, they are game as fuck and hungry to make money. They remind me of us back in the day, fearless. Si's the brains behind it all and he's ready for anything. He's determined to be the main family in Manchester, and says that when he is – which he thinks won't take him long – we'll be able to stitch most the north between us. He loves the hustle just like we do. I spoke to him this morning and he's on about arranging some dog fights too. He's said he's got a pocket bully that would rip any dog apart in seconds. The punters will love that, blood all over the show. What do you think? Is it something we want part of or what, so I can give him the heads-up.'

Marco liked to think he was as hard as they came. He'd ended more than one human life without flinching, but he drew the line at dogs. 'I'm up for anything that can earn us a decent slice, but I'm not a fucking dogfighter. That's for sick fucks – people too scared to fight people. Get on the blower to him and tell him we're up for as many boxing bouts as he can arrange – his guys versus ours – but I'm not putting animals in the ring. Did you say he's from Manchester? We could have ourselves a nice little allegiance.'

'Yeah, he's got a top crew behind him too, already runs a lot of the bars and clubs down there too, he was telling me.'

'So arrange for us to take a trip to Manchester and let's see if he's telling it like is. It's a win-win for us. If he's being honest and he's on the up, then we make cash together. Or if he's giving it all Billy Big-Bollocks and is actual small fry then we take over whatever he has and get a toehold in Manchester.'

Kes looked edgy; he'd just told him he was an alright lad, why would he even think about ripping him off? They needed men like Si they could call on whenever they needed extra manpower.

Marco's mobile phone started ringing and he shot a look at the screen. He rolled his eyes. 'For fuck's sake, like I need Monica pecking my head again. She's after booking a holiday. "A nice break," she says. I don't need a fucking rest. I need my life back, the way it used to be.' Marco cancelled the call, stood up and started to pace about the room. His phone started ringing again and this time he picked it up and roared down the line. 'What the fuck is up with you, woman, I'm busy, I'll ring you back later.'

Kes knew when to keep his mouth shut and this was one of those times. Silence filled the room until Trisha walked into the office. She'd often come here and do some paperwork for him before he was banged up, but she'd got used to sitting on his side of the desk while he'd been inside. No one else had dared sit in Marco's seat – but she was family, she told the guys. Blood. But she wasn't going to push it now. No, she went straight to the small desk at the other side of the room and logged on to the computer. Knowledge was power, she'd heard her dad say often enough, and she'd learned just how true that was while her dad had been away. She just had to show him she was ready to step up.

Chapter Sixteen

Danni sat watching Steve as he spoke on the phone. Roddy and his boys were on their way, and they were going to see if they could put this beef to bed for once and for all. Steve ended the call. 'I hope I'm not making this any worse than it already is. Hopefully they can just show the Royals we've got back-up, rough them up a bit, you know, give them a few slaps and everything will go back to normal. A few warnings – tit for tat – that's how we used to settle things.'

Danni folded her arms tighter around her body. 'I've got some men coming to replace the windows in the next hour or so too.' She looked at makeshift jumble of boxes and table tops they'd shoved over the gaps until it had got light. 'I'll feel safer when they are back in, Steve, just be careful with what you tell Roddy to do. The Royals have their rep for a reason, and I have a bad feeling about them. I know you want to stand up for us, but Roddy and the boys are no match for these clowns. I think we should ask

Jamo to speak with the Farrows and see what they are saying first.'

Steve sucked hard on his lips and came and sat down beside her. 'I hear you, but I just can't sit back and let someone else handle them. Let's see what Roddy says tonight when he lands. Will you make up the spare beds because I told them they could stay for a few nights if they want too.'

Danni jumped up from her seat. 'Bleeding hell, I'd better move my arse then.' Danni went to Steve's side and pecked him on the cheek. 'Stop worrying, everything will turn out right. I hate seeing you all worried like this. It's usually me who is the worrier, isn't it?'

He tried to smile but it seemed like the corners of his mouth were glued down. 'Go on, babes, you get going. I'll finish cleaning this glass up. Alice should be here by now, she can give me a lift. I'll just bung her an extra few quid.'

Danni was gone.

It was late afternoon and Steve was stood behind the bar talking to Jamo. The door opened behind them, loud voices washing in. Steve's face lit up. 'Yes, the boys!' he shouted as Roddy walked in.

'Get them beers lined up, Stevie boy, we're gagging for a few cold ones.'

Steve watched five men line up at the bar; big, stocky geezers, all built like units. Jamo was eager to introduce himself and the moment he got the chance he stretched his hand out to Roddy. 'Jamo's the name and I'm the one who has been looking after Steve here while he's been in Manchester.'

Roddy shook Jamo's hand as did the rest of the firm. Steve filled all their glasses, eager to fill them in on what had been happening. They were all ears and after he'd told them the score, he knew he had their backing. Roddy kept his voice low and jerked his head slowly. 'Well, let's see them come in today while us lot are here. I'll rip their heads off and shit down their throats.'

Alice came out from behind the bar, unbothered by the men's big talk – she was well used to blokes claiming they were tough guys. She looked exhausted. 'Clean as a whistle, Steve. I'm off now but tell Danni we will be in later to have a chat with her about the darts team.'

Steve was too engrossed in his story to have a proper conversation with her, just a few words. 'Yep, thanks, love, I'll tell her when she gets back from shopping.

The day turned into night and Roddy and his boys were sat in the pub, tucked away in the corner. The hours had ticked by, Steve clocking every punter the moment they entered. He knew the Royal brothers would be in eventually – back to the scene of the crime – to see if their boys' work on the windows had tamed Steve into paying.

Finally, *bingo*, in walked Ben and Bert with a few of their boys. Steve eyeballed Roddy so he knew their mark but they let the brothers pick their spot. Just as predicted, the Royals didn't strut up to the bar, instead taking to an opposite corner instead. They made no attempt to hide their gear and within seconds the drug deals started to take place. Steve tried to keep his expression neutral though beads of sweat were forming on his forehead. Jamo swigged the last of his pint and sneaked off out of the door, his survival instinct stronger than any sense of loyalty.

Steve waited a few minutes longer, then jerked his head over at Roddy; his eyes wide open, breathing fast. Roddy took one last survey of the place and stood up from his seat, followed by his boys. Danni stood next to her man behind the bar. 'Steve, you keep out of this too. Remember, you are the landlord and you could lose your licence. This is why you got your old gang in – let them do the dirty work.'

'Just go upstairs, babes, and leave us to it. It is what it is now, Danni, no turning back.'

Roddy stood tall in front of Ben Royal now, his men behind him, weighing up the others sat there. 'Can I have a word, mate?'

Ben lifted his head up slowly and took the measure of the man stood in front of him. He smirked. 'What's up, pal?'

Roddy inhaled deeply, his chest expanding fully. 'You see, Steve, down there behind the bar, well, he's my mate and I hear you have been giving him some shit.'

There was a moment's pause then Ben stood stock-still, not needing to say a word. Then his boys behind moved as one. It was hard to see what happened first: the table flipped up in the air, shouting, screaming filling the space. The other customers in the pub knew this was no drunken squabble, instead running outside to seek safety. Shards of glass were spraying around the room and Steve ducked down behind the bar to save himself being hit by a bottle that had been launched at him. Steve knew it was all-out war, his pub needed protecting. He reached for the iron bar he kept below the bar and clutched it tightly in his hands. It was showtime. The adrenaline pumping, Steve found the kind of energy he'd not had in years and vaulted over the bar, swinging the iron bar around him, just like he'd done back in his hooligan days. He roared at the top of his voice, eyes bulging from their sockets. 'Come on then, you pussies, if you want a piece of me, have it.'

There was a man running straight at him, he had to think on his feet. It was do or die time now. Old habits die hard and Steve whacked the iron bar at the man's arm. He was ready to swing again but not this time; someone gripped him from behind and in seconds he had two men on him, holding him back, dragging him down, booting and kicking him. Steve fought with all his strength, with no shot of overpowering them but taking all his energy just to cover his face with his hands, rolling around to stop the force of the boots hitting him in the gut. Curled on the ground, he realised he never stood a chance, nor did Roddy and his boys. These lads were trained, drilled, ruthless. The Royals had wiped them out, all of them on the floor now. Ben stood over Roddy and growled down at him, lifting him up with one hand from by the scruff of his neck. 'Never, ever, try to take me down, bro.' He ran over to where Steve lay now and screamed at the top of his voice at him. 'The price has just fucking gone up now, you daft prick. I want five ton, not three. Make sure the next time I'm in here it's ready for me or the next time I come back, you'll be leaving in a fucking body bag, you and your Mrs.'

The men scarpered. One of them went behind the bar and opened the till and took whatever he could, stashing it in his back pocket. Ben beckoned Bert, who'd stood leaning against the wall, watching throughout, and the brothers sauntered out like it was a walk in the park.

Steve scrambled to his feet and made his way to Roddy. He could tell his mate was in a bad way and looking around at the rest of them, the others were no better. 'I'll ring an ambulance for you.'

Roddy's eyes flickered and his voice was a whisper. 'No dibble, just give me a minute and I'll be fine. Just check out the rest of the boys.'

Steve's anger was fading now, replaced by guilt for summoning his mates into this carnage; this was not what he'd wanted to happen. He'd expected a few sore heads, maybe a man or two down but not this kind of whitewash. This was all his fault; he should have just paid the bloody money like Jamo had told him to. All he could hear was moaning and groaning around him. Danni ran into the bar and covered her mouth as she took in the chaos. Steve looked over at her. She'd never seen him cry before.

'Get the keys and lock the pub up, hurry up before they come back.' His voice sounded like it belonged to a broken man.

Danni rummaged behind the bar looking for the keys, her eyes flicking one way then the other. She sprinted to the double swing doors and with shaking hands she locked and bolted them. Her heart was drumming, she wasn't thinking straight, darting one way then the other, not sure where she was going or what she could do to help. Once she'd checked all the men were dragging themselves to their feet, she stood with her back against the cold wall and closed her eyes for a few seconds. As her pulse slowed, Danni helped Roddy up to a seat. His nose was clearly broken, blood and pulp splattered across his face, and he was bleeding from his mouth. The rest of the gang didn't look much better either, all cut and bruised, wincing as they tried to right themselves. Danni ran to get a few pot towels from behind the bar and pressed one to Roddy's head in the hope that it would stop the bleeding. He cringed as she applied pressure to the open cut.

It was soon clear that Roddy's pride was hurt as much as his head, and he sat sipping a glass of cold water. 'Fucking solid them lot were. He didn't even give me a chance to get my blade out.'

Steve patted Roddy on the knee. 'Mate, I was like you, I was swinging the bar about and before I knew it, I was on my arse. Maybe we are too old for this game now.'

'I think you're right, ruthless they are, on another level.'

Danni passed the hot cloths about now so they could all clean themselves up. Roddy's head was still pouring blood and he knew a trip to A and E was on the cards if they couldn't stop it. He dipped his head low, deflated as he spoke to Danni and Steve. 'I'm going to head back up to our ends and get this head sorted. I'm gutted we couldn't help you, pal. We're talking bigger than we ever were here, we need to face it we're not tooled enough for them. If we try and have them again it'll be shooters, you know it.'

Steve rubbed at his arms as the hairs stood on end and a cold chill ran down his spine. 'I know, I know,' he mumbled. 'Just get you lot back home out of the way. If the police come in asking any questions then I'll just tell them a fight broke out and I never knew any of the people involved.'

Roddy was obviously eager to get his arse out of here. He gripped Steve as he walked him to the front door and whispered into his ear, so nobody could hear him. 'My advice would be to get the fuck away from here, sooner rather than later, because they'll be back and what then?'

Danni unbolted the doors and stuck her head outside the door, making sure the coast was clear. She nodded to the men as they limped off into the deserted street.

Danni locked the door again and let out a sigh. She looked around the pub at the mess and anger filled her body. What was the need for all this violence? Greed it was, sheer bloody greed. Protection rackets were just thieving from anyone lower down the food chain in her eyes. Nicking from other crims was one thing, she knew turf wars were eternal, but she had no time for the kind of low lives that targeted people and businesses trying to make an honest quid.

Steve slumped down on the bar stool, head in hands. She tried to find the words to reassure him. 'Come on, love, don't get upset. Roddy will be fine, as will the rest of them. Not their first rodeo, is it?'

'Someone could have died tonight, Danni. I should have known better and just paid the money they wanted.'

'No, you shouldn't have. They are arseholes who are preying on who they think are weaker people. They will get their comeuppance, trust me, people like that always get what's coming to them and when it happens I for one will be stood watching with a big smile on my face.'

Chapter Seventeen

Monica Reece stood looking out of the big window, waiting. She was always like this when she knew her husband was on a job. Her heart was racing at the thought of getting that dreaded knock on the front door. She'd already faced the knock that told her he'd been arrested, she'd survived his sentence and now, in her bones, she felt his luck was running out. Would the next knock be the one that told her Marco had been found dead? How many times had she told herself that she was walking away from this life even if her other half didn't? And yet, here she was doing the same as she always had. Waiting.

Marco had been her world since she was a young girl. His own upbringing was not something he liked talking about, though she knew he'd grown up poor – properly poor. He told Monica of the nights when he lay in bed dreaming not about football or holidays or any of the things most kids are meant to dream about – but instead just about eating nice food and having a full fridge to come home to. There was no such luck in his household and when his mum became ill it was every man for themselves. His father had apparently tried to look after them all the best he could, but it was only a matter of time before he found himself another woman and got on his toes with her and left them all. Marco had gone to see his father a few times and begged him to help his family out, give them some money to buy food or keep the heating on, but the man turned his back on them all and told him never to darken his doorstep again. And so Marco never did. He was just sixteen years old when he found another life, another way of supporting his mum and keeping a roof over their heads, a world that was shadowy and full of lies, betrayal and greed. A whole network of illegal gambling he'd never known existed. But, he'd told her, the main man had taken a shine to him and took him under his wing. Marco was the runner for that bookie for years, first carrying money here and there, then taking bets. It opened his eyes to a different way of living and from then on he'd known he would never be poor again. Marco grafted for the bookies in the area and the money he was earning was like nothing anyone he knew had ever earned before.

As he'd worked his way up the organisation he saw that beyond the betting was another level – the fixing. Soon he was part of the hustle and bunged money on the winner to show his favoured clients he was in it with them. It was a win-win situation. Then he crossed paths with her. Monica was the daughter of Frank Scarton, another big bookie in the area. Monica had loved him from the moment she set eyes on him; he was cheeky, edgy and showered her with the best money could buy.

Marco had treated her like a princess, although he was wise enough to realise he had to – if he hadn't Frank would have cut his balls off and made a necklace out of them. Getting married was Monica's dream, and Marco was perfect – the rising name on the scene, someone she'd never have to pretend or lie about where her family money came from. He'd already told her he loved her and spoke about their future together from their earliest dates. But his work always came first even back then, leaving restaurants to take calls, missing nights out to collect debts, disappearing for weekends at a moment's notice. She should have known this life more than anyone, her own father lived it too and her mother had spent years begging in vain for him to step away from the life he lived. But Frank had never listened to anyone and when his body was found by a dog walker one dark windy night, it was Marco that Monica turned to. For comfort, for security, for revenge.

Marco had known if he avenged Frank's death it would not just win him Monica forever, but also give him the throne where Frank used to sit. And so Monica never asked him exactly what had happened to her father, who had done it or what happened to the perpetrator. She just knew it had been sorted. It was the look in his eye when he came home one night with traces of blood on his hands, and lay restless beside her night after night.

Monica and Marco had got married when she found out she was pregnant with Trisha. It was one of the best mob weddings Leeds had seen; anybody who was anybody was invited, the wedding party went on for days. It had sealed their position as the city's bookies. Lending and loaning, staking and gambling – and demanding it all back with interest. It had seemed like the good life – until the cracks started appearing.

Trisha came into the house now and made Monica jump. 'Bloody hell, I nearly had kittens. I thought you were staying out tonight?'

Trisha giggled. Her mother was so jumpy, scared of her own shadow sometimes. 'Don't tell me you've been sat looking through that window all night long waiting for my dad to come home? Get your gladrags on and get out yourself instead of sitting about waiting on some man.'

Monica shuffled about, swiped her hair back from her face. 'No, I've just been watching a film.'

'Really? And where is my dad again? Mam, I thought you were putting your foot down, telling him it's you or the life he lives with the boys. Men do my head in and I for one will never need a man to put food on my table. I'm a strong woman, Mam, one who knows the script.'

Monica swallowed. Trisha was right, she had said she was going to be different this time around now Marco was out, but here she was, doing the same as always, stood at the window waiting. She was deflated as she replied, 'It's not that easy, Trisha, he can't just walk away from the business like that, it takes time.'

Trisha let out a sarcastic laugh. 'You're just living his life, not your own. Mam, when my dad was in prison, I was so proud of you. You didn't need him then, did you?'

Trisha shook her head and came and sat next to her mother. 'My dad needs you – he wouldn't be able to do a thing for himself, he's always relied on you to give him a good home. But he needs to be careful, Mam, I've already heard rumours that he's dicing with death, stepping on people's toes going too far, too fast since he got out.'

Monica scratched at her skin on the side of her face and red blotches started to appear. 'You're old enough to hear the truth, sweetheart. I'm just not sure he loves me like he used to. Something has changed and it's not just prison. The way he looks at me is not the same, the way he kisses me is not the same. I'm scared he doesn't love me anymore. Well, not scared, I just know I need to start looking out for myself and not him.' There you go, she'd said it, finally told someone how she was feeling. It was her truth and now that she had got it out, she realised how close to the bone it really was. She looked directly into her daughters' eyes. 'A woman knows, call it a gut instinct, call it intuition. You just know when your man is no longer interested in you anymore. You're a grown woman now, you know what I mean. You might feel invincible when you're young, but you're never too young to be wise to what getting in too deep with a fella can mean.'

'Shut up, Mam.' Trisha grimaced but looked thoughtful. 'But yeah, I hear you. And yes, I'm old enough to know that sometimes what Dad says and what he does are two different things, anyway.'

'You're telling me. I didn't let on to anyone when it happened, but you might as well know if we're being honest: just before he got nicked he sat me down and told me it was over, told me he no longer loved me. Do you know how much that hurt? It ripped my insides up, and those words have never left my head.'

Trisha winced. 'So why are you still here? Cart the prick then, bin bag him. He's my dad, sure, but you don't have to pretend he's a saint to me, Mam.'

'Look, you were still a kid when he got charged. And then when he got sent down, he said he was sorry for what he'd said to me and that he didn't mean it. His head was all over the place he said, and he didn't know if he was coming or going.'

'But still, why would he say he didn't love you? That's sick that is, playing with people's feelings like that. You should have kicked his arse to the kerb and let him rot behind them bars because that's what I would have done if he had been my man.'

'You don't just give up on the man you love, Trisha. You're forgetting your dad is the only man I have ever known, it's always been me and him, I meant that "until death do us part" bit.'

'Get a grip, Mam. You're living in old fashioned times. Life is not like that these days – putting up with shit for the sake of it; sure you might have been raised in "you've made your bed, so you lie in it" times but the world has moved on. Women have choices these days and they have a voice. Come on, tell me, what were your dreams when you were growing up? What did you want to do because all I've ever heard from you is about being a wife and being stuck in the house all day at my dad's beck and call. Who even are you, Mam?'

Monica stuttered. 'To be a wife, that was my dream, to have a family and look after you all.'

'Mam, I'm nearly twenty-five years old and I don't need looking after no more. I haven't needed looking after for a long time, to be honest. I stand on my own two feet and live my life, not nobody else's. You and Dad raised me strong: I can tackle anything that stands in my way, and I mean anything that stops me getting what I want.'

'I'm pleased for you, Trish. But that's not me. I don't want no big career; I just want peace in my life, security, stability.'

'But, looking at you now, Mam, you're not happy and you should do something about it. Life is for living, you know. Book a few days away and go and find yourself, find out who you want to be and where you are going in life. It's not all about a man, you know.'

Monica was lost for words. Trisha had always known her own mind. Even from being a young girl she was never afraid of voicing her opinion, she was strong and not a pushover like she was. She had Marco's blood flowing through her veins, for sure. Monica reached over for her vape and sucked on it hard. She had never been a big smoker but lately she needed a blast of nicotine to calm her nerves.

Trisha realised that she had gone in hard on her mother and tried to backpedal. 'Or we could do it together, Mum. Why don't we both bugger off to the sun for a few days, just me and you, lying there doing nothing. Sometimes you need to recharge your batteries and focus again on what is real and what is not. Look at me when I split up from Zac. My head was all over the place and I never thought I would smile again.'

Monica agreed and sucked again on her vape. She'd never warmed to her daughter's ex. 'They were bad times for sure. You know your dad wanted to send the firm around to Zac's house and sort him out. I had to beg him not to.'

Trisha scoffed. 'The way I felt at the time, I wouldn't have minded him getting a few slaps and maybe a kick up the arse but I'm glad they didn't. I needed to sort it out myself. The only person a woman can ever count on is herself, do you know that?' Trisha continued, quieter now. 'Zac was sleeping with someone else, Mam. I've never told you this before because I felt embarrassed that I was blinded to it.'

'Bleeding hell, why on earth didn't you tell me all this was going on? I would have supported you. Cheating is pure snake behaviour.'

'I know you mean well, I didn't need supporting, Mam. I don't want to go into it, but I had the last laugh on Zac and his slut. Let's say, he'll never mess with me again.' Trisha winked at her mother. 'All is fair in love and war, right?'

Monica studied her daughter carefully and she knew whatever had happened she wouldn't have liked. But she'd had a lifetime of knowing when not to ask a question – she'd got this far on the principle of 'don't ask, don't tell'.

Marco finally crept into bed next to his wife in the early hours of the morning. She kept her eyes closed and didn't say a word. She could hear the drawer opening at the side of him and closing again slowly. She lay still. Marco reached over and put his warm hand on her back. 'Are you still awake, Mon?'

'Yes, why?' she said in a tired voice. 'I just want to say sorry for how I have been speaking to you lately. I've just had a lot going on in my head, that's all.' His excuses were all familiar to her, and her stomach turned knowing it was always just about him and the way he felt. Trisha's words were running through her head, and she turned over to face him and blurted it out. 'I'm going on holiday with Trisha. I need a break from all this shit.'

'What shit?' Marco looked astonished that his wife had spoken back to him. He shut the bedside drawer with a slam and faced her fully.

Monica knew she would have to choose her words carefully. She took a deep breath. 'Marco, for years I've been living your life and not my own. I've stood by your side and been the best wife I could be. I want peace now, a husband who wants to spend time with me, not this – late nights and half-truths.'

Marco was stony-faced. 'If you want to go on holiday then go. You can't see me stopping you, can you? I've always given you everything – including your freedom. Do what you like, what do I mind?'

'Exactly, Marco, you just don't care about me anymore. It's all about you, just like it's always been.' She sat up and folded her arms. 'Remember when before you went to jail you told me you didn't love me—'

Marco butted in. 'Not this again, how many times have I gone over this and explained to you that I didn't mean it. I didn't know where my head was at.'

'No, you listen to me now, Marco. Those words left your mouth, and you meant them at the time alright. And I know why you changed your mind when you got nicked. Oh yes I do. So that this dickhead here—' She stabbed her finger into her chest. 'So I stood by your side and ran around making sure your empire was alright.'

Marco dragged the covers off and sprang out of bed. 'I'm too tired for this, I'm going in the spare room. I don't know what's up with you lately, but sort it out before I do.'

'Oh yes, you piss off when the going gets tough,' Monica hissed. 'Maybe I should have done that when you had rough times, eh? You go, Marco, but these problems will still be here in the morning and this time I won't be sweeping them under the carpet like I usually do. I'm doing me from now on, watch this space.'

Marco slammed the bedroom door shut behind him, nearly taking it from its hinges. Monica lay staring out at the crescent moon, most of it in shadow. Her breathing was settling now. Things were changing around here, this time she was sure of it. She was no longer going to be anybody's doormat, especially not Marco's. He'd spent years cheating on her, using her to keep house – and she'd looked the other way. She'd always thought her wedding vows were a bond of gold, like the gleaming band she wore on her finger. She realised now they'd become shackles. Now it was time to break the chains.

Chapter Eighteen

The Fox was busy. But every time the door opened, Steve's heart skipped a beat, heart in his mouth as he scanned the faces of every punter walking in. Jamo had been in touch with the Farrow brothers and they said when they had time, they would call in for a 'chat'. But he knew they likely had bigger fish to fry and if they were earning big dough, did they really want the headache of this little boozer on their hands, especially if it came with the hassle of beef with the Royals?

As the door banged again, Steve was relieved to see it was just Josie who had walked in. She came straight to the bar and banged her carrier bag down. 'Alright there, Steve, I'm just going to get rid of my swag if that's alright. Nothing too flashy, only make-up and a few packs of razor blades tonight.'

Steve raised his eyebrows. In all fairness this was the least of his worries tonight. 'Yeah, knock yourself out. Danni will be down soon, she was just finishing blowing her hair.' It was darts night and Steve knew his missus would be glamming up to hide her own nerves.

Josie looked herself up and down and squirmed. 'Bleeding hell, she never said it was a fashion show, I've just got my jeans on.'

Steve chuckled to himself and watched as Josie went about her business flogging everything she'd lifted that day. Next Alice arrived, nipping behind the bar to grab her darts. As always, she was dressed up, hair with a fresh bouncy blow, make-up on. 'I'm excited about tonight, Steve. Hopefully we can bag our first win now we have some new blood. I'm going to tell Betty and Jasmine they are on the bench tonight and give Danni and Josie a game. I'm braced for a bit of moaning. Betty can be a right one when her feathers are ruffled but it's for the good of the team. Nice for the pub's reputation too, don't you think?'

But Steve was away with the fairies, not listening to what she was saying. She walked to his side and nudged him. 'Oi, cloth ears, did you even hear a word I said then, or what?'

Steve was back in the moment. 'Sorry, love, I was thinking. I hope Danni keeps her cool.'

'She'll be golden,' Alice said, waving at Frenchie who'd dashed in. At least she had no kids tagging along tonight, her babysitter must have turned up. 'I'll have a pint of lager, Stevie lad. I need something to calm me down. The kids' dad has just been giving me abuse, calling me a bad mother because I'm going out to the pub tonight and expecting him to watch his own ruddy sprogs. You should have heard the mouth on him; he called me slut and slag and every name under the sun, saying I was just going down the boozer to get a shag. It's a bit rich considering he's done every bird between here and Glossop. One pissing night of babysitting, that's all I asked for, not much considering I've not seen sight or sound from him for months.'

Alice shook her head. 'You're a good mother, Frenchie, and don't let anybody tell you anything different. He's just a sperm donor who walked out on his kids, I hope you told him that.'

Frenchie swigged a mouthful of beer. 'You can bet your life I did. I told him about his little knob too. In fact, I told everyone on the street who was listening. I mean, come on, I had to come back with something didn't I? You should have seen his face when I shouted it out, he was as fast as lightning getting in the door. He had the cheek to bring his new bird with him too. She's lucky I never called her out too, utter shag-bag she is.'

Alice chuckled and shot a look over at Steve, who was gobsmacked, not used to the constant drama of Frenchie's life. Josie was back now, and she threw a packet of blades over at him. 'There you go, pal, perks of the job for you, freebie.' Steve smiled over at Josie and picked the box up. She might have nicked more toiletries than he'd had hot dinners, but he could tell she was a kind soul and that she was only doing what she could to keep her head above water. He'd never really understood poverty until he got to know real communities – the kind of places where families chose between money on the meter or food on the table, and it was worse now than he'd ever known it. One look around the pub and it was there for him to see how much people struggled to live and provide for their families. It was why times were harder in the trade – barely anyone could afford to come in every night for a drink on their way home from work like they once had. The folk who could afford to still come were the lucky ones.

Josie ordered her drink and reached for her darts on the bar. She nodded over at Alice and Frenchie. 'Come on then, let's chuck a few darts and get warmed up. A lot is riding on this match for me. My Stef said if I lose, he won't be watching the kids again. On my life, it's cost me an arm and a leg to get him to babysit tonight. He's a cheeky bastard he is, I've got to bring him a kebab home too.'

Frenchie was already on her way to the vault. Steve walked through to them and put Josie's drink on the bar. He put one for Danni there too, hoping she'd be down any minute.

Danni's cheeks were flushed as she came to join the girls, who'd all arrived by the time she came down. Betty had a face like a smacked arse and Jasmine looked none too happy that she'd been dropped from the team tonight. Betty spoke in a stroppy tone, 'Alice, I hope this is a one-off because I've been on this team from the beginning. This is my one little treat a week.'

Alice could see she was upset and edged closer to her, eyes still watching Josie throw her darts, warming up. 'We just need to win a couple of games, get up the league a bit and then you two will be back in. Danni is going to give us some tips and help us with our stance and that.'

THE HUSTLE

Alice watched as Josie walked off and Danni stood up next. Danni positioned her dart in her hand, unsure if it felt right. She was twisting and turning it, rolling it around her fingers, the thick scar tissue rubbing against the cool metal. Her eyes widened as she flicked her hair over her shoulder. She licked her lips slightly and focused, her head fully in the game now.

Steve watched from behind the bar.

Boom, three arrows, one hundred and eighty. Betty looked at Frenchie and then Alice and then Jasmine. She made the sign of the cross against her body and whispered under her breath. 'Thank you, Lord.' Josie went to examine the darts board and turned around, laughing her head off. 'Bleeding hell, Danni, a full house. I better pull my socks up and do the same.'

Alice was up next, she was really trying her best, but anyone looked hopeless in comparison. Danni was by her side though, a few words of guidance: 'Don't grip the dart too tight, relax and keep focused. Only look at the place where you want the dart to go, switch off from everything around you.'

Alice tried again and this time she did exactly what Danni had told her. As the darts hit home with a thud Alice grinned: a great score, the best she'd had in a long time. Frenchie was eager to have a go too, there was no way she was being left behind. Alice punched her clenched fist into the air as Frenchie launched her last dart.

'Super, smashing great, keep out of the black and in the red, nothing in this game for two in a bed,' she roared, laughing.

The girls were pumped, it seemed like everything could only get better. Steve called Danni over and gave her another drink. 'I'm so proud of you, babes. I know I keep saying this, but you look great up there, full of confidence and, well, it's pretty sexy, let me tell you.'

'Give over, Steve. It's bloody darts. I love the game but it's hardly a turn-on, is it?'

'What? A powerful woman with every man's eyes on her? I don't care what it is, I'm buzzing for you.'

But the banter and the warm-up was over. Danni watched as the door opened and the away team came marching in. Danni had to hand it to them, they looked the dog's bollocks, all dressed in matching red shirts. Steve eyeballed her and whispered under his breath. 'You win tonight, and I'll buy the full team new shirts. I promise, no cheap shit, top of the range.'

Danni shook his hand. 'I'll take you up on that offer.'

Steve watched Danni walk away to meet the visiting team.

The guests were number three in the league and confident they were going to win here tonight. Alice was bustling about setting everything up for the game, Danni remembered she had to play landlady as well as team player and got the food set out for after the game. But she couldn't draw it out any longer. Her first proper match since – she looked at her thumb and remembered Marco's face the day he maimed her – since her old life ended. As Steve let

'The Eye of the Tiger' boom out of the speakers, Danni knew she had to put her past out of her mind. It was game on.

The match was soon in full swing, and The Fox team was smashing it. The away team were shocked, stood whispering to each other, clearly having been told their opponents were a walkover. None of the players noticed when the double doors opened and in walked four men. They scanned the place before sitting down in the corner of the bar. The main man was clearly sat at the back, a lackey going up to the bar to order.

Si Farrow loved a game of darts and when he watched Danni hit triple nineteen, he nudged the guy next to him. 'Check out that bird, she's shit hot. Fucking hell, you don't usually see pub players – let alone women – who are that good.'

Si was fascinated by the game now and even when his lieutenant brought his bottle of beer over to him, he was still focused on what this mystery woman was scoring. Danni was still smashing it, needing double eighteen now to win the game. Si hushed his crew. 'Be quiet, will you. Just let me see if this woman can finish the game off. Fuckin' class, she is.'

Danni inhaled deeply and closed her eyes for a split second. She concentrated on the number she needed, pictured a line between it and her hand, and finally the dart left her hand. Si got up out of his seat to get a better look as shouting and clapping broke out. Frenchie was jumping about in the air with Josie celebrating the pub's first ever win in the league.

Si sat back down and spoke to the man at his side, his brother judging by their similarity. 'Top girl she is, wasted playing darts here, let me tell you.'

As the celebrations continued by the board, Steve had clearly been warned about who these punters were. He was at the table now and he reached his hand out to Tim then Si. 'Thanks for coming, I wasn't sure if you would. I know how busy you must be.'

Si played his cards close to his chest. 'Pull up a chair and tell me the script. I haven't got long, so straight to the point, aye.'

Steve flushed and blurted everything out: their fresh start, the Royals, Roddy and the beating. He'd figured it wasn't worth playing the big man with this lot and spinning them a yarn – they probably had kids dealing on every street corner who'd tell their bosses the truth anyway.

Si sat stroking his chin, looking faintly amused. 'The Royals are jumped-up wankers. So, they want five ton each week from you?'

'Yes, at first it was three hundred but when I confronted him with my boys, he smashed the place up and said the money had gone up now.'

Si laughed, the others waiting on him to speak. He rocked about on his chair and slurped a mouthful of his beer. 'Greedy fuckers! I'll sort the Royals out, but,' he paused. 'I want three ton a week for it.'

Steve's eyes flickered. As much as he wanted to tell this prick to go and take a running jump he knew he would only be cutting his nose off to spite his face.

Si explained further. 'Listen, pal, for me to help you out here I'm going to have to piss Ben Royal off, and he won't like that as you already know. I'll put two of my boys on your door for a few weeks and once Ben sees I've boxed this place off, he will do one. But it all costs money. I have to pay my boys, don't I? I won't be coining it in from you – you pay, I pay the lads. You get a pub that doesn't get torched, and I get to show Benny and Berty that they should stay in their box.'

Steve glanced over at Danni. He'd brought her here, now it was on him to keep her safe. He reached over and shook Tim's hand. At least he would sleep tonight knowing they were now protected. Si cracked his knuckles and nodded his head over at the darts team. 'So, who's the chick hitting them big scores?'

Steve smiled. 'That's my Danni. Good, isn't she?'

'More than fucking good, mate, one of the best I've seen in a long time.'

Alice had walked over to Steve, buzzing with adrenaline. 'Steve, we won, the girls have won their first game. We will be the talk of the league. I'm so happy, on my life, I usually go home from here in a mood after a game, but not tonight. I'm going to celebrate with a few gins.'

'On the house they will be, Alice. You girls have done me proud, tell the rest of them to get what they want too.'

Steve shepherded her away from the Farrows, and, as he pushed Alice's glass under the optics, he saw Si and Tim already heading out the door, but not without a backward glance at Danni, which made something twitch with fear in Steve's gut.

Danni ran to Steve's side and snuggled into him. 'Bloody hell, I didn't think I still had it in me, you know. My hand was shaking on those last few darts, I thought I was going to fold.'

'No, you're bigger than that, babes. I knew you would show everyone here tonight just how good you are. A class act, love, I'm super proud of you.'

She kissed the side of his cheek and went back to join the girls in their celebrations. Josie quickly checked the wall clock behind the bar and necked the rest of her drink. 'Crap, I'm going to have to get off. I told Sef I would be no later than eleven bells, he'll be fuming if I'm late. I promised him I'd put out too – if I'm late he'll spit his dummy out. He's probably lying there covered in baby oil already, waiting for me,' she giggled.

Danni cackled with laughter. 'You're a right nutter, you know that? But I tell you what else, I feel alive tonight, on top of the world. I haven't felt like this in years. It takes me back to being a teenager, you and me, feeling invincible. It makes me realise what a shadow of myself I've become. A miserable cow who was scared of her own shadow. Thanks for helping me be me, love, even if just for a night.'

Josie bearhugged her. 'Stop being stupid, I haven't done anything special. If anything you've helped me get out of that bleeding house of an evening and reminded me that sometimes, even folks like me get to win. And none of this "one night only" nonsense. Look how good you were tonight! Now we're back together, I'm not letting you go. We can take on the world.'

Danni felt a wave of emotion grip her body. Her eyes filled up. 'Honestly, you do make me feel that sometimes, Josie. I've decided I'm going to see my mam too. I owe it to myself to see what she has to say. I need closure, why she just gave up on me.'

Josie inhaled deeply and nodded her head. 'Yes, you do what you have to. You've been running for far too long, I reckon, afraid of all the shit that went down when you were younger. But one look at you tonight, and I'll tell you something for nothing: you're no victim, Danni Cox.'

Chapter Nineteen

Kes sat facing Marco Reece. There were a few other men sat with them in the pub, slumped back in their seats like they'd come off a battlefield. Kes had an angry wound under his left eye, and most of the others had bruises and cuts too.

'The Murphys didn't know what fucking hit them last night. We dealt with them good and proper, didn't we?' Marco rolled his shoulders, satisfied that one of the newer families scrapping for a piece of the scene in Leeds had been put in their place.

Kes winced as he answered, not meeting his boss's gaze. 'We did, Marco mate, but listen, I reckon we need to back off for a bit now and recover. Look at us all, Joey can hardly stand up today. That geezer swung a baseball bat right across his back and look at Marv, he's bruised to fuck. We're lucky they weren't tooled up properly because if they were it would have been another story for us all.'

'Would it fuck, we were strong. I could see the fear in their eyes; they knew they were outnumbered and it was going off big time.' Marco looked around at the boys.

Kes lifted his eyes up and addressed the group. 'We need to make sure we are on guard now, because they are shady bastards and they will not take this lying down. We need to be ready when they come back at us, because…' He shook his head and sighed before he carried on speaking, 'They will come for us the moment we turn our backs, and they'll come team-handed and ready for war.'

Marco stood up, face red with rage, hating the fact that he could see fear in his boys' eyes. 'We'll deal with anything that is flung at us. Everyone else, beat it. Kes, you need to sort your fucking head out, lad. Since when have you been the person who hesitates at taking somebody down? This is our world, where we rule. How else have we all creamed money in for years. Anyone comes at us, we come back bigger, stronger than ever. It's the way we have always worked. We've kept the firm going while I was inside, now's the easy bit – show people I'm back.'

Kes realised that he sounded like he'd lost his mojo and pulled it back. 'I'm scared of no young guns, and I'll be at the frontline as I always am. I just think these days it pays to think big, get connected. I spoke with Si Farrow again last night to arrange our little visit. He's game as fuck and so are his boys.'

Marco sat playing with his pocket-knife. 'Yeah? Well let's get on with it. After all, Mon's fucked off on holiday for few days with our Trisha. On my life that woman lately is doing my nut right in. Do you think she's got another bloke on the go or what? I've been inside a long time, not all women wait.'

Kes gulped, hated being put on the spot. 'No way, pal. Monica is a one-man woman, she wouldn't entertain another man, she doesn't roll like that.'

'I'm not so sure lately, Kes. She's changed since I've been home, something in her eyes tells me she's had enough.' Marco ran his finger along the blade he always carried.

'Come on, the woman has been by your side for years and you have told her that you will walk away from this world one day.' Kes could recognise the restless tone in his boss's voice.

'Yes, I did tell her that but when I'm ready, not when she tells me. Look at the life it's given her anyway? If she's just waited till I'm out to try and bin me, I'm not having it. When I was in jail I saw some men fall apart when their Mrs sent them Dear John letters. There was a man across the landing from me, big guy he was, tough as fuck. Anyway, his girlfriend carted him, and he stayed behind his door for weeks on his jacks. Mate, you should have seen the state of him when he finally came out from his pad. He'd lost stacks of weight and he was a shadow of his former self. His head was never the same after that and when I spoke to him, he told me that he didn't have a clue she was sleeping with someone else, no signs, no nothing.'

'Well, you don't need to worry about shit like that; your Mrs is faithful, nobody has heard anything about her playing away from home and come on, who'd go near her when she's your wife. It'd be like signing your own death warrant, shagging Marco Reece's bird.'

'I'm just saying, Kes, putting it out there. Never say never. She's never gone away without me before.'

'Your Trisha is with her, so I don't think she's going to be meeting any men, do you? Stop being paranoid. Do yourself a favour, send her a bunch of flowers to her hotel and tell her how much you love her, she'll be over the moon with that and come home all loved up again, wanting to renew your vows and all that bollocks.'

Marco looked Kes directly in the eye and sucked on his cheeks. 'That's the trouble. I'm not sure if I do love her anymore. Before I got lifted, you know I'd told her it was over. And I meant it – my plan was to make a go of it with Leigh, but then I got nicked and she turned out to be a snake, nicking my money. I knew I needed something safe, and I had to backtrack. Come on, I needed Monica back then to sort my shit out while I was inside, didn't I? Our Trisha too, she made sure everything ran smoothly. She's got a good head on her.'

'So you're telling me it's over with you and Monica then or what? You don't want her eyeing up other fellas but you don't know if you want her?'

'Look, it's complicated, alright? I love her, but not like I used to. She's just always been there with me, hasn't she? She married me knowing my world – I don't care if it's double standards; she knows the men in this game sometimes have a bit of fun on the side. Her job was to keep home, raise me a kid and not peck my head about what I got up to when I wasn't home. And she got everything that money could buy in return.'

Kes reached over and looked at his boss. 'Mate, you don't need woman trouble when we have all this crap going on around us. Sort out your business, and the women can wait. I know you want Leigh found and once she is you say you will be able to concentrate on what you really want, but, like I said, Monica is a diamond and letting her slip would be something you will regret for a long time. Just give her the attention she needs and watch this space. She'll fall back into line no problem, just you wait and see.'

Marco smirked over at Kes. 'Wise words, mate. I might take you up on that and send her some flowers. Happy wife, happy life, and all that.'

Kes had gone quiet again. His boss had always got what he wanted – money or a blade convinced most people. But though he talked a good game, Kes knew his words felt hollow. Love was the one thing you couldn't threaten, trap or buy. But there was no way he was telling Marco that. Not if he wanted to keep his life.

Chapter Twenty

Danni walked slowly along the road where she used to live, flashbacks of the young girl she used to be flooding her mind. This was the place she used to play on the street with her friends: hide and seek, British bulldog, knock and run. Plenty had changed – the place looked rougher than she remembered, quiet apart from a few kids zipping past on electric bikes. But she still knew the place. Finally, Danni stood back from the house. Her breathing was fast as she came to a halt at a rusty gate and turned to look up the path. Just seeing her old house gave her palpitations. Danni held onto the rickety wooden fence and gripped it tightly to stop her legs from giving out. Maybe she'd made the wrong choice in coming here today, was she even ready to see her mother again? She'd felt so strong when she'd won the darts match and told Josie she was doing this. But in the cold light of day she felt anxious and alone. So many emotions were taking over her body. Danni walked one way then the other, debating her next move. If she scarpered now, no one would have to know she'd lost her bottle. But she'd know.

Taking a steadying breath, she opened the gate and walked down the garden path before she changed her mind again. Looking around her, she clocked the garden and the state of it; tufts of parched, overgrown grass, old furniture smashed up in the corner, dead plants in clumps of old sticks. Slowly, she walked over to a garden pot and lifted it up. It was dirty and cracked. Her eyes clouded over; she'd made this pot at school, painted all the bright-coloured flowers on the side of it that now were faded. She placed the plant pot back down on the ground. She went to the front door and knocked softly.

Danni stepped back and looked up at the windows for any sign of life. Nothing. She knocked again, but this time she rapped harder on the letterbox. A man came to the front door now and sneered at her. Was this it? Maybe her mother was long gone from this place, some other down-on-their-luck tenant taking her place. Danni didn't know whether to be relieved or disappointed. She looked at the guy.

He was scruffy; long, greasy hair, unshaven and the tang of stale beer coming off him. He rubbed his knuckles into the corner of his eyes, then stared at her. 'We don't need anything so piss off. I'm sick of you lot posting crap through the front door and forever knocking and trying to sell us something. How many times do you need telling we are not interested. Solar panels, double-glazing, cleaning stuff – does it look like we want any of that crap? Go on, piss off before you feel my foot up your arse.'

'I'm not selling anything!' Danni growled over at him, steeling herself to ask about her mother before giving up. 'Is Julie in?'

The man looked her up and down and dug his hand down the front of his trousers. 'She's asleep, why, who are you?'

Danni stuttered, not sure of what she was going to say next. She'd tried to prepare herself for seeing her mum again but, in the moment, words failed. 'Can you tell her Danni is here to see her... I'm her,' she finally managed. 'I'm her daughter.' There, she'd said it.

The man shrugged and left the door open slightly as he went back into the living room. She could hear him speaking but couldn't make out what he was saying. A minute later, he was back. 'She said come back later; she's sleeping.'

Danni felt the lie like a punch to the gut. She should have expected this. Well, she wasn't hanging around. 'Tell her I won't be coming back. I'm at The Fox pub, edge of here and Harpurhey, so if and when she can be arsed, or if she grows a conscience, she can come and see me if she wants to.'

'No need for the attitude, love. I'm just passing on the message, that's all.'

Danni turned around and started to walk out of the garden when she froze on the spot. She crossed the muddy grass and picked up her plant pot. She turned to the man still stood at the door and spoke through clenched teeth. 'I'm taking this with me because it's bloody mine.' Danni walked out of the garden, and never looked back. Why had she even thought there would be some great big reunion where her mother told her she loved and cared about her when in her heart she knew it would never happen like that, never in a million years. Danni walked down the busy street and held the plant pot close to her chest. This was hers, a part of her childhood, happy times. Faded and dirty, maybe, but still hers. There was no way she was ever going back to that house, ever. And, as for her mother? She'd had her chance and messed it up. It was obvious the bottle still meant more to her than her daughter.

As she trudged away, Danni gave Josie a ring and asked to meet for a coffee. She needed a friend, someone who knew her past, what she had been through, someone who wouldn't judge. She made her way to the cafe on the market and Josie told her she would be there as soon as she'd finished her morning shopping to order for her regulars. Just not paying for it. Danni felt comforted by the warm fug of the cafe, its chipped tables and the clatter of metal teapots making her feel safe again. She ordered the drinks and sat gazing out of the window, people watching. She wondered which of these passers-by harboured secrets too – broken hearts, broken families, broken promises. So many people hid so much – but everyone had to find a way to get up each day and keep living.

The door opened and in came the windswept Josie. She bustled over to the table and stood back, looking through the window. 'Danni, just keep your eyes on that man there, I'm sure he just followed me from Cash Generator. I lifted a couple of old iPhones from the cabinet when he wasn't looking and I'm sure he's on to me. He must have checked the camera because when I walked out, I could hear him shouting after me. I've just dusted him and had him chasing me around the market for the last ten minutes. He's a quick fucker too so I bet he'll put his beak in here. Sit here while I go to the lavs for a few minutes.'

Danni kept her eyes on the man outside; he was walking one way then the other, scanning the street. Sure enough, a minute later he walked into the cafe. Instead of going up to the counter, he ran his eyes over every customer. Danni didn't meet his eyes but was glad this man wouldn't know her from Adam. She sat back when he finally turned on his heels and left.

Josie reappeared from the back, fidgeting, nervous. 'Has he pissed off yet?'

Danni craned her neck. 'Yes, he's just walked back the other way. The coast is clear.'

'Thank god for that. He was going to get a slap if he tried gripping me, but I'm on a caution already.' Josie plonked herself down at the table and pulled the two phones out of her coat. 'This is a good day's graft for me. I'll get fifty quid each for these.'

Danni knew Josie stole to help her family, but she knew from bitter experience it was no life always watching your back. She was sure she could have got a little cleaning job or something – she felt guilty now wondering if she'd come back sooner, maybe they could have both kept each other straight, found normal jobs, normal lives. She'd had a taste of that in Huddersfield and now she was back in Manchester she realised how precious that simple life had been.

Josie rubbed at her eyes. 'I'm coming down the pub later for a practice. I told Sef we won, and he was really chuffed for me, told me to carry on because he said I looked really happy – and it's down to you, Daz. I was telling Sef about you, and he didn't believe me that you were hitting them high scores nearly all the time.'

Danni blushed and sipped on her hot coffee. She looked over at Josie and began to speak. 'I've just been to my mam's house.'

Josie sat up straight, alert, eager to hear more. 'Go on, what did she say? I hope she begged on her knees for you to forgive her – leaving you in care without a letter, a visit or even a sodding text message.'

Danni played with her fingers. 'I didn't even see her. Some random guy opened the door and when I told him who I was he went back in the house and told her I was outside.'

Josie was hanging on her every word, eyes wide.

'He came back and told me she was kipping and that I should call back later, like I was some door-to-door salesman. What the hell, Josie? I told him I wouldn't be coming back, and I was at the pub if she wanted to see me. How can she just sit in that house and say stuff like that, when her only daughter – her long-lost only daughter at that – is standing outside? I've only got one answer. She must have been hungover, or still pissed as always.'

'Rotten she is, Danni. I know she's your mother, but I just feel like going around there and giving her a mouthful, ask what's she playing at, she should have been running out to see you, making up for lost years.'

'Exactly what I thought. Don't get me wrong, it would have been hard for her to see me after all this time, but she should have at least made the effort to come to the door.'

Josie reached over the table and squeezed Danni's cold hands. 'It rips my heart out – now I'm a mum it's even worse than when we were kids. I could never in a million years treat my kids like she's done to you. But it'll catch up with her. She'll turn up at the pub, mark my words. She will walk in there one day soon, and be crying her eyes out. And, if I was you, I would tell her to turn straight back around and piss right off.'

Danni sat thinking for a few seconds, blinking away the tears that were forming in her eyes. She'd got this far without a mother's love. She told herself the fresh rejection only hurt because she'd allowed herself to hope. But she didn't have time to let that pain out now. She decided to change the subject; Josie loved some drama. Danni moved in closer. 'Did you clock those guys talking to Steve the night we won our match? They're the Farrows. You must have heard of their reputation. They're going to sort the Royals out and put them in their place.'

'Top one, you need to have someone with some muscle looking out for The Fox and I've heard Si is a good lad.'

'Not that bloody good: he wants three hundred pounds a week for it, to protect us he said.'

'Christ alive, even the cost of a bleeding protection racket has gone up these days! But come on, it's a small price to pay for peace of mind. And you better be prepared, it's going to kick off properly when Bert and Ben know that Si and Tim have taken you under their wing. The

Royals won't take that news lying down, let me tell you. Just tread very carefully, snidey pricks they are.'

'I know, it's Steve I feel sorry for. Coming here and making a life in Manny, making some proper wedge, was always his dream. To see him struggling is not something I ever wanted to see. He thought he could have sorted it out his way, but look at what they did to Roddy and his boys, they were badly hurt.'

'It's a different game around here, Danni. You know that. Sounds like where you were before, a nice quiet gaff, you didn't get any bother but you're in the thick of it around here. Everything has a price; it's a dog-eat-dog world.'

'I know that, I lived it, but come on, we run a local pub not some big business that's raking it in. We were just trying to play it straight.'

Josie sighed. 'There's no such thing round here, D. And you'd better tell Steve to keep the fuck out of it when the Royals and the Farrows are sorting it out too. There will be blood spilt for sure. I know he'll want to stop anyone getting hurt in his pub, but it needs to happen so Ben gets the message and backs down. It's the accepted way between these big families, so word Steve up so he doesn't get involved. No heroics, you hear me? And that goes for you, too.'

Danni played with the cuff of her coat and looked over at Josie for longer than she should have. It was time to tell her the truth, tell her about Marco. She swallowed hard and checked around the cafe to make sure nobody could hear her. 'Josie, I need to tell you something else too. I just need you to know everything about me because one day I will need you by my side when he comes looking for me.'

Josie's expression changed. Nobody messed with her friend, nobody. 'Who will be looking for you? Don't you remember what I always said when we were kids? Friends stick together. You fight one, you fight us all.'

Danni slowly stretched her fingers. She nodded at where her thumb ended, a serious look in her eyes. 'The man who did this to me. I know I told you it was an accident what happened to me, but I wasn't telling you the whole truth.'

Josie fidgeted in her seat. There were some stories that once you knew, you'd never be able to forget.

Danni continued. 'Marco Reece. He was the guy I was with before Steve. The man I was in love with, the man who did this to me. Thank god he's banged up now, but I know it won't be forever. He's a main head up in Leeds and everyone round there knows who he is. He runs the high-stakes gambling across the city, people win and lose a fortune at the matches he puts on – but if you owe him money? Then he's one nasty bastard.' She winced. 'And I don't mean like when we were bunking school, watching old-timers bung their pension on the horses or pissheads spending their dole on the fruit machines. The people at Marco's nights drop more money than I'd ever seen.'

'Christ, Daz, how deep did you get in that world?' Josie was wide-eyed.

'It was bit by bit. I see that now – that's how these men work. I thought I was tough – I'd made it through care, I'd escaped Manchester, I was earning enough money to live with my darts. But he was one smooth operator. He saw me when I was playing darts. I was hustling; you know, getting cocky, boozed-up fellas to bet they could beat me. Anyway, he said I was wasted on the small-time stuff, took me under his wing, and I began to hustle for him. Started making serious cash – but he kept the majority of the money. He only gave me a tiny bit of what was earned and that's how it always was. I didn't care back then, I thought he loved me, but when I found out he was married it all changed and I wanted out. That's when the violence started; he controlled me, told me who I could speak to and where I could go.'

Josie couldn't hold her tongue. 'The dirty no-good bastard, I hate him already. I've met his sort before. I'd have them whipped and beaten if it was down to me.'

Danni carried on talking, words that clearly hurt her to share, but desperate to be said – things she'd kept quiet for too long. 'I knew I needed to get away from him. But I had nothing – no papers, no money, no family. And when the Old Bill started investigating, I took my chance. Normally he was dead careful – all his dough went straight into a safe, or one of his grafters took it to all the little businesses he had laundering for him. But he was in a tight spot – he had to leave some with me. I'm not proud, but I took his money, Josie, fifty grand. I was almost free when he caught me. Almost safe. He chopped my thumb off; he knew it would ruin the only thing I'd ever been any good at. And he told me he was coming back, would take another finger each day I didn't tell him where his dough was.'

Josie was sat chewing on her fingernails now, shocked at what she was hearing.

'Luckily for me he got nicked the same night. And they were never granting that shady sod bail. I know when he's out he won't rest until he finds me, nobody has Marco over and gets away with it, nobody. I met Steve just after I left Marco and he's been my safety net ever since then. I wasn't sure about coming back to Manchester – I thought maybe he'd have watchers down here as well as on his home patch, but maybe Steve was right. Maybe facing one part of my past has given me strength to face whatever else is coming at me and, to be honest, I'm sick of hiding. When he gets out, I'll be ready.'

Josie looked gobsmacked. She sat staring at Danni. 'Fucking hell, you're a dark horse you are. Check you out, having the gangsters over. And there was I thinking I was a bad girl for robbing a few perfumes and some steak dinners.'

Danni offered a gentle smile, but she spoke again with a serious tone. 'Josie, one thing I'm deadly serious about is he will not care about hurting anyone else if it means he gets to me. It's why I've never had friends, not since you and me, really.'

'So you lifted fifty grand from him? I can see that's not pocket money. What did you do with it, lady? Tell me you're not a fucking gambler too?'

'No chance! Yes, I've spent some of it – I needed it to live when I left Leeds. I had nothing else – no bank account, no savings of my own. I've got a fair few Ks left, but I think even if I gave that back, he'd still want a finger for every grand I spent.'

'Shit, Danni, fucking hell. I'm glad you told me about this, but it's sent a chill up my spine if I'm being honest. If anyone comes round here asking questions, I'll say nothing. Good on you anyway, for taking what you were owed. He's no better than a pimp in my eyes. They should leave him in jail to rot, if you ask me.'

'I know, Josie, but the reality of it is that, one day, he's going to come looking for me. I don't want you caught up in anything dangerous, but I figured it was more dangerous for you not to know. And if I'm being honest, there's another thing you should know…' She blew out a massive breath before she continued. 'I have a gun. I stole it from Marco.'

Josie went white and shook her head before she dragged her fingers through her hair. 'A fucking gun, this is some heavy shit. Have you ever used it?'

Danni shook her head. 'No, have I bleeding hell. I just knew one day I might need it, so I hid it away and brought it with me when I knew I was leaving. It has two bullets in it too. If he ever comes at me with a machete, I need to be prepared.'

Josie blinked. 'I will always have your back, Danni, but even for me this is a bit deep. I would smash anyone's head in for you, no worries, but to deal with a man like this, Marco did you call him? I don't think I'm in his league.'

'I'm not asking you to do anything, Josie, but this way, if I ever go missing, and if they get to me then they'll probably have got to Steve too, then at least now you know the truth and you can tell someone. I don't want to be another crime statistic. A murder case on the news that everyone forgets the next day.'

Josie swallowed hard. Her voice was low when she replied, 'Friends forever, Danni. Good times and bad.'

A single tear ran down the side of Danni's cheek and she wiped it away quickly. 'Thank you, Josie, thank you for saying that. One real friend is worth more than all of Marco's dirty money.'

Chapter Twenty-One

Steve was a bag of nerves. Jamo had told him he heard on the grapevine the Royals were coming into The Fox tonight for their payment. This time Steve wasn't leaving anything to chance. He'd coughed up the first instalment to the Farrows and Si and his crew were already scattered about the pub. He'd worded Steve up, telling him no police must be rang, whatever happened; that was the deal for their particular brand of 'help'. Knowing neither the Farrows nor the Royals would mess around, Steve had told Danni to stay upstairs out of the way and, in truth, he wished he was up there with her too. He poured himself a double brandy and added a bit of Coca-Cola to take the edge from it. He took a deep breath and necked it in one. Jamo clocked him and chuckled. 'You better give me one of them too, mate, my arse has fell out too and my nerves are shattered.'

Steve poured Jamo a drink and passed it over to him. He might not have looked like a fixer, but the guy had helped him out and keeping him in the know with what was going on in the area was worth the odd free drink or two. The pub wasn't that busy tonight, just a few older guys sat gabbing in the corner of the room discussing the footy. Steve just wanted this over with, to get on with his life and run his business the way he'd imagined. He hadn't signed up for all this ball-ache and admitted if he'd have known this was going to happen, he would have stayed put in the old place – sure, that life wasn't making him rich, but at least he slept at night. Jamo sipped at his brandy, trying his best to make it last, none of his usual endless chitchat as he watched the doors edgily. Steve turned the music up; it was like a morgue in here and he decided he needed some background noise to take away the eerie quietness.

Then it was go-time. Ben and Bert Royal walked into the boozer, five other guys behind them. Jamo was gone in an instant, he headed straight to the toilets and Steve knew that was where he was staying until whatever this was over. Steve shot a look over at Si. Why was he still sat there like he didn't have a care in the world, he thought, he should have been up on his feet smashing this prick's head in. For a moment he wondered if maybe there was still a chance for this to end without blood. Was the threat of it enough?

Ben nodded his head at Steve. 'Beers for the lads, mate.'

Steve gulped, bent down and fetched the bottles of lager out of the fridge and placed them on the bar. Maybe the Royals were so confident this was their gaff they hadn't even noticed the Farrows. Before he could tell Ben how much he should pay, he growled over at him. 'Have my money ready in ten. I'm just going to have a drink with the boys, and I'll be back.'

Steve shot another look over at Si, still nothing. He stood there and watched them going to sit down. He was sure now they hadn't clocked Si and his brother yet. Steve filled his own glass up again and necked it in one, his hands trembling. Then he saw it. Si stood up and walked over to where Ben and Bert stood, Tim close behind. Of course, when the Farrows stood up so did their boys too, always two steps behind. Steve moved to the end of the bar, ready for a quick getaway. The atmosphere was crackling and even the other punters in the pub knew something was going down. Steve mouthed over to them to go and sit in the vault until all this was over. They asked no questions, clearly even the old boys knew the script well.

Si towered over Ben. 'Alright, big balls. What you lot doing here?'

The Royals made a good effort to hide their surprise but Steve could see Si and his boys were the last people they thought they would see in this pub.

'What's up?' Bert replied as he glanced behind Si to see who was backing him. It clearly wasn't a coincidence or a social call.

Si was doing the same, weighing up where everybody was and positioned himself where he could defend himself if anyone tried to surprise him. He bent his head down slightly and spoke through clenched teeth. 'We can do this the easy way or the hard way, Bertie Boy, it's your shout, but I'm running this pub now, not you.'

Ben was about to stand up when Bert pulled him back down. He'd read the room already and knew the odds were against them. Si was team-handed and if this kicked off, they would be the underdogs. Ben leaned forward and bit down hard on his lip, frustrated, knowing he could do nothing. Bert nodded his head at Tim, not ready just yet to hand over this boozer without comment. 'Tim, I don't come near your area, so why are you disrespecting me by coming to mine. You do your shit and I do mine, we don't cross the line.'

Tim spoke up from behind his brother. 'I heard you were getting a bit greedy. So this is our pub now, bro. I don't have to explain what the set-up is here so drink up and fuck off. I'm only going to tell you once, so think about it. Not that thinking comes easy for you, dipshit.'

Bert lost it and sprang from his seat like a jack in the box. He went nose to nose with Tim Farrow, pushing him with his head, eyes bulging from their sockets. Steve held his breath. Si moved in a flash, dragged Ben towards the door with two other men, and went in heavy on him, booting and kicking him. 'This is my pub, if I see you or any of your muppets in here again, you know the score, don't you?'

Bert was being dragged to the door too now, four men on him, so the rest of the Royals crew were surrounded. They knew there was no point putting up a fight when they were this outnumbered. Ben Royal roared at the top of his voice as he was flung outside the boozer and landed on his arse. 'You fucking watch, Farrow, I know where your mam lives and your sister, you'll pay for this, just you watch.'

Bert and the rest of his firm were together now and they were looking around them for weapons, anything to launch at the Farrows. Ben found half a brick and launched it over at Tim in the doorway, missing him by inches. Si didn't flinch, stood as cool as cucumber next to his brother. 'You know where I am if you want me, you bunch of pricks. Anytime, anywhere, you just shout me if you fancy your chances.'

Bert yelled back at him as he wiped the blood from his nose. 'Snidey pricks, ambushing us. We'll be ready next time, just you wait and see. We'll catch you slipping, bro, and when you do, I'll be right there making sure you pay for this.'

The Royals jumped into their cars and spun off, hanging out of the car windows shouting insults at Si and his boys as they drove off. Bert made a gun with his fingers and pointed at Tim. 'You're getting it, prick, just you watch, you're getting it. You're going down.'

Si pulled his shoulders back and inhaled deeply. A decent day's work. He checked in with his boys to make sure they were alright and there were no serious injuries. This could have been a whole different story if the Royals had known they were coming. The guys they'd had with them today were clearly just the foot soldiers, lads really, just trying to look hard and make up the numbers. But Si knew Bert and Ben had a team of proper headcase guys, the ones they used for serious enforcing. If they'd been there, it would have been a blood bath, guns, machetes, baseball bats, anything they could hurt each other with. And next time he knew they were the ones the Royals would bring.

Si jerked his head at his boys to come back inside the pub. 'We'll stay here until closing time just to make sure they don't come back. Now let's have a beer and celebrate.'

Steve didn't look anywhere near celebratory when the Farrows came back into the pub, smiling and swaggering now their fight was won. His words were stuttered as he spoke to Tim. 'Is that it now, are they going to come back? Did they get the message?'

'They might try their luck here again, but two of my boys will always be in here for the next week or so and they'll shout me if I'm needed.' Si held a hand out to Steve. 'Wages please, and like we said, every week the same: three ton. I think you've got a bargain, if you ask me.' He let out a menacing laugh as Steve took a wad of notes from the till. Turning to go and sit back down, he shouted over to the landlord. 'Steve, lad, send the beers over for the boys to show your appreciation, yeah? And keep them coming. On the house, right?' he smirked.

Steve was gobsmacked, the cheek of this guy. £300 from the till and at least half as much again through the taps. But, he thought, at least he wasn't calling the glazers, the fire brigade… or the ambulance. He texted Danni and said the coast was clear if she wanted to come back down.

The night since had been quiet, and everything was back to normal on the surface. Josie and Danni were playing darts in the vault and Si wandered in for a game of pool, still keeping watch on the darts game from the corner of his eye. He nudged his mate Davy. 'That bird is fucking mint, just watch her.' They both stopped playing pool, eyes on Danni as she threw her darts. Si grinned wolfishly at Davy, 'Told you didn't I, class she is.'

'Nah, Si, it was a fluke,' Davy scoffed. 'Anyway, look at the weird way she throws, and did you clock her hand? She's missing half her ruddy thumb! I bet I could beat her.'

Si said nothing but walked over to the oche, still holding the pool cue in his hands. 'Good evening, ladies. My mate here thinks he can beat you. I've been watching you and, may I say, I think you're the dog's bollocks. Personally, I don't think he would stand a chance.'

Danni looked awkward. 'We're just practising.'

Josie watched another guy enter and, realising who it was, she went and stood at his side, hands on her hips. 'Alright, Timmy, I've not seen you in a long time, what have you been up to?'

The younger Farrow brother had to look twice at Josie to see if he remembered her and he smiled when he did. 'You know me, ducking and diving as always. Are you still the best shoplifter around these ends then, Josie, innit?' He chuckled.

'That's me. If you need anything, give me a shout. I mean that. There's no security guard in the city that can catch me. I can get you anything that you want… within reason.'

Tim smiled and nudged her in the waist. 'If you're offering. Perhaps you can get me some nice bedding for my Ma Dukes. Not that cheap shite either – my mam likes that Egyptian cotton, hotel stuff.'

Si interrupted. 'This isn't bleeding QVC. What about this darts match, then?'

Josie looked at Danni and gave her a cheeky smile. 'She'll play him.' She nodded back at Davy. 'But it has to be worth her while, how much does he want to throw on the game?'

Si liked the cheek of this girl. He rubbed his hands together and shouted his pal over. He loved a bet. He put the deal on the table. 'Davy, she will play you, but it will cost you. Put your money where your mouth is, mate, and make it worth her while to whip your arse. Give us all a good laugh.'

Davy was clearly still adamant that he was going to wipe the floor with this match. He looked Danni up and down, writing her off; a look she'd seen before when she was hustling. 'How much, love? Come on, you make the shout if you think you will win.'

Josie decided to dive in and chance her hand: go big or go home was her motto. 'A ton, put a hundred pound on it and my mate D will show you how it's done.'

Davy looked surprised at the figure, but also like there was no way he was backing down. The sly grin on his face suggested he already felt he had this in the bag. A few darts against a woman with a bust-up hand? Easy-peasy. 'Yep, I'll throw a ton in, but don't be crying when I take your money, girls.'

Josie burst out laughing and went and sat down with Si to watch the game. Danni spun her darts around in her fingers, confident now she had warmed up that she would beat this guy. She started off gentle though – nothing too flashy, kept her score well under one hundred.

Si was mesmerised by the game, or was it Danni he was fascinated with? Davy played his darts – not a bad score – and the onlookers stopped their chatting as they realised a decent contest might be on.

Josie whispered to Tim: 'You watch my girl now she's in the zone, look at her concentration.'

Another three darts, and this time Danni let her precision show.

'I'm watching, don't worry,' he replied. 'Let's see what your pal can do.'

A flush of embarrassment hit Davy and he looked eager to throw his darts again, prove that he could smash through whatever beginner's luck this woman had, but his darts landed wide of every big number he tried.

Danni knew from experience to avoid showing off, no point pulling a nine-darter against this guy. So she let the match play out but soon the chance to go in for the kill was too much to resist.

Boom, full house.

Danni held her hand out. 'Better luck next time.'

Davy wouldn't shake, but grudgingly handed the money over, a sore loser.

Si clapped his hands together and invited Danni to come and sit with him. 'Davy, go and get the drinks in while I have a chat to this champion here. What are you girls drinking?'

Josie didn't need asking twice. 'I'll have a vodka and lemonade, a double,' she said as she gave Si a cheeky wink. 'And you, Danni, what are you on?'

Danni was a shy person by nature and all the years that she'd spent hidden away from the world hadn't helped her confidence. It was only ever in front of a dartboard that she felt she could relax. Sitting here with the Farrows felt like pulling teeth and she couldn't wait to get away. 'Can I just have a lemonade please? A half? I don't really drink unless it's a special occasion.'

Davy went to the bar. Si stared at Danni, intrigued by her. 'So, tell me, how come you can play darts like that?'

Danni avoided any eye contact and dipped her head low. 'I don't really know, I used to play as a kid and practice a lot. I've not played for years due to my accident.' She gestured to her hand, no point hiding it when everyone always stared, anyway. 'I've only just got back into it so I'm still a bit rusty.'

'You look fine to me. Say, have you ever thought about earning some decent money doing it? I know a few guys who can set up games for big money if you're interested?'

She didn't need to think about her reply, but tried to keep her voice casual. 'No, I just do this for fun and that's how I like it.'

'Well, give me a shout if you change your mind. Like I said, serious money to be earned.'

Josie could see Danni was uncomfortable with the conversation and changed it quickly. 'Is your mam still living on the Smedley estate, Si?'

'Yes, she'll never move from there, I've asked her lots of times to up sticks but she won't, she's set in her ways. Plus since my dad died, she won't leave all her friends behind.'

Josie nodded her head. 'Yes, sorry about your old man. I lost my mam not too long ago too. It's hard, isn't it?'

Si nodded his head slowly. 'Knocks you for six, Josie love, doesn't it. Anyway, let's not talk about doom and gloom tonight, let's celebrate Danni's win over Davy-boy.'

Davy came back holding the drinks and placed them on the table. He seemed to be seeing the funny side of things now. He congratulated Danni and shook her hand. 'Hats off to you, you won fair and square. I thought I was good, but you are on another level.'

Eager to avoid another invitation to play, Danni excused herself and headed for the loos. Steve grabbed her arm as she went past. 'I've not seen you all night. Are you OK talking to the Farrows like your best mates? What have they said? And watch out for that Si. What's his game talking to my woman all night? He'd better not be coming on to you?'

Danni burst out laughing. She'd hidden herself away so much she'd never seen this jealous side of Steve before. 'Is he hell! In fact, he was asking me to play darts for money. Little does he know I've been there, done it and got the t-shirt.'

'I know we need to keep them sweet, but I hope you know he's trouble he is, Danni. I hope you said no…' Steve started, then froze, clearly having a brain wave. 'Or maybe we should use this to our advantage. You could tell him you will play for the money he takes from us each week. I know you're meant to be keeping a low profile, but…'

'Exactly. I mean what if the Farrows set me up against someone Marco's boys are running. I've only just come to terms with the fact that playing in the Harpurhey pub league is probably small time enough for me to not to get noticed. But we don't really know the Farrows, or the circles they mix in. But I know it won't be pretty, they're not small fry kind of guys, are they?'

'But that's the beauty of it.' Steve was warming to his own idea now. 'You'd be doing it on behalf of the toughest guys in town. If – and it's a big if – even if Marco is still running a racket from inside, or has his crew doing it – no one is going to mess with anyone the Farrows are backing.'

Danni raised her eyebrows high, maybe he had a point. She leaned in and kissed Steve on the side of his cheek. 'I'll ask, but for now, let me go to the lav!'

Danni stood looking at her reflection in the mirror. She flicked her hair back over her shoulder and smiled at herself. 'Welcome back, Danni,' she whispered to herself before she went back into the bar. Tonight had been an eye-opener for her, every day she was getting stronger and stronger.

Danni went back over to join Si and sat facing him. The money he took from this place each week was worth the risk in her eyes. She eyeballed him and took a deep breath before she spoke. 'You know that you said about earning some money from playing darts, well…'

Si didn't even let her finish, he was straight on her.

'I'll make sure you earn real till, I promise you.' Si looked made up.

Danni flashed a glance at Josie before she continued. 'I'll play one game a week, but not some big flashy match. No, I'll play for the debt on this place each week. The three hundred pounds Steve pays you. If I win you drop the fee that week. If you win, then I'll up it to five hundred pounds that week.' She sounded cool as a cucumber but inside she was doing the sums and panicking. What on earth was she thinking? If this went badly, it was a lot of money to fork out each week. What if the takings were low, what if they couldn't pay? She'd not thought this through. But Si Farrow didn't look like the kind of man you welched on.

Si held his head back laughing, he liked her brass neck. He sat thinking for a few seconds before he spoke again. 'It can be arranged, but I won't be playing you. I'll bring somebody in.'

Danni tried to keep her voice casual. Who would he bring in to play against her? 'So who will I be playing? Have you got someone in mind or are you going to be trying ringers each week?'

Si shrugged. 'I'll need to make a few calls before I say. But I'll try and get it sorted for a few days' time. We can do it when the pub closes. If I get the guy I'm thinking of, he won't want everybody watching him, knowing his business. Is that good for you?'

Danni nodded. The fewer people who knew about this, the better. She stood up. 'Right, see you in a few days then. Josie, are you coming with me? You can help us collect a few glasses and give Steve a break?'

Josie said her goodbyes and followed her friend. 'Bleeding hell, Danni, do you need your head testing?' Josie piped up as soon as they were out of Si's earshot. 'This could all go tits-up and then what?'

Danni pulled her to a quiet area of the pub and kept her voice low. 'I have no other choice really. If we're bleeding three ton a week to these boys we'll be dead in the water here anyway. Steve has risked everything for us over the years, so if I can help make our life easier here then I have to step up to the mark. I have a few days to practice so I should be fine. It's just hitting the bullseye that freaks me out, I just can't master it like I used to.'

Josie looked directly at her friend. 'Well, I'll be right by your side when you're playing for support. We've missed a lot of years when we should have been stood shoulder to shoulder, but you've got me now.'

'Thanks, Josie. It means a lot. I just hope I pull it off.' Danni considered this.

'You have more guts than me, girl, for sure,' Josie said. 'Look at how you cleaned up against that Davy fella.'

'I know, but who's this guy Si Farrow has in mind to call? I bet you anything it won't just be some cocky kid from his gang. No, I can feel it – he's going to bring in the big guns.'

Chapter Twenty-Two

Monica was back from her holiday, had just walked into the house dragging her suitcase behind her. Trisha was paying the taxi outside, the front door was left open for her. Monica flopped down on the sofa. Her tan stood out against the white velvet couch. Her skin was gleaming, a rich golden-brown colour, showing off her blue eyes. This was how you were meant to come back from holiday, she thought – looking good, feeling chilled. But the minute she'd set eyes on her home, all her troubles filled her mind.

Trisha slammed the door shut behind her and sat down on the sofa next to her mother. 'I don't know about you, Mam, but I'm done in. That flight has taken it out of me, bloody two hours delay didn't help either. I thought Dad might have picked us up instead of us having to get a taxi.'

Monica sucked on her vape. 'No, he wouldn't take time away from his precious boys or his work. But I'm not going to rise to it. Like I said before, I'm focusing on me from now on. Let him do the same. This holiday has opened my eyes to a lot of stuff that I've been sweeping under the table for years, things I should have dealt with a long time ago.' Monica looked like she was on a mission. She stood up and kicked her shoes off. 'I'm brewing up, do you want coffee or a tea?'

'I'll have a milky coffee, Mam.' Trisha studied her mother, a confused look in her eyes. What on earth was she up to?

Marco strolled into the house just after ten o'clock that evening. He'd had a haircut while Monica had been away and looked fresh in a pale-blue shirt and dark jeans. He clocked his wife sat in the armchair and went over. 'Come on then, give me a cuddle, I've missed you, I have.'

She opened her arms as Marco leaned over and though she could feel her husband in her embrace, her eyes filled with sadness. She used to be full of excitement when her man came home each evening, she'd always jumped up out of her chair and run to him. That wasn't the case tonight, she felt cold as she hugged him robotically.

Marco sat down and took his shoes off. 'You look well, babes, was it hot out there?'

'It was sweltering, the hotel was lovely, and I would stay there again. It just gave me time to think, you know.'

'Well, maybe we'll go together the next time.'

Monica looked over at him. 'So you have missed me then?'

'Dead right I have, I've got no clean shirts and I've been eating out most nights.'

So, there it was right in front of her eyes; she was just a bloody cleaner for him, someone to cook and skivvy for him.

He kicked his legs onto the sofa and looped his hands behind his head. 'So, are we back to normal services from tomorrow then?'

'Meaning what?' she hissed over at him.

'I mean, has a bit of sun cheered you up? You're not going to piss off and leave me on my tod again? I've had some mad shit going on and I like you by my side to know you're safe when I'm beefing with pricks.'

'I don't know, Marco, that depends on you.' Monica was in no mood to sweet-talk him.

He tried a softer approach. 'Babes, you know I don't function properly without you. I know I hurt your feelings before you left but I'm sorry. I just get angry and don't think before I put my mouth into gear, do I? And I know it's been a lot getting used to me back out of the slammer. You probably needed some girl time, that's all.'

'Girl time? Yeah, you could say that. It's definitely girl time.'

'And what do you mean by that?'

But Monica had already started to walk into the kitchen. 'Nothing, it means nothing. I'm making a drink; do you want one?'

'You bet I do, this is what I've missed for sure.'

Monica went into the kitchen and rammed two fingers up at her husband behind the door. 'You've missed me bloody slaving about after you, that's all. Lazy git you are, bleeding sponger.' But there was no point saying that to Marco right now. She had to stick to her plan.

Monica was rummaging about the bedroom when she heard Marco coming up to bed. She closed the bedside drawer and quickly scrambled under the covers and pretended to be asleep. She could feel his warm body next to hers and his hand flopped over her waist. He was clearly restless.

'Mon, are you still awake?'

She answered in a croaky voice. 'Not really, but what's up?'

'Nothing, just wanted to know what all that cryptic shit was about earlier. You've been a bit off with me tonight and I just wanted to check we're alright, that's all. You know it cuts me deep inside when we are not right.'

Monica rolled onto her side and faced him, looking deep in his eyes; his bedside light casting his face into sharp lines of light and shadow. He was a handsome man, still. But neither he nor her were getting any younger. Too old for lies and bullshit, that was for sure. 'Are you still in love with me, Marco?'

Shock flashed across his face before he regained his cool. 'Yes, I don't even know why you'd ask. I'll always love you until my dying breath.'

She used a different tone now. 'But are you *in* love with me? I know you care about me, I'm the mother of your kid, and as you've made bloody clear tonight, you need me to keep fucking house. But do you still fancy me, want me like you used to?' There was a heartbeat's pause. 'Mon, we have been together a lot of years, and you can't expect me to do cartwheels every time I see you. We're past the point where we're at it like rabbits – what do you want me to do? Bend you over the sofa every time I come home? I love you, end of. I'm here, ain't I?'

Her next question rolled from her tongue with ease. She studied him as it hit home. 'Tell me the truth, Marco. Have you ever cheated on me, been unfaithful since we were wed?'

This was a question too far. Marco snapped and stood up at the side of the bed. 'For crying out loud, you should have stayed where you were on holiday if this is your thought process. What a bleeding daft question to ask, and at fucking midnight too. In fact I won't even dignify it with an answer.' He started pacing to and fro across the bedroom.

And there was her answer right there. She could always tell when he was lying to her, his eyes skated about, his voice was high-pitched, he paced. Yes, he'd been unfaithful alright. If she hadn't known about it for years she might have felt wounded, but instead what she'd lost was her last thread of hope that her husband would be honest with her.

Marco left the bedroom and slammed the door behind him, she could hear him shouting as he walked down the landing to the spare room. 'Back two minutes and already kicking off. I don't even know why I bother. Women. Fucking hysterical.'

Monica folded the duvet under her chin. Normally, when they argued, she'd give him a night in the spare room, they'd both cool off and then she was always the one to make up. She'd go in with tea and toast in the morning or tell him she was just hormonal or some other line to smooth things over. Well, that life was over. No more peacemaker. No more little woman, waiting and placating. She knew what her dad would have told her: what doesn't kill you makes you stronger. It was time to prove it.

Chapter Twenty-Three

Danni had been feeling sick all morning; her nerves were shattered, her stomach turning like a washing machine on full spin. A long soak in the bath was usually her cure for most things but she still felt dreadful. She was thinking of pulling out of the match, why had she listened to Steve? She'd just got caught up in the moment and now she was sorry she'd even opened her mouth. She came out of the bathroom and knew Steve could tell by her face that she was hot and bothered.

'Babes, just do your best. If we have to pay the extra money, then so be it. But I have faith in you and what you can do with them darts in your hands. Honest, you are shit hot. Si Farrow's ringer won't know what's hit him. You were made for this.'

'I'm glad you think so because I'm shitting myself, Steve. This guy is one of the best round here from what Jamo's heard on the grapevine. I'm just a bloody has-been hustler with a gammy hand who should have known better. I wonder if I speak to Si, he'll understand that I just can't do it. We'll just have to pay up instead. The pressure is too much. Since I've agreed to this match I've not slept properly, I feel like I'm going to spew. On my life, I'm going to have a bloody heart attack at this rate.'

Steve was by her side, holding her in his arms. 'Babes, the ball is in your court. Or the dart, rather.' He attempted a weak smile. 'Look, if it's too much for you then, like you say, we'll just walk away. Si can shout and scream all he wants but he can't make you play, can he? Sure we've got to shell out a couple of hundred extra but it's not worth you getting sick over. I'll tell you what…' He pulled fifty pounds out of his pocket and passed it her. 'Go and get your hair done today and take your mind off it all, get your nails painted too. Get out of this place for a few hours and clear your head – whatever you decide after that, I'll back you.'

Danni lifted her head up to look at him. 'You're a good one you are. I don't know how you even put up with me and my moods sometimes. But you're right, I need to keep myself busy and not sit about this place all day thinking about it. Is Alice still downstairs, do you know? She said after she'd finished cleaning she was going to have a few games of darts. Practising, she said, for the next league match.'

'I think she's still here; and you might as well know, I did let it slip that you were playing a special match after hours tonight and now her and Frenchie want to come and watch it. She did say Betty and Jasmine too.' He cringed as the words left his mouth knowing she would be hacked off.

Danni shook her head. 'Bleeding hell, Steve! Si said just a few people to watch tonight and now you've gone and opened your big mouth to the world and his wife.'

'He's got a few of his lads coming and I just thought the girls could come and support you too, to even things out.'

'This just gets worst by the minute, this does. I'm going downstairs. No doubt Alice will grab me now and want to know all the details.'

Alice was sat waiting for Danni in the vault. Her darts were on the table and she had her phone in her hand. She grinned as Danni walked in. 'I'm so excited about tonight. A proper money match. I've told Steve that I will make a curry and Betty said she would bring some cakes along too. Frenchie is sorting a babysitter out and Jasmine said she wouldn't miss it for the world, so all your girls are behind you, supporting you every step of the way.'

'For crying out loud, the full crew are coming! I appreciate the thought, Alice, but if it wasn't for Steve and his big gob, I'd be doing this on the down-low. 500 bigs is a lot to lose if I balls this up. And with people watching.'

'Danni, babe, we're not putting any pressure on you – we just want to cheer you on. Plus now I've seen you in action, I think you could take on anyone.'

'I just hope I don't let you all down, Alice.' Danni tried to feel some of her friend's confidence. 'A lot is riding on this, more than just the money, if I'm being honest, and if I mess up, I'll never forgive myself.'

Alice leaned in. 'Don't be saying that, love. You've given us all hope where the darts are concerned. Your Steve has told me our new shirts are on the way. Who'd have thought it a few months ago – we were a joke till you came along. We all respect you, Danni, and for a lot of us – including myself – it's the first time any of us have ever won anything or been part of something like this. It means a lot to us girls, more than you will ever know.'

Danni reached over for the darts and walked over to the board. She turned her head to Alice and spoke before she threw her darts. 'It's the bull that's freaking me out. I'm more or less confident with everything else.' She took her stance and concentrated on the bullseye. Three shots; each of them missed. She plucked her darts out of the board in silence. She stood at the oche and tried again. But the darts lodged anywhere but in the red circle. She ripped the darts from the board and stomped back to Alice, flinging the darts on the table. 'Absolutely shite I am, what's the point in playing this match if I can't hit the bull for love nor money. It's my hand, I can't play like I used to.'

Alice sighed. 'Look, I've seen you hit every number on the board. If you can hit treble twenty, you can hit the bull. You've changed the way you play, of course, I get that. I don't know what you were like before, but you're still top class. If your new style means you can throw a dart, you can throw at the bull. It's not your thumb that's the problem, it's your head.' Alice could see Danni frowning, but wasn't taking no for an answer. 'So I'll see you later for another practice. Steve said it's going to be a late one tonight, so I'll try and have a nap this afternoon before I come back and then you can get warmed up proper.'

Danni gripped her coat and handbag from the table and headed for the door. 'I'm off to get my hair done, hopefully it'll calm me down and stop me having a fit with all these nerves. If I'm still breathing, I will see you later tonight.'

'Yes, you go and relax, we need you with a level head for tonight.'

But Danni was already gone.

It was mid-afternoon and Jamo was talking to Steve when the door opened and a woman walked in and headed for the far end of the bar. Steve was used to welcoming in all punters, but this woman looked like she needed a hospital more than a pub. Her skin was yellow, her teeth decayed and brown, cheeks sunken and hair like rats' tails. She shot a look at Steve and snarled at him, 'Are you bloody serving or what?'

Steve looked at Jamo. Normally if someone new walked in, Jamo would clock them the moment they entered, and give Steve a sense if they were trouble or harmless. But Jamo just wriggled about in his seat, his voice low. 'Mate, please tell me you can smell that too, is it her?' Jamo pinched his nose together and pulled his jumper up over his nose as he continued talking. 'Tell her to hurry up and drink her drink and get gone.'

Steve thought it was a bit rich, Jamo complaining about anyone else's personal hygiene when most days you could see what he'd had for breakfast by looking at his shirt, but he had to admit there was a reek around this new customer. Still, if she showed him the colour of her money, he couldn't refuse her a drink, he supposed. He moved along the bar but stood back slightly. 'What can I get you?'

'I'll have a double whisky with one cube of ice.'

Steve went to make the drink and tried his usual small-talk. 'Is it still cold out?'

'Perishing it is, I've got three jumpers on today to keep the cold out.' The woman looked thin as a rake despite the layers.

Steve passed the drink over and the woman handed a crumpled ten-pound note to him with shaking hands. She was looking around the pub like she'd lost something. He wondered if she was looking for Josie and her knock-off bargains. Steve passed her the change and she spoke again, still looking shiftily about her. 'Is there anyone called Danni here? Heard she worked here now.'

Steve looked the woman up and down. He knew Danni was petrified of someone from Marco's gang tracking her down, but this woman didn't look much like a criminal mastermind. Maybe she was from a charity shop that Danni had been in and she'd told her to come and collect the old clothes that she had bagged at the top of the stairs. 'She's out at the moment, but can I help you?'

The women's eyes looked red, full of burst blood vessels and watery. 'I'm her mother and she told me she would be here if I wanted her.'

Steve didn't know what to do, where to look or even what to say. This was not what he'd expected. He stuttered.

'She'll be back later on if you want to wait for her or I can tell her you called?'

The woman swilled the drink about her mouth before she swallowed it and banged the empty glass on the bar. 'No, I won't wait. I have places to be. Just tell her Julie her mother came in to see her, it's her own fault if she's not here, isn't it? I'll probably catch her another time.' The woman walked out from the pub and slammed the door shut after her.

Steve ran his fingers through his hair. There was not a chance he was telling Danni that her mother had been in the pub today. She had enough on her plate with the darts match tonight, never mind seeing her mother after all these years. No, he was keeping schtum for now. She'd not seen the woman in years from what Danni had told him – another day wouldn't hurt.

Jamo watched her leave. Once he was sure she was gone he let out a laboured breath. 'Get the air freshener out, pal. On my life she smells like she's been dug up. Why has nobody told her that she stinks? Surely, she has family who she lives with, friends?'

Steve knew he should keep schtum and not breathe a word to Jamo about who the woman really was. No, this was Danni's secret to share – or not. He walked back towards his best customer. Jamo was drinking more than usual today, he must have had his benefits. He pulled a twenty-pound note from his pocket and placed it on the bar.

'Are you doing any pub grub today, Steve? Just a few chips and a couple of rounds of bread will go down nicely.

I've not been shopping yet and just need something to keep me going until I can get to Asda.'

'I can rustle up a few chip butties for you, our kid. You just keep your eyes on the bar for a minute while I bang the chip pan on.'

By the time Danni was back, Steve had closed the kitchen. He was relieved to see the afternoon at the hairdresser's seemed to have done the trick and she was smiling. Her hair was cut shorter than usual, and she had a deep purple colour threaded through it. It suited her, Steve thought, her skin tone looked warmer. 'Whit-woo, babes, your hair is lovely, it suits you. Makes you look foxy.'

'I only went in for a cut, but the stylist tried a new colour on me. I like it, to be honest. I needed a change and, the way I've been feeling, looking different is just what I need. Anyway, how's it been in here, it looks like there are a few in?'

'It's been busy, love. I've done some food today, earned decent cash from toasties and chip butties.'

'Great. I will go upstairs and put my bags in, and I'll come back down and help you with some of these glasses. Any other regulars in?'

Steve gulped, his palms sweaty. He hated lying to his partner and it didn't sit well with him not telling her about her mum, but he couldn't afford for her to spiral. Still, he'd always said honesty was the best policy. He was just about to shout her back over and confess what had happened when Jamo yelled from across the room. 'Steve, get the cards out, a few of the lads fancy a game of Queenie.'

Steve turned on the spot and went to find the cards. Maybe it was for the best that he kept his mouth shut for now. He needed his woman stress-free and ready to win.

Chapter Twenty-Four

In the end, it had been over in minutes. After closing time, Danni had ushered out the last of the regular punters then scarpered upstairs to steady her nerves. Her instinct to run was kicking in. All she'd have to do was grab the suitcase from below the bed, tiptoe out the back and get in a cab and that would be that. Another failed chapter in the life of Danni Cox.

But something inside her told her she'd waited a lifetime to get back to Manchester. And why should she let a darts match run by some local thugs chase her off? All she had to do was throw a few darts, win the match and save her and Steve this week's money for Si and Tim. She'd done this kind of shit three times a week in her hustling days. The only difference was those were the days before she'd met Marco. And, in truth, it wasn't the darts match, or the Farrows that were causing all this stress. It was the thought of word getting back to Marco. Her thumb pulsed at the thought.

She heard the door banging downstairs. Was that her opponent arriving? No, she could hear Josie's laugh echoing up the stairs. The sound gave her courage and she tried to tell herself she had a home advantage. Plus she looked like a new person after her dye job. So she'd waited until Alice had come up and knocked on the door of the flat, then had a swig of gin for luck, then headed to the vault.

The small back room was crowded. Not just with her girls, but the Farrows had clearly brought a few of their guys with them too. And in the middle of a cluster of people, a lanky ginger guy with a cockney accent. Someone she'd never played before, never even set eyes on.

Some people hated playing strangers but Danni had relaxed immediately. A darts hot-shot from down south? Happy days. She was much happier against some kid than anyone who might have recognised from her old days. It was all she'd needed to switch into match mindset.

It had been another boozer, not too far from here, where she'd first picked up a dart. Underage, alone and bored, Wilf had taught her everything he knew. Danni still thought of him sometimes, wished she could thank him. But, in the end, it wasn't so much the game itself he'd taught her – she'd been a natural at that. But it was the attitude he gave her. He'd taught her that she was never really playing her opponent, that was where most people slipped up. No, Wilf had taught her to forget about the world, and just play the board. That was when Danni first fell in love with the game. You didn't need anyone else, just you and your darts.

She did the same now, the noise in the room fading, the faces blurring. She barely acknowledged anyone else – the girls whistling and clapping, the Farrows' boys goading her. She'd shaken her opponent's hand, and in a matter of minutes, eleven darts later, she'd shaken it again, the winner.

Si Farrow wasted no time in marching over; the bubble was burst and Danni was back in the pub. The sounds, the smells, the cheering. Was he going to keep his word? She'd half expected him to knock the tables over and demand a rematch, but he just clapped her on the shoulder. 'Nice work. I could get you more of it. In fact, I'm going to a fight tomorrow night, with some very important people watching. Serious cash being dropped. Just so you know the kind of crowd I can get you into. Think about it, why don't you? Same time next week?'

But Danni hadn't answered. Hadn't told him how her life had been ruined once already by Marco giving a very similar speech. Hadn't told him how she'd decided tonight was a one-and-done. She'd been saved by Steve walking over, and had decided she'd wait till morning before telling Steve and Si that the deal was off. She couldn't put herself through this every week. That ticking clock she always felt inside ticked a little louder on nights like this. She'd got away with tonight, she thought. But next time, would she be so lucky?

Chapter Twenty-Five

Marco sat with Kes on one side, Tim Farrow on the other. The Reece family had never been one to trust new contacts quickly and tonight had been a test. A bare-knuckle fight with a couple of real scrappers – they'd all earned a good amount of money from the hustle, and trust came easier when the cash was flowing.

Si Farrow walked over, his swagger full of confidence. Kes passed over his cut from the deal. 'Nice one, mate. I might have a few other ideas in the pipeline for you too, Marco. I've got some real hot property on the Manchester darts circuit. It's going to be big money stuff. But leave it with me for now and I'll shout you when I've boxed it all off.'

Kes smiled over at Marco, pleased these new brothers he'd introduced to his boss had come good. His boss loved a darts match – or had done until Leigh fucked off. Marco looked over at Si and licked his gums. 'I've got some other things going down too. I need a few people taking down who owe me money from when I was in jail. Are you up for it or what? I'll give you half of each amount you get back. Debt collection is par for the course in my game, and now I'm out I need people to know I'm calling in what they owe – no messing.'

Marco passed a book over and Si opened it, looking at the names. There was serious money to be earned here and he could sub-contract these jobs out to his younger boys, who were even hungrier than he was to earn.

Marco spoke in a firm tone, keen to show he meant business. 'Get the money back and let them know that nobody fucks with me. Take more than they owe too, I want interest, even if you have to take rings and chains from their wives and kids, I don't give a fuck. I'm not arsed, as long as my money is back and they get the fucking message that they can't mess with me.'

Si studied the names and the addresses and stared at the page for a lot longer than he should have, puzzled by one name that was written in blue bold ink, over and over again. Kes cut him short before he could say anything. 'That fighter of yours is an animal. When he split the other guy's cheek, it was like Tarantino stuff. The punters loved it you know, sick bastards some of them are, love all the blood and the guts. But it makes them put some silly bets on – great business when there's a new kid in the ring.'

'I know. He's only a small fucker and people underestimate him, but he's ruthless.'

Marco cut them short. 'Look, I want you and your boys here with us on Friday night. We have some shit going down in one of the clubs and we need extra manpower, what do you say, are you up for it?'

'I am if the readies are right. I don't do something for nothing, I'm a businessman just like you are.' Si held his gaze.

Marco screwed his face up. In his eyes these Farrow blokes should have been chuffed that someone like Marco had asked them and their boys to join forces with him. He rolled his pen around in his fingers.

Kes shot a look over at Marco and knew he had to step in before this got heated. 'If there is money involved then you and your boys will be cut in. Marco just wants your presence felt for now, nothing more, nothing less.'

Marco could feel Tim's silent presence just as much as Si's big talk, and he knew the quiet one was someone who needed watching, he reminded him of himself when he was younger, someone who watched and held no fear whatsoever, game for anything or anyone.

Si stood up. He pulled his mobile phone out of his pocket and made a quick call. 'Ready, park at the front and I will be out in a second.' He folded up the book Marco had given him and rammed it in his back pocket. 'Shout if you need me, Kes, otherwise let me know where the meet is on Friday,' he said as he started walking out of the door, Tim at his side. Before he left, he shot one last look over at Marco and smirked to himself. He was gone.

'That prick needs watching, Kes,' said Marco when the brothers had left. 'We use them where and when we need back-up, but we tell them fuck all. I have a gut feeling about them; they'd sell their own nan for a bent fiver.'

Kes frowned. 'No way, the lads are sound. You're just paranoid.'

'Watch and learn, Kes. I've been in this game since you were swinging around in your dad's ballbags and know a dodgy bastard when I see one. Mark my words on this.'

Kes had lasted this long in Marco's empire mainly because he knew when not to argue. 'I'm going for a few scoops, Marco, if you're coming, or are you heading home?'

Marco checked his watch and reached round to the back of his chair for his coat. 'I'll have a couple with you. Pointless going home anyway. Monica is probably out again. I know she's making a point, but why has she picked now to kick off? You know the kind of shit women do, Kes? No clean shirts, no food cooked and, as soon as you walk into the room, they walk out.'

Kes burst out laughing. He knew that his boss wasn't exactly what you'd call a modern man, but he also knew which side his bread was buttered and when to play along. 'You don't have to tell me about being in the doghouse, pal, I'm always in it. This new bird I'm seeing is loony. She wants to know what time I'll be home, who I've been with, and who I've been talking too. I've had to put her in her place a right few times but this one has balls, doesn't back down.'

'You need a strong woman behind you, lad. That's what you've needed for years, someone to clip your wings. You should say "I do" again.'

'Not happening, not now, not ever. I've been there and done that, love is not for me, hurts too much. I can't deal with the heartache. Or the bills.'

A look flashed across Marco's face. Quickly his tone changed. 'Anyone found the whereabouts of that thieving bitch Leigh yet? I put a price on her head, and nobody is coming up with anything. She is not fucking invisible, how hard can it be to find her?'

Kes hunched his shoulders. 'Like I've told you before, I think she's pissed off abroad. That money she took from you was enough to keep her going for a good few years on the Costa del Crime.'

'No, she's not that sort. She's a homebird at heart. And anyway, it's easier to find a crook in Benidorm than it is in Bolton these days. Nah, she's still around, I swear on it. Up the money on her head, put another ten grand on it.'

Kes opened his eyes wide. Surely, no woman was worth this much hassle, he thought. If his boss had asked him, he'd have just told him to go and get himself another bird to take his mind off the other one. That's what he did when he went through a break-up. What makes you ill, makes you better or so they said. How could he convince Marco that all he needed was a knee trembler with some new piece. He chose his words wisely. 'Marco, when you fall off a horse you get back up and ride again. Take it from someone who knows, women who'll appreciate you and what you can offer them are ten a penny so don't waste your time – or your dough – on the one that was foolish enough to do the dirty on you.'

But Kes didn't realise that it wasn't just the love he'd once had for Leigh that was like a drug to him, it was the fact she'd dared defy him. No woman ever had before or since. And he couldn't forget that.

Monica sat in the hairdresser's having a curly blow. Debbie, the hairdresser, had been doing her hair for several months now and they'd become quite close. Debbie examined her work as she switched the hairdryer off so they could chat properly. 'I'm sick of men, Monica. Every one I bloody meet is either married or a weirdo. That guy I was telling you about last time, the one with the nice car and his own business? Well, I've only gone and found out he has a wife and kids at home. He's so lucky I've not knocked on his bloody door and told his wife all about him. On my life, I never had a clue, he ticked all the boxes for me – and he even stayed over a few nights a week. Dirty, conniving bastard I called him when I found out. And do you know what the tosser had to say when I confronted him?'

Monica urged her on, enjoying hearing about someone else's love life rather than worrying about her own, for once.

'He said it was good while it lasted and he was more man than one woman could handle. I slapped him right across his face before I told him to do one. And, to add insult to injury, the guy still texts me telling me he misses me, the cheek of him. I wouldn't mind except the arrogant wanker actually was the best shag I've had in a long time. At least if he couldn't make me promises, he could make me scream!'

Monica chuckled. 'Bloody hell, you don't half get them, Debbie. How many is that this year? I don't know why you don't stay single and send them all marching. I'm seriously thinking about trying the single life too. It could be the way forward, you know.'

Debbie paused. She'd never heard her client speak this way before. 'Is everything alright, doll? You've only just got Marco back out of the slammer, what's he done now?'

Monica swallowed. It sounded scarier now she'd said it out loud. She backpedalled. 'Nothing major, Debs. It's more what he hasn't done, than what he has. I don't feel like I'm anyone's number one, if you get me? I mean, I've been married since forever, and it would be nice just to think about myself for a change instead of running about after some bloody man. If he thinks he can come back home and treat me like a skivvy, he's got a surprise in store. I've downed tools. No more waiting in, cooking, cleaning and ironing, until he can actually show me I'm more to him than a housekeeper.'

Debbie nodded. 'Well I've taken myself off all the dating apps, plenty of knobheads, it should be called because that's all I've met on the internet, weirdos and lying wankers. Maybe we are better off alone.'

Monica smiled as Debbie switched the drier back on and carried on blowing her hair. She stared at her reflection in the mirror and examined every inch of her face. She was older than she pictured herself, eyes darker, sadness held in them that nobody else could see but her.

'There you go, lovely, all done. You look like a million dollars. Where are you going, anywhere nice?'

'Just going to Manchester for the day tomorrow. A shopping trip.'

'Oh, that will be nice. I love a night out in Manchester. The last time I went we ended up in the village, it was a cracking night. The music was brill, and there wasn't one bit of trouble.'

A night out without any trouble sounded like heaven. Monica stood up, flicked her hair over her shoulder and had a last look in the mirror. 'You always make me feel so much better about myself, Debs. Can you book me in again for next week, round about this time?'

'I sure can and have a great time in Manny.'

Monica paid Debbie and walked out. She dug her hand in her bag and dialled a number. She stood frozen for a few seconds before she spoke, checking around her to make sure nobody could hear her. 'I'll be in Piccadilly at eleven, can you meet?' She listened carefully to the voice at the other end of the phone and then ended the call.

Chapter Twenty-Six

Danni was up and cleaning. She'd always needed to have her home spotless – right from the day she got her own place. After all the years living in chaos at home and in care, it calmed her mind to have her home in order. Even when she was hustling for Marco and he'd offered to get a cleaner in, she'd wanted to do it herself. It made her feel clean again, washing away the dirt and mess. But it had got harder. Steve was one scruffy man. Wet towels on the floor, clothes flung anywhere, plates and cups left abandoned on every surface, it drove her crazy.

Steve walked into the front room of the flat looking flustered. 'Have you seen my car keys, I've got to go to the wholesaler today, then I've got money to bank, and I need to be back here to open. Bloody hell, I'm stressed.'

Danni hugged him. 'If you actually hung your keys up when you came in, you'd avoid all this bother. But look, calm down. If you want, I'll open up and then you don't have to rush about. Go and get that barnet cut too, you look like you've been dragged through a hedge.'

Steve ran his fingers through his hair and agreed. 'Tell me about it, every time I plan to go and get it cut something happens. Are you sure you will be alright opening up?'

'Yes, come on, its only opening the doors and pulling a few pints until you get back. Jamo will be in as soon as I open the doors anyway so I won't be on my own, will I?'

'Yeah, that's right. Oh, do me a favour, tell Jamo that he needs to pay his tab. It should have been paid on Friday, but he came up with some excuse, so give him a nudge today and tell him until it's paid, he can't have any more tick.'

'Look, you're the one who agreed he could have a tab, so you tell him it's time to clear it.'

'Fine. I'll sort it. Anyway, keys, have you seen them?'

Danni looked at the coffee table. 'There, right where you left them. Mind you, you wouldn't have seen them under all that crap you left with them. Honest to god, when you were growing up did your mam not show you how to pick up after yourself?'

Steve shook his head. 'I did bits, but nothing major. Mam done it all, that was just how it was back then. She ironed and cooked for me too and when I finally left the nest it was sort of expected that I'd meet a girl who'd do all that. But before you start pecking my head, I know, times have changed. I'm a reformed character. I can use an air fryer and I unloaded the dishwasher this morning.'

'Give the man a medal!' Danni laughed. 'All I can say is, it's a good job I came along otherwise you would have been lost in all that shit you leave lying about. When I moved in with you it took me months to sort your house out, proper hoarder you are.'

Steve sniggered; knew she had a point. 'Right, I'm off. I'll be back as soon as I've finished running about. If you need me, ring me, anything at all.'

Danni started to walk into the hallway and turned and spoke to him before she left. 'I'm going to be fine, Steve, don't stress.' Danni went into the bedroom and began to get ready for the day. Josie was coming to the pub today for her dinner. They'd been like hinge and bracket since they'd met up again. They rang each other every single day and Danni had started to realise some of the things she'd missed in life – things other people took for granted. Friendship, support, trust – all new to her. Some of those things had been lost to her from her years in care, some Marco had stripped from her, and some she'd denied herself by hiding away for so long.

Danni heard Steve leaving. She inhaled deeply and pulled the old suitcase from under the bed. Funny how a whole life could fit in one case. She'd only taken one bag when social services had taken her, so childhood memories were few and far between, then there was barely anything from her time in care. Her hand dipped inside the suitcase and she pulled out a small white piece of paper that was stashed in the stitching and opened it slowly. She stared at it, thinking, before she folded it back up and stashed it back where it was originally. She couldn't afford to go further down memory lane now. Instead, she shoved the case back and looked at herself as she was now, pushing aside thoughts of the lost girl she used to be.

No, she was older and wiser now – and ready to face what each day brought. She combed her hair and she was ready for action.

Jamo looked miserable today, had done since the moment she unlocked the doors and let him in. Danni noticed he wasn't talking much today. She pulled a pint and took it over to him and placed it on the bar. 'There you go, Jamo, that one's on the house. What's up, you don't look your normal bubbly self?'

Jamo lifted his head up. 'It's Bruce. My dog, he died last night. He's been with me for years and, to tell you the truth, he's the only true friend that I've ever had. He's not been well for a few weeks, and I knew he was old, but I couldn't bear thinking this was it. But the last few days he's just been lifeless, you know, lying there, not running about like his normal self. Anyway, last night, wherever I was he was by my side, and I knew that wasn't like him. He must have been telling me in his own way that he was saying goodbye. I woke up this morning and the poor thing was lying next to me in bed as cold as stone. Broke my heart, it has.'

Danni covered her mouth with both her hands. 'I'm so sorry, Jamo, that must have been horrible for you. I've never had a dog, but from what I hear, they're more loyal, kind and trustworthy than most humans.'

His eyes clouded over as he replied. 'It's done me in, Danni. They say dogs are man's best friend and it's so true, he was.' A single tear ran down his cheek and he wiped it away. 'I never usually get upset, didn't even cry when my old man died. It's just knocked me for six, that's all. I'm properly on my jacks now.'

Danni felt for Jamo. He was a bit of a chancer, sure, but under all his chat and banter he just wanted what most people wanted – a bit of warmth and companionship, to not feel alone. She knew what would cheer him up. 'I'll tell you what, when I open the kitchen, I'll make you a nice plate of chips with one of those steak pasties that you like, what do you say to that?' Jamo was just about to speak when Danni stopped him. 'It's my treat too. I know you've hit hard times lately so it's the least I can do. You helped me and Steve when all that crap landed on us with the Royals and I won't ever forget what you've done for us.'

Jamo nodded. 'Thanks, love, you're a star. At least I know my Bruce is no longer in pain. Isn't that how most of us would choose to go – quietly, in our sleep? Hopefully the daft thing just fell asleep, dreaming.'

Danni kept an eye on Jamo all through the lunchtime rush. He seemed lost in thought most of the time, and with no Steve or Alice helping behind the bar, Danni was run ragged. Perhaps that was why neither Jamo nor she saw the tall figure enter until they were right next to them.

'Afternoon,' Si Farrow said.

Danni turned her head and raised a half-hearted smile, not sure why he was in the pub. Him and Tim had made sure one or two of their boys kept checking in, but it was usually just underlings. Not the Farrows themselves. What did he want? The debt was squashed, wasn't it? She'd won fair and square. Had Steve not told him she wasn't going to be playing every week?

Si ordered a drink. 'Bottle of Bud please.'

Danni bent down and with shaking hands she passed it over to him, hesitating as she asked him for the money. She wasn't sure if she should even be asking him to pay for his drink. Si passed her a tenner and still she could feel his eyes burning into her as she turned around and went to the till. She counted his change out and closed the register. Once she'd given him his change, she wasn't sure what to do next. 'Steve's just nipped out, he should be back soon if it's him that you wanted to see.'

Si swigged a mouthful of his beer and eyeballed her. 'I don't need to see him. I just called in for a bit of quiet time.'

She still wasn't sure what to say to Si – didn't want him to ask about the arrows. 'Is it still raining outside, or has it brightened up out there yet?'

'Still pissing down, that's Manchester for you though. Where is it you came from before here?'

Danni went bright red. 'I've lived all over the show, I'm a bit of a free spirit.' She was just about to speak when Josie came bursting into the pub looking out of puff.

'Fuck me, I've just been chased from the shopping precinct again. Two of them were on me this time. I've just dusted them.'

Si started laughing and ordered a drink for Josie. 'You make me laugh, Josie. You've never changed, have you? Are you not too old to be getting chased around town by security guards?'

Danni was off the hook and got her friend a half of coke, glad of the distraction. Josie sat next to Si now and he turned to her. 'So how do you two know each other then?'

Josie was a proper loose cannon, and Danni flinched, not sure how much of her life Josie was going to spill. She got the feeling Si Farrow would never forget any useful bit of information – or hesitate in using it against people.

'Oh, me and Danni Cox go way back! We were friends when we were younger, we all used to chill together with Mary Jones, who lived off the square. You remember her, don't you? The one who married her mam's ex-boyfriend?'

'Oh yes, I heard about that. Bit sick if I'm telling the truth.'

'I know, I said the same, but she seems happy enough and who are we to judge anyway. But yeah, D and I? We were thick as thieves. Nutters we were, Tim. We spent hours upon hours in Danni's gaff playing darts when we were bored, and I always knew then that this girl right here was something special with them darts in her hand. Once Danni left the area, I never really played again to be honest.'

'Didn't realise you were a local lass, Danni.' Si looked like he was filing the information away in his mind. 'But you've been away for years, am I right?'

'Been away far too long!' said Josie. 'But we're making up for lost time. And look, she's only just back and she's already got The Fox on track to win the women's darts league. She's one dangerous customer with a dart in her hand, Si.'

Si grinned. 'You can say that again. She's mint, never seen anyone throw darts like she does. I'm hoping I can earn her a right few quid if she's up for it. I can set up games, make sure the purse is alright for us both.'

Danni jumped in. 'No, I'm not into that. I've told Steve a hundred times. Darts is just for fun from now on. I'm just going to play for the darts team and see if we can win this bloody league. But I don't want anything bigger than that.'

Si shot a look over at her and licked his top teeth. 'We'll see. Just food for thought, isn't it?' He necked his drink and put the bottle on the bar, still holding eye contact with Danni. 'Take care, ladies, have a nice day.'

He walked out of the pub, ruffling Jamo's hair on the way past. Josie waited until she was sure he was gone and giggled. 'He's defo got the hots for you; did you see the way he was looking at you. He was all over you like a rash.'

'Shut up, no he wasn't.' Danni had to admit she'd felt uncomfortable when Si's eyes had lingered too long on her lips, flicking down to her cleavage. She was used to punters having a quick peek when she leaned over the bar, but there was something hungry about the way Si had looked at her. Like she was prime steak.

'He definitely was, I was watching him, he fancies you rotten.'

Danni looked over at Jamo and made sure he couldn't hear what they were saying. 'Why was he asking you that stuff anyway?'

'Just asking how we knew each other, that's all. See, he's doing his groundwork on you. No wonder he wants you to play darts for him – he wants to get you into the feather with him. Oh my god, what would you do if he put it on you?' Josie grinned.

Danni glared at her friend. 'I would tell him to piss off. I'm way older than him, he's still a kid in my eyes.'

'Age is just a number, pal. Look at Mary, her fella is twenty years older than she is.'

'Josie, it's not happening so just forget about it.'

Josie was still laughing, not giving up. 'I bet he's a cracking shag, you've seen his muscles, haven't you? I bet he would throw you all about the bedroom and go all night long, like some bleeding stallion. C'mon, don't say you don't ever think what a younger man could do – you could ride him all night!'

Danni finally burst out laughing. Josie had no shame.

'Where's Steve anyway?'

Danni checked the clock behind her. 'I was thinking that myself, he should have been back ages ago. He was only going to the bank and having his haircut, it doesn't take this long, does it?'

'Making himself gorgeous for you, I bet!' Josie chuckled as she slammed a bag onto the bar now and started to pull out legs of lamb and steak. 'Anyway, I'm meant to be making some dollar. Gotta pay for my supper somehow! I'll just get all this sold and then I can relax. We can have a few warm-up games of darts when Steve comes back, it's a big game tonight and I want to make sure I'm at my best.'

Josie worked the pub selling her swag. The regulars loved it and even a few new faces put their hands in their pocket for a bargain. Danni could hear her friend giving it all that about the price of food, and she knew she wasn't wrong. Most people who came in the pub had no money left by the end of the week to buy proper meat for a Sunday dinner – the kind of families who used to have a nice cut of beef were now scrimping and saving. Josie's steaks and joints were getting snapped up by people who'd got fed up of their weekly shop going up faster than their pay packets.

Even Jamo had chirped up a bit now and he ordered another drink. As Danni pulled his pint he sat talking to her. 'Sorry I didn't clock Si Farrow earlier. I'm not myself today. But those Royals have been quiet you know. I half expected them back in here either demanding money or calling out Tim and Si's boys.'

'Me too, but Si said he's sorted it so I will take his word for it. Si said he would put a couple of lads on the door each night and, in all fairness, he has.' Danni had got used to seeing the lads hanging around outside.

'Sorted then – for now – but, believe me, the Royals never take anything lying down. This could be the quiet before the storm.'

Danni rubbed at her arms, and you could see the blonde hairs there standing on end. Jamo was right and she knew it. Maybe they shouldn't relax just yet. Steve always told her he could handle himself, but was this too much? Oh yes, Steve had been a right one in his day and every now and then he would let slip some of what he used to get up to but when she questioned him on it, he always told her that was behind him now. She, of all people, knew sometimes the past was better left where it was, but she also knew he wasn't telling her everything about the days gone by. Maybe that's why they'd lasted so long. Each of them had enough to hide. But she felt a chill now as she thought of Jamo's words. It was true, the Royals might have tried all their usual stunts to get her and Steve to cough up – broken windows, threats, even some beatings – but if they felt they were fighting the Royals, they'd move up a gear, when the time was right.

At that moment Steve walked back into the pub, soaked to the skin, and stood there dripping wet. He shook himself down like a dog who'd just come in from the rain.

Danni looked at him. 'I thought you were going for your haircut; you've not even had it done, you've been ages. I wanted to practice darts for tonight with Josie, she's been waiting for me to finish up serving.'

'Nightmare day, babes. I got a flat tyre, got that sorted, finally got to the bank and it was closed so I had to fly over to another branch and don't even get me started with the wholesalers.'

Danni could see he was stressed and backed off. The punters always thought it was all laughs and free beer running a pub but, in reality, it was an endless job, no evenings off, no downtime. Steve dragged his wet coat off and slung it over the bar. 'Give me ten minutes to get some dry clothes on and I'll be back downstairs.'

Danni rolled her eyes. 'Go on then. But don't hang about. Josie is on curfew and she needs to be home to do the kids' tea, isn't that right, Josie?'

Her friend grinned. 'It sure is. I'm a shoplifter by day, a mother until they get to bed, then I'll be back here to be a crack hot darts player!'

Steve was already heading to the door. 'Back as quick as I can, ladies.'

Chapter Twenty-Seven

Danni was stood with the girls ready for the evening's match. Alice was up next, and she was playing the captain from the Hammer and Nail pub. She'd played her before and always lost. Danni had clocked immediately that she was a right cocky cow, always preaching about how good she was, convinced The Fox team were a bunch of no-hopers. Frenchie and Betty, Jasmine and Josie were all sat near, eyes fixed on the dartboard. Twenty, nineteen, and one. Not a bad opening score. Frenchie punched her clenched fist into the air and shouted out. 'Go on, girl, get in there.'

Alice lost her match – but only just. And as the evening wore on, the games were even, and it finally was Danni's turn to throw. Frenchie had played a blinder of a game and Betty had lost, as usual. All eyes were on Danni, everyone whispering about the new landlady and how she was going to win the league with her girls. The other pub's captain came and stood closer to the oche, ready to witness triumph or defeat.

Then, just as Danni changed her stance and readied to take her shot, she saw Si Farrow and his boys rolling in like they owned the place. She refocused and her breathing slowed. She rolled the dart around on her finger and the scarred end of her thumb. The soft thud of each dart hitting the board in perfect rhythm. A full house. The onlookers were clapping and yelling, but as Danni grabbed her darts she could admit to herself what she'd never tell the girls. It didn't feel like luck or fluke or even a surprise, it felt like she was back where she belonged, doing the only thing that had ever come naturally to her.

All the players shook hands after the game, but anyone could tell that the away team had more than a touch of the green-eyed monster. This had been sold as an easy match. Si wasted no time in strolling over. 'Danni Leigh Cox, you're one of the best out there. And if you won't keep playing for me, you should think about turning professional. I have a mate who could help with that, he's a scout.'

Danni froze. Did he really just say her full name? Where had he been digging into her past? 'Thanks but no thanks, Si. Like I've said before, just playing in the league is good enough for me. I don't want any pressure. Anyway, I'm too old for the pro stuff – it's all kids these days, taking over.'

Steve started shouting her from behind the bar and Danni was delighted to have an excuse to leave Si. But when she saw Steve's expression, her face fell. What had happened? 'What's up with you?' she asked as she weaved through the people to reach the bar.

'Danni, your mam has just walked in. She's in the other room and she's just sat there on her own with her drink. Shall I say you're out or what? I said I would check, so you tell me – do you want to face her?'

Danni froze on the spot, not sure of anything anymore, it was as though time was standing still and she couldn't hear anyone. She could see Steve's mouth moving, but his words fell on deaf ears. Danni shivered and tried to focus. Steve was still talking.

'Yes, no, what do I tell her?'

Danni could feel her chest tightening and her heart fluttering. 'Is she drunk?'

'She's definitely had a few. But she didn't seem incoherent, like…' He trailed off as if he was about to say something else. 'Look,' he finally continued. 'At the end of the day, she's your mother but she hasn't acted like one for years, so you decide what will bring you peace, and I'll back you. But if you want my advice, whatever you do, you should put this to bed once and for all.'

'This is proper messing with my head, Steve. I know she's my mother but I'm not wasting my time with some lush. It doesn't matter if I tell her I love her or hate her – if she's pissed out of her mind she won't remember what I say. Or she'll start with some drunken chat and do my head in, and I'll end up saying something I might regret. Go and suss her out will you? Please, love? I need a minute to think what to do. I wasn't ready. I'm not sure I will ever be ready.'

Josie was at her side as Steve walked away. Her friend could see she was upset. 'What's up, kid, what's happened?

You just won a match with a one-fucking-eighty and you look like someone's pissed on your chips!'

Danni stood stock-still, on the spot. Josie held her arm and guided her to a seat nearby, dragging another chair up next to her. 'Are you going to tell me or what?'

Danni spoke in a whisper. 'My mam has just turned up; she's sat in there.'

'Well, that's good, isn't it? You said you wanted to see her,' Josie went gently.

'I did, but now she's actually here I'm not sure if I want to. It's digging up the past, going over shit that happened years ago. I don't know what I want – it's not like seeing her will make up for what she did, for all the lost years. I don't know if I want to slap her or hug her.'

'Danni,' Josie said in a soft voice. 'You know I love you. And Christ knows, you've been through some shit and you're old enough to make your own choices, but the fact you already went round there once tells me you need to see her. Whatever you want to say, that's up to you, but I think there's a part of you that won't find peace till you set eyes on her again. Trust yourself – you'll know what to say when the moment comes. It's time to bite the bullet and go and see her.'

'I wanted her to come looking for me so bad when I was first in care. She had years to come and see me, Josie, bloody years and years. And now she shows and I want to run. I'm angry, mixed up, I don't know if I'm coming or going at the minute.'

'Well, if I was you, I would go in there with my head held up high and sit down and talk with her. At the end of the day, like you said, it's in the past and though you've got the scars, she can't hurt you anymore; you're a grown woman now, not a scared little girl she can ignore.'

Danni's whole body language was tense. Slowly, she lifted her head up and looked at Josie. 'You're right, what the hell am I scared of? It's her who should be hanging her head in shame, not me. Skulking here like she's still got all the power.' Danni jumped up from her seat and walked out of the door into the next-door room.

Steve clocked Danni enter and stood behind the bar, watching her every movement. Danni walked across the pub, immediately locking eyes on the figure hunched at the far end of the room. Steve had said she'd 'had a few' but even from this distance she looked battered, head falling one way then another, eyes closing and then jolting open again.

Danni took a few steps forward and stood at the edge of the table where her mam was sat. She took in a steadying breath before she spoke. 'Hello, Mother.'

As Julie lifted her head up, Danni stood tall looking down at her. Julie swigged a large mouthful from her pint and placed it back on the table. Her words were slurred when she answered. 'You're here then? You look well, Danni. Older, sure, but you've not changed.'

'Neither have you, Mother, still pissed as always.' Danni was surprised at the tone of her voice. She hadn't realised how much anger was wrapped up with the hurt.

Julie looked like she'd been stabbed in her heart as the words fired from Danni's mouth. Danni sat down next to her mother and opened fire. 'So come on, let's hear it. Let's hear what you have to say about where you've been all these years; no contact, no letters. You didn't even come to the door when I came round the other week.'

'Well isn't that a fine way to talk to your mother? You always were a sour child, complaining about everything when you were a kid. Whining if I had a little drink, tried to have a little fun. If I knew this was how I was going to be treated, I would have stayed at home, Danni.'

'Maybe you should have because looking at you now, nothing has changed, you're still the same old selfish bitch that you always have been. I mean, what woman ignores her kid in care and leaves her to rot? I've thought about meeting you again for years, Mother, and I thought I would cry and you'd hold me in your arms and tell me how sorry you were, but nothing's changed, has it? You're still that self-centred woman you have always been. You've always cared more about where your next drink is coming from than where I was.'

Julie clenched her teeth together tightly and leaned closer, steadying herself with a bony hand on her shoulder. 'You don't know shit about my life. I let you go into care because I had my own shit going on. My mental health was bad, still is. I couldn't look after myself, never mind you. Yes I'm an alcoholic, have been for a long time, ask anybody around here. They all know; I'm honest about it. I was drinking a lot when the social workers took you, I admit – but I drank even more when you'd gone.'

'You gave up on me, never came to see me once. I waited and waited for a visit from you. I sat at the window at Christmas and on birthdays thinking you would turn up to take me home, you never did.'

'I didn't know what bleeding day it was, Danni. I drank to block it all out. I've been in and out of hospital for years, my liver is knackered, and the doctors have told me if I carry on drinking, I won't see the year out.' Julie shivered.

'And yet...' Danni paused as she pointed at the glass on the table. 'You're still drinking.'

Julie pushed the glass away from her and looked at Danni, her eyes flooding with tears. 'I need help. Do you think I've wanted to end up like this? I know I'm a disgrace but I'm in a dark, deep hole and I can't get out. I have tried, you know.'

'Have you, Mother? Because I'll tell you something for nothing, shall I? If my daughter was in care because I couldn't look after her, I would move heaven and earth to get her back. Part of the reason I've never had kids was the fear I'd turn into the same kind of mother you were.'

Julie gritted her teeth together tightly, eyes screwed up tight, a look Danni remembered always used to come before her mother laid into her. 'I came here to see you to try and mend the wrongs that I have done but you're still that mouthy kid who never knew when to keep her big trap shut. You don't know how hard it was, it's all you, you, you.' Julie suddenly lurched and swung her spindly arm to slap Danni.

Danni caught the blow and squeezed at her mother's wrist. 'I'm not a kid anymore, Julie, drink your drink and go back to the gutter where you belong.' She flung her mother's hand back towards her and snarled at her. 'There we go – same as it ever was. I remember when you used to belt me as a kid – you'd say it was for anything, for not making you a brew, for coming downstairs when you were entertaining one of your dodgy blokes or that time I robbed a butty from the corner shop when there was no food in the fridge. You didn't care about me then, you probably never will. I don't even know why I came to find you in the first place. I've survived on my own this long and I should have kept the past in the past.'

Julie slammed her palm down on the table causing her drink to spill. 'Danni, it kills me to hear you like this. But you're right. I was a shit mum. I know I left you alone, didn't keep you safe. I know I let you go. But I never stopped loving you though. I made mistake after mistake when you were growing up and I regret that every single day. I thought I'd missed my chance to ever make it up to you. But you're back in Manny now. You're here. Just when I was ready to give up on life. What if it's a sign? A last shot?' She reached out and this time not in violence. She clutched her daughter's hand. 'Help me get sober, go on, let me try. Now you're back in my life I will have a purpose, something to get me up out of bed each morning. Help me, Danni, please.'

Danni shook her hand loose and stood up. 'Nice words, Mam. And I can't tell you how much I want to believe them. But I can't let you break me all over again. I don't know how we start to build something back between us. But let me tell you this, if you want to get clean, then do it. Do it for you. If you come back and see me when you've had a week sober, and still want us to try again, I'll listen.'

Julie reached over for her drink and swigged the last mouthful from her glass before she slammed it on the table. 'Fine. I'm going now, Danni. You know where I am if you want to come and speak to me, but I won't hold my breath. But I'll do it you know, I'll show you I'm not all bad, I'll show the lot of you.' Her voice was loud as she stood up and growled at the other people in the pub before she left, unsteady and shaky.

Danni was white as a sheet. Where had all that emotional stuff just come from? Had she overreacted, been too nasty to her mother? It was all so raw. The questions were firing around her head when Josie came and sat down next to her, passing her a double vodka and lemonade. 'Get that down your neck, girl. Go on, neck it and stop yourself from bloody shaking.'

Danni lifted the glass and downed it in one. She looked over at Josie. 'I think I went in too strong on her. I just couldn't help it. On my life, all my emotions took over me and a ball full of fury burned in my stomach. It was like I was a young girl again and she was attacking me like she used too. The cheeky cow tried slapping me too. She would have floored me if I would have let her.'

'Mad that is, you would have thought she would have been here with her cap in hand begging for forgiveness from you, wouldn't you? I can't imagine ever raising my hand against my kids – even though I threaten it when they're being little buggers.'

'I just saw red and, to be honest, I feel bad now. She was telling me she's been ill and her liver is packing in, and I never listened to a word she said, I just opened fire on her. I hated her, I wanted to hurt her like she'd hurt me. What's up with me, Josie? Why did I act like that? I should have been more understanding.' Danni looked broken.

'You just flipped out, it's understandable. You just told her straight. Nothing wrong in that but maybe next time you should let her have a chance before you go in on her all guns blazing.'

'I know, I know, but what if there's not a next time? I'll leave it a few days and see how the land lies before I do anything else.' Danni stopped as the door flew open. Was her mum back to go at her again? It was worse: Ben Royal had just walked in with a few of his boys and he looked like he was searching for trouble, his eyes scanning the boozer.

'Fuck me. Look over there. The Royals are in and Si is sat over there, not good is it.'

'The Farrow boys will already be on the blower for back-up, trust me. Ben and Bert won't chance their luck, they know the score.'

'I hope you're right. Today's been dramatic enough without World War Three breaking out under my own roof.'

'Well sorry, babes, but I can't stick around to watch it. Sef's already rung me twice wanting to know what time I'm home. He said the kids are doing his head in and he's ready for flipping.'

'He should be bloody proud of you – that was a top match tonight, Josie. If we carry on like this, we will be the top of the league in no time.'

Josie looked around the pub one last time before she stood up. 'Right, I'm here for a good time not a long time so I better get going before Sef and the kids are banging on the pub's door,' she chuckled.

The girls gave each other a hug and a kiss on the cheek and Josie was gone. Danni was about to go and collect glasses when Ben Royal came and sat next to her. Her heart skipped a beat and she automatically looked over at Si to make sure he could see her. But he wouldn't catch her eye.

'Alright,' Ben said.

'Yes, all good thanks,' she replied. Ben cracked his knuckles and shot a quick look around at his surroundings. 'So, Si and Tim are looking after this place, right?'

She hesitated and nodded her head. Ben moved in closer and opened his eyes wide as he spoke in a quiet voice. 'I just hope you've made the right choice and the Farrows can protect you like they say they can. Shit happens around here, love, especially in the dark of the night.'

Was this a threat? 'It's not my name above the door. If it was up to me we'd have neither of you families creaming our hard-earned cash just to protect us from yourselves. No, I don't make the rules round here. More's the pity.' What a sell-out she felt, passing the buck to Steve.

Ben laughed. 'Maybe you should have a voice and start making the decisions around here, just saying. See what happens when you try and go solo. Everyone needs a guardian angel, darling.' Ben stood and went to join his boys, leaving Danni sat on her own with her head in a spin. She waited a minute, determined not to show he'd spooked her, then went to tell Steve what he'd just said. These threats and warnings didn't feel hollow, and he'd probably want to let the Farrows know something was going down. But she realised as she walked over to the bar that the Royals and the Farrows' turf war didn't scare her the way it had done a couple of days back. Sure, they could cause some serious trouble, ruin the business, hurt people… but after speaking to her mother, Danni realised no one would ever be able to hurt her that badly again. Her mam had abandoned her, her fella had maimed her. She'd been through it all and was still here. She stood tall now. After all, she knew one thing about tough times: if you're going through hell, keep going.

Chapter Twenty-Eight

It was the dead of the night, around three o'clock in the morning, and Steve and Danni were fast asleep in bed. Loud banging noises outside roused them. Steve stirred first and rolled on his side, still half asleep. Then banging on the front door meant Danni woke up, eyes wide. 'Steve, somebody is at the door, listen.'

There it was again. Steve jumped up out of bed and ran to the window. 'It's my car, D. It's on fire!' He rushed around the bedroom and nearly fell as he tried to put his jogging bottoms on. 'Bastards, I'll string the fuckers up if they think they can mess with me like this.'

Danni was at the window now too, her body shaking as soon as the cold night air hit her skin. 'Is this the Royals' next move?'

'Of course it damn well is. Si should have had this place boxed off. What the fuck is he playing at? Ring the fire service. Come on, hurry up before it blows. I'd better go down there, try one of the pub extinguishers on it.' Steve sprinted out of the bedroom.

'Be careful, love!' Danni shouted as she gripped her mobile phone and dialled 999.

Steve watched as the fireman swiftly put the fire out. They'd turned up in minutes, but not fast enough to stop a few of the residents coming out to gawk. They were out filming and pointing.

Old Max from across the street had come over to Steve and spoke in a low voice. 'I'll have all the footage on my CCTV but I'm not telling the police that, it's just for you to look at.'

'Nice one, Max, I'll have a look when this lot have pissed off. It's not like it will make a difference though; the muppets who did this will be masked up.' Steve knew the score with this kind of world. He'd never really told Danni about his life before he met her, told her he was a football hooligan and that was it. But the truth was, he was into crime from being in his teens; torched cars, armed robberies and, when needed, he'd stabbed a few guys up. But that was in his early days, before he got out of that life and got back on the straight and narrow.

The fireman walked over to Steve and shook his head. 'Petrol bomb, mate, we think. There has been loads of them lately around this area. You've not got anything of real value in the car, have you?' The fireman moved in closer and made sure nobody else could hear him. 'Only strange thing is, the burnt-out cars we usually see have been nicked, and torched after joyriding, ram raids or worse. The fact they've not done any of that suggests it's personal – more about you than the motor. Off the record, but I'd watch your back.'

Steve stood thinking as he watched the grey smoke circling in the air at the side of him. 'I'll string the fuckers up if I find out who's done it.'

'I would do the same, mate, lock them up somewhere and kick the living daylights out of them. Scumbags they are.'

Steve nodded his head in agreement remembering when he'd done exactly the same thing to someone who'd had him over. The fireman moved away and Danni came out and stood with him, her eyes never leaving the smoking vehicle.

The fire service left after about half an hour. With no one injured, this was small fry in this part of the city. Steve gave Max the nod and he followed him back inside his house. 'Danni, go back in and I'll be in soon. I just want a word with Max here.'

Inside his house, Max zoomed in on the cameras, his silver-rimmed glasses hanging on the end of his nose. Steve peered at the screen; he could see the toe-rags now, all dressed in black, faces covered. Both of them sat watching every movement the attackers made. A man was swinging a baseball around, smashing the back window. They could see him reach inside the car, a bright light held in his hand. Then the explosion went up and they watched the guy go flying into the air from the blast and land on his arse, they could hear him moaning and groaning as he stumbled to his feet and started running off into the distance, his mate with him. Max scratched at his grey hair. 'I bet he's hurt himself, you know; he'll be burnt from that blast for sure.'

'I hope the fucker has burnt his bollocks off; though he only looks like a bit of a kid. I would have loved to have got my hands on him. He would have shit himself. Trust me, I would have kicked the fuck out of him.' Steve was furious.

Max shook his head. 'There is no protection around these parts, lad. The streets rule us all and we live by their law, nobody else's. The police do piss all, they know what's going on but pretend they don't. I know you're new round these ends but us residents are sick to death of all the crime in the area, but what can we do? Nobody listens and when and if they do they want names and addresses, official statements and all that. No one who wants to live is going to step up and spill the beans, are they? The last person who tried that was nutty Norman who lived four doors down from me. He was fed up of it all and made a statement to the police giving names and all that. They terrorised him after that, windows plugged, his car petrol bombed like this, and they even had the cheek to rob his house too. The old man had nothing of any worth either, just a few quid here and there. Honest, he told me himself that after he woke up and he saw somebody at the end of his bed while he was sleeping, it put the fear of God in him. He said he would never ever report anybody again. He had to get the council to move him before long. The police say they will protect you, but come on, they do fuck all, they just feed you to the lions and piss off, leaving you to fend for yourself.'

Steve was listening but he stood tall. 'Well, they've messed with the wrong person this time, let me tell you. Sometimes you have to act like they act, don't you. Don't get angry, get even I say.'

'Yep, just be careful though, Steve, and don't tell a soul what you've seen on my CCTV because I want no part of any of this. I live a quiet life and I want to keep it that way.'

Steve patted the top of Max's shoulder before he started to make his way to the front door. 'My lips are sealed, pal, and thanks again. It's not like we've got a face or a name to go on, but it just puts me in the know now, doesn't it, knowing some prick out there is out to get me. The next time you call in the pub, shout me and I'll sort you a few drinks out on the house.'

Danni sat in the kitchen drinking a hot cup of tea, both her hands hugging the mug for comfort. 'I've made you a brew too, Steve, I put an extra sugar in it for you. You look like you've seen a ghost.'

'I need more than a cuppa, love, I'm raging inside. What the fuck is going on? First thing in the morning I'm getting on to Farrow; he should have been protecting us, not letting us get attacked like this. The guy is a fucking plastic gangster, full of shit he is.'

'I bet it was just a warning – more for the Farrows than us.' Danni tried to calm him.

'I'll show them what a fucking warning is, Danni.'

Danni reached for Steve's hand. 'Steve, you tried to sort this yourself and you even brought some footie boys down here and you said yourself this lot was too much for you. Don't be getting involved, just let Si sort it like he said he would.'

'The footie boys were no match for the Royals, but don't think I don't know people bigger than them because I do. I'll get proper backing – guys from Liverpool, Sheffield, Leeds. If this is the way they want to play it, I'll fight fire with fire. I'll petrol bomb the Royals' mam's gaff. That will show them then, won't it?'

Danni looked panicked. 'We should just pack up and leave this place. We never had anything like this where we were before. It's a different world here and even though I thought I could hack it I'm not sure now, the place is full of people who would stab you in the back the moment you turn away. I know there are good people here too, but, come on, everyone is caught between the gang bosses and their foot soldiers.'

Steve looked like he had something to say but changed his mind. 'Go on, finish your drink and get back in bed. We need to be up in a couple of hours and we can't be caught off guard again... Or next time there'll be blood.'

Chapter Twenty-Nine

Marco looked like he had the worries of the world on his shoulders. Monica walked into the living room, clocked her husband and went to leave again. They'd not spoken properly for weeks. Marco had been working late and she'd been staying out of his way. He looked scruffier than she'd seen him in a long while. Usually she made sure his designer gear was box-fresh, but he looked like he'd been dragged through a hedge.

'Have you calmed down yet, woman? Got some HRT or whatever you need to sort your napper out?' Marco gestured to his get-up. 'I've been having to buy fucking new shirts every day to look the business at work. I said I was sorry, paid for you to get some sun. So have you got off your bony backside and done the washing yet?'

Monica smirked over at Marco. 'No, sorry. I've been busy, you know, busy just like you've been.'

Marco scoffed. 'Busy doing what?'

'Doing whatever I'm doing. I don't ask you about your day anymore so don't ask me what I'm doing – or who I'm doing it with.'

Marco jumped up from his chair and ran at Monica. He gripped her by the throat, her eyes bulging from the sockets. 'Listen, you cocky bitch, I've heard just about enough of your shit. If you don't like this life anymore, then piss off. Do you think I need you by my side to survive? I've never needed anyone, not now, not ever.'

She was wriggling about to try and break free and she hissed at him. 'Don't you worry. I will piss off, but when I choose, and just for the record, Marco, you do need me by your side. You might think you don't at the moment, but I'll say this only once; be careful who you meet on the way up because you'll meet them again on the way back down.'

He loosened his grip on her throat; she'd unsettled him. He flung her to the side of the room where she landed on the sofa, hair falling onto her face. 'If you're going then go now. See what life's like when you've got to earn your own dollar.'

'I'll go when I'm good and ready, Marco, but rest assured, I'll take half of everything. I've been the good wife for years and never asked questions, never asked for more than what you gave me, but no more. I'm taking what's mine.'

Marco ran his fingers through his hair. 'I asked for a bleeding clean shirt, that's all. And I get this kind of response. I'll tell you what, leave today and I'll hire somebody to do all the stuff you think is so vital.'

'Are you going to hire a new wife too, Marco, or have you already got one lined up?'

Marco turned back and faced her. 'Are you having a laugh or what, why would I get married again after you?'

'Is that so? You just like the kind of women who you can see when you want, don't you? Well, you get what you pay for in life, I suppose.'

She was talking in riddles now and Marco couldn't hide his confusion. 'I'm going to get ready. Nutter you are, off your bloody head.'

Monica rubbed at her neck, bright-red marks appearing there. 'I'll show you, Marco, just you watch.'

Marco sat in his BMW waiting. Another black car pulled up next to him. Marco nodded his head at the driver and Ben Royal climbed out. He looked around him and got into the passenger seat of the BMW.

Ben smirked. He'd heard lots of stories on the grapevine about this guy and this was the first time he'd ever met him. His Uncle Sam had met Marco in jail and had vouched for him.

Marco got straight to the point. 'So, speak to me, your uncle has been on the blower to me, and he said you're hungry for work?'

Ben ran his tongue across his pearly-white teeth and faced Marco. 'I hear Si Farrow and his family are backing you?'

Marco nodded his head, not sure what was coming next. 'You don't want those wannabes as your muscle. My brother and I can provide any back-up you need, we can give you ways into the Manchester scene, and we won't fucking backstab you. Si is a wanker and he's a grass, not somebody you should want to have around when you are doing serious stuff.'

Marco nodded, he had thought the same, had a gut feeling about Si too. 'And you're here for what reason? Warning me off the Farrows out of the goodness of your heart?'

'Fuck that!' Ben laughed. 'Nah, I want to do some business with you, earn a nice stake and take Si Farrow down. He's from my neck of the woods and he's done me dirty a few times. It would be a pleasure to see the gobshite get what's coming to him. Him and his sidekick of a brother.'

Marco studied Ben. 'So, you want to take Si down, how do you plan to do that?'

Ben sat forward and the words fired out of his mouth like a loaded gun, eager to get Marco onboard. 'We let him think you're glad of his help. Set up a job somewhere – neutral territory – you blow some sunshine up his arse, let him feel like the big guy, then we catch him with his pants down. The Farrows think they are untouchable, stepping on everybody's turf. He's a dead man walking, the clock has been ticking for a long time for that family and I'm more than ready – with your help – to take everything that they have. We'll go bang down the middle.'

Marco looked curious, pound signs virtually flashing in his eyes. But did he want all the mither, the chance of blood on his hands? He wasn't sure if he was too old for all this. But some young, hungry kid who'd do all the heavy work and then cut him in? That sounded sweet. Ben twisted in his seat, facing Marco now, waiting on an answer.

But Marco stared out of the car window. He spoke with his back half turned away. 'OK. I'll set something up. Let you take him down, but,' he paused. 'I want more than half a cut. If you fuck this up, or squeal, it's my name at stake and if this gets out that it's me who stuck the boot in then it's bad press that I don't need.'

Ben looked outraged. 'I'm no rat. Just tell me where and when and I'll show you.'

'Fine. Si is arranging a darts match, there are going to be a right few heads there. A big purse. It's the ideal time to take him down, plus, if he's gone then his cut is too. I want it done quick, no eyes on him, plan it properly so nobody sees fuck all. Once he's out of the picture then we can discuss what our next move is. I'm what you call a silent partner in all this. Nobody knows I'm backing you and I want to keep it like that, do you understand?'

'My uncle said you were old school – more about getting the job done than showboating, so no bother, I'll not be dropping your name about.' Ben held his hand out. 'It's a deal, you just send me the details, make sure I've got time to do a recce and I'll do the rest. Si Farrow is going down this time and never getting back up.'

They shook hands. Ben inhaled deeply. 'Right, I'm getting off. You have my number, so just bell me.'

'Tell Sam I said hello and to keep his chin up. It's a fucking hellhole in these nicks at the moment, shitholes they are, fucking all of them. Only the strong survive.'

Kes sat with Si, waiting for Marco to arrive. He should have been there over half an hour ago. Si was playing about on his phone, forever asking where the main man was. Kes was stalling, wanting to get this next hustle signed and sealed before the day was out. 'So, tell me again about this match – why you think it's going to be shit hot?'

'Well, instead of knackered all-timers with beer bellies or spotty teenage hotshots, it's a woman. A fucking good one at that.' Kes' ears pricked up. Could this be Leigh? Surely she'd have gone further afield than Manchester?

Si carried on. 'She's just some landlord's bird, runs a shitty pub team, but I reckon Danni could beat all-comers.'

Kes stood down – he'd checked all the pub leagues in the north in case Leigh had been playing in those and there had been no sign of her for years, this Danni chick must be some newcomer. 'And have you asked her to play for us and told her the score?'

Si hesitated. 'She's been telling me no for time, but I've got something up my sleeve that might be a big game changer. Everybody has a jugular, pal, and I've just found hers.'

'You're a cunning one, you are, mate. I know Marco's not letting you into the inner circle yet, but he's a paranoid fucker lately; he's got shit going on, women problems.'

'Don't we all, mate. Where is he anyway? I've got to go soon so I just want a venue and time for this darts match. I'll bring this chick along with me, but I need to know where and when.'

'Calm down, he'll be here soon. He's probably just got sidetracked.' Kes was used to keeping people sweet until Marco rocked up.

'Time is money in my world too, Kes.' Si stood up, fed up with waiting about. 'Right, I'm getting off. Give me a buzz when you know the details and I'll make sure we are there. I want everybody betting big on this match because if she plays like I've been seeing, we can rake the cash in. Does Marco know who she will be playing? Get an old school darts player – pints and pies, you know the type – everyone will pick him over some bird, then we won't even have to pay him to throw the match, my girl will walk it.'

Kes sat back, thinking for a few seconds. 'He knows some guy who was semi-professional once. All the bets will be on him winning. I might shove a few quid on him too then, even if your lass bottles it, I'll be laughing either way.'

'Don't waste your money, Kes lad. This woman is the real deal.'

'Fine. I'll ring you with all the details. Give me a couple of weeks to set it all up. Get a decent book going. Marco will be game for it too so don't stress out, and if this works out, then I reckon you're properly part of Marco's firm.'

'Right, speak soon, man's got money to earn.' Si was gone.

Not long after, the door opened and Marco walked in with a big smile spread across his face.

'Fuck me, what's made you smile? Has Monica let you out of the doghouse or what?' Marco smirked and made his way to his desk; he sat down in the black leather chair and looped his hands behind his head. 'All comes to those who wait, or that's what they say anyway.'

Kes was intrigued. 'Go on then, fill me in what's made you smile?'

Marco rubbed his hands together, not uttering a word.

Kes tried a different tack. 'Si's been here waiting for you. He wants the next hustle on as soon as. Apparently, he's got a woman who plays darts like he's never seen before. Don't bite – it's not Leigh, I checked. I've told him we're on it, so pull your finger out of your arse and let's start earning some decent money again. The wind has changed, Marco, I can feel it. We're back on the top and it's our job to make sure we stay there.'

'Oh, we will stay there now, Kes, mark my words. Like I've always said, I'm two steps in front and one behind these pricks who think they can come for my throne.'

Chapter Thirty

Danni stood at her mother's front door and flicked invisible dust from the top of her shoulder. She was nervous, not sure how this was going to pan out. Nothing was ever easy in Danni's life, she should have known that by now, and today was no different. But she'd decided she was different this time. She was going to stay cool, not let emotion carry her away. She'd brooded on that awful conversation with her mother – and knew she couldn't leave it like that. So she'd decided to give it one last go. See if Julie had stayed off the bottle for more than a few hours, and if so, let her have her say and see if she could help her turn her life around. God knows, she'd needed enough second chances herself.

Danni knocked again and could see somebody coming to answer the front door. The door opened and Julie stood there, plainly surprised to see her. She looked different though; hair brushed, clean clothes, even a touch of colour in her gaunt cheeks. 'Danni!' she gasped.

Danni responded with a gentle smile, and she couldn't wait to get her words out. 'I'm sorry about the way I spoke to you the other night. You have to understand where I'm coming from. My head was mashed and I wasn't thinking straight.'

'I'm the one who should be apologising,' her mum answered. Then Julie opened the front door wider and invited Danni in. 'I've not cleaned up yet so excuse the mess.'

Danni walked inside and she nearly gagged; it smelt of wet dog and bin juice mixed together. Danni tried not to recoil and walked into the living room, gobsmacked at the state of this place. It still had the same wallpaper that she remembered from when she was growing up. In fact, nothing much had changed in this room – it was all just older, tattier and filthier. The misery of this woman's life was embedded into everything in this room, the addiction, the drinking, the despair – you could read it all from the sad state of the place.

Julie rushed to the armchair and lifted the piled clothes and empty cans from it and placed them on the already-full dining table behind her. 'Do you want a drink of anything? I've only got tea though?'

Danni stuttered, 'No thanks. I'm not staying for long, I've got to go shopping. I just thought I would call and see how you are.' There was no way she would have drunk from a cup in this house, no way in this world.

Julie sank her head low and played with the tattered cuff of her sleeve, her voice shaky. 'I've not been good, if I'm being honest with you. But I've not had a drink for three days now, it's probably the longest I've been sober in a very long time. Seeing you has given me the strength to want to change, D. I'm not saying I'm out of the woods yet, but at least I'm trying. I've been to the doctor's too and he's given me some tablets to help with the detox. He's given me the phone number of a support group too, but I'm not ready for that yet. Even leaving the house feels too much. I just feel shaky all the time and at my wits' end. I don't know if I'm coming or going.'

'I know you must feel like crap now, but you're actually doing it – drying out. That's amazing. I'm glad you've managed it – each day is a big win right now, especially with the doctors telling you your liver is packing in.'

Julie dropped her head low. 'It's like everything is landing on me like a ton of bricks, I've not stopped crying for days. I know the booze was just hiding how I really felt. I told that idiot I was with to get his shit together and piss off too. He was only here with me because he had nowhere else to stay. I can see that now. Look at my arms where he dragged me about, the bloody bully.' Julie rolled her sleeves up and you could see the black and blue bruises all over her thin arms.

Danni looked around the room and she sighed, felt itchy just being sat here. 'I'm no doctor or shrink, you need to listen to them. But what I can do is make a difference here. I'll help you get this place straight if you want. I'm a good cleaner and it shouldn't take that long.'

Julie smiled, the first time Danni could remember her looking that way. 'You sure are. I remember how you used to clean this place up when you were younger.'

Danni choked up. The days she was left here alone, just a kid, cleaning up to try to keep the place liveable, to make sure she had somewhere to sleep or wash.

Julie coughed to clear her throat. 'I know it's only early days, but can you ever find it in your heart to forgive me? I've made some horrible mistakes in the past but all I can say is that I will try and make it better. Look at me, I've only just found you again and already I want to be sober. I've never ever wanted to be sober since you've been gone. And don't think you were never in my thoughts because you were. I cried all the time about you, but I knew I was in no fit state to look after you. I tried you know, tried to get clean, but it never happened. Look at my hands now, after just a few days.' She held her hands out in front of her; she was shaking uncontrollably.

Danni reached over and took her mother's cold, thin hands in hers. 'Stop worrying now, Mam. It is what it is. We have to take every day as it comes. I know I want to help you but it's going to take time. I have to sort my own head out too, Mam. I've got my own problems, but I'll be here to support you where I can.' Danni felt lighter just saying the words. Maybe they could start to build some kind of relationship back.

'And that's enough for me for now,' Julie replied. 'I just need to keep busy and keep away from the booze. It's ruled my life for as long as I can remember, and I know it doesn't love me back.'

Danni looked at Julie and she just blurted it out. 'Come and stay with me and Steve at the pub. There's a spare bedroom there and I can keep my eye on you.'

Julie's eyes were wide. 'Danni, I'm an alcoholic, do you think a pub is the best place for me?'

The penny dropped and Danni let out a laugh. 'Sorry, Mam, I never thought about it like that. Maybe you're right. But, for a start, let's get this place sorted out and then at least you will have a nice place to live. A clean home is a happy home, or so they say.'

Julie hesitated but she went in for a hug. Danni felt uncomfortable, it didn't feel natural, not yet. She pulled away quickly. 'I'll take my coat off and get cracking. The shopping can wait for now. Have you got any cleaning products?'

Julie raised her eyebrows. 'I don't think so, I've probably drank them all, knowing me,' she chuckled weakly. 'I might have a bit of bleach under the sink in the kitchen but I'm not sure.'

Danni shook her head. 'Right, I'll nip to Asda and get some cleaning kit and a few bits for you. Should I check the fridge and see what you need?' Before Julie could reply, Danni had stood up and she was in the kitchen. Danni rushed back into the living room, covering her mouth. 'Bleeding hell, the fridge is full of mould.'

Julie hung her head in shame. Danni could see she was getting ready to burst out crying and she reached over for her coat and slipped it on with speed. 'I'll be back soon, do me a favour while I've gone, open some windows and let some fresh air in.'

Danni crossed the road outside as a black car drove slowly past her. Maybe she was being paranoid, but it spooked her enough to keep looking back to make sure the car wasn't following. Danni sped up and walked faster towards the shopping centre with her head down. Her mam's house was a hellhole and all that was on her mind was getting the place cleaned up. She'd pick up some cleaning products and groceries, as well as some new mugs so they could actually have a brew without thinking it might give them the black death. She couldn't believe her mum had been existing in that place – nobody should have to live like that. She was going to try her best to give her mother a fresh start.

She'd called Josie on the way and met her friend in their usual cafe. Josie had brought a bag of new bedding for mate's rates. Josie was full of gossip as ever. 'Have you heard anything about who blew Steve's car up?' Josie moved in closer, aware people could be listening. 'The word on the street is that it was Bert Royal who paid a scrote from the estate. He showed his mates the burns on his hands, the little shit.'

'What have we come to that kids are doing this kind of stuff, Josie? Steve is gunning for the Royals properly now, you know. I hate to think who he's been calling.'

'If I was you, I would let sleeping dogs lie. You don't want that family on your back, trust me.'

'I know what you're saying, but what if we're in too deep now? I don't want to scarper now I've just started trying to see my mam again. Though like I was saying, she's been living like an animal, Jose. It's proper grim.'

Josie sighed. 'If you want, I'll come and help you clean your mam's. I can only stay a couple of hours but many hands make light work and all that.'

'You're a diamond, Josie, but be prepared, it's a shit-tip like nothing you've ever seen before. It's manky from top to bottom. I'm even thinking about getting Jamo in to decorate for her. You know it's the same wallpaper up as when I was a kid. Just yellow from fag smoke and half hanging off.'

'Shut up, that's years old. I remember that stripy stuff from when I used to come round.'

'Tell me about it, everything's ancient and absolutely stinks. I've not even been upstairs yet; I dread to think what's up there.'

'At least she's trying, Danni, it speaks volumes that she wants to change.'

'I'm not holding my breath, Josie. You know more than me that my mam always lets me down. But at least I can say I've given her a chance, and tried helping her, can't I?'

'Yep, do your bit and see what happens.'

The friends paid up and got a taxi with all the shopping; Danni had spent a bomb getting all the stuff she needed. She sat staring out of the taxi window and, once again, a black car caught her eye. She craned her neck to get a better look, but the car was gone. Maybe it was her mind playing tricks on her, but it looked a lot like the same one as earlier.

Five hours in total it took to clean the house from top to bottom. Danni had been online and ordered a new mattress and a second-hand sofa from the charity place nearby was being delivered later on that night. She collapsed on a flea-bitten chair and let out a sigh. 'That's it! When the sofa comes, just throw those new cushions on it and then it's all done. I've spoken to a guy I know. He will be here tomorrow morning to start the decorating.'

Julie kept looking around the house in disbelief. 'It doesn't even look like the same house. Tell Josie when you see her that I thank her from the bottom of my heart for her help too – she put a proper shift in. I thank you both. It makes me feel so much better already. I will try and pay you back towards the bed and the sofa. As soon as I get my benefits, I can give you fifty quid.'

'Don't worry about it, the charity shop gave me a good deal. The lads said they will carry it in too and take this old one away, so that's good, isn't it?' It was just as well, they needed the space. Danni looked out the window at the pile of black bags in the front garden. Her and Josie had filled sack after sack with empties and old takeaway boxes, as well as all kinds of foils and bongs; her mum had clearly been letting all kinds of wasters come in and crash there when she was off her head. But now the floor was clear, and the surfaces cleaned, the house was starting to look like a home again.

'I will sort out all the old photographs too. I have a box of photographs from when you were a baby, when you were growing up. I've never let them go you know. It was all I had left of you, and I always looked at them and sobbed my heart out.'

It was nice to hear that her mam had a heart after all, but Danni was still keeping her at arm's length. She'd hurt her before and she wasn't allowing her to do it again. It was early days and Danni knew her mother could switch at any time. She checked the time on her wristwatch and stood up. 'I have to go now, Mam. I've made you a sandwich and put it in the fridge for when you get hungry. Try and eat something, it will make you feel better.'

'I can't keep anything down at the moment, I'm not used to eating much. The doctor said I will be like this for a few weeks so I'm just taking it day by day for now.'

'Well, it's there if you need it. I will call again tomorrow and see what this guy I know, Jamo, is saying about the decorating. He's a nice lad, he never shuts up, but his heart is in the right place. He's just down on his luck at the moment so that's why I gave him some work. You will like him, he's a right character.'

'Thank you, Danni. It means a lot; I know I don't deserve your kindness but I'm happy we are talking again. Maybe one day you can find it in your heart to forgive me.'

Danni's eyes clouded over and the ball of emotion that had been stuck inside her ribcage for years kept threatening to burst. She smiled tightly at her mother before she left. 'I'll see you tomorrow. Try and get some sleep, you look knackered.'

Danni was crossing the road, almost home, when a car came speeding down the street, running a red light, and she only just managed to jump out of the way, falling to the pavement as it sped past. She was screaming at the top of her voice, but the car was already burning away down the main road. Danni looked down at her knees, felt a burning pain and saw blood trickling down her leg. A woman came rushing to her side and helped her up from the floor. 'I seen that, are you alright, love? They nearly knocked you down, I bet it was another drunk driver. Or high. People take all sorts of crap then get behind the wheel these days. There have been three accidents here in the last few months.'

Danni creased in pain as she used a nearby lamppost to get to her feet.

'I couldn't make out the driver,' the passerby said. 'It was a black BMW, I think. I'm not that good at cars but I'm sure it was a BMW or a Merc, maybe.' The woman helped Danni to her feet and stood with her for a few minutes. 'Do you need me to ring you a taxi to get home?'

Danni took a few deep breaths. 'No thanks, it's just knocked me for six, that's all. I'm fine, just a few cuts and bruises.'

The woman said her goodbyes and Danni was left alone. She hobbled across the road towards The Fox. Steve was deep in conversation with Si Farrow, but broke off at once. 'Are you alright, Danni?'

Danni rested her arm on the bar and rubbed at her knee. 'Some nutter has just nearly run me over. On my life they just missed me by inches. A passerby saw it all. I wish I got the numberplate. Check the CCTV, Steve, would you?'

Si was over straight away and he looked closer at her injuries, shaking his head. 'Women! I bet it was someone on her mobile phone or putting on fucking lipstick and they ran the light. Don't get your knickers in a twist. I've had bigger cuts on my dick, love. It's just a few scratches, nothing to worry about.' He burst out laughing and Steve was chuckling too now.

Danni gave him the evil eye. 'I'm going upstairs to get cleaned up, Steve. I'll leave you two idiots to carry on laughing about my near-death experience.'

Steve knew which side his bread was buttered and tried to make amends. 'Aw, don't be like that, we're only joking. Stop being a mardarse.'

Danni was convinced he was showing off in front of Si.

Steve scrolled the app on his phone that showed the CCTV footage from outside. 'Nah, D, it's not caught anything, it must have been just round the corner. Si's right, it'll have been someone off their noggin – then burning rubber to avoid you phoning it in. Here, love, get a drink down you before you head up, it will help take the edge from the pain.' Steve went to pour her a drink and Si seized the moment to catch Danni.

'Right, I'll say this quick. You and me – it's a darts dream team. I set up the big money matches, you do the arrows. It will change your life.'

Before he could finish, Danni stopped him dead in his tracks. 'How many times have I told you that I'm not doing it?'

Si leaned in closer to her and whispered into her ear. 'That was then, and this is now. I'm not asking you anymore, I'm telling you. One game then I'll be off your back. Would be a shame if we couldn't come to an understanding. If my brother and I had to tell the Royals they were welcome to do what they like to this place. And you.'

Danni felt the air change and the way this guy was looking at her had changed too. This was a threat he wasn't even bothering to disguise. He'd backed her into a corner. 'I would hate to see anything happen to Steve either. A nice guy he is, very nice guy.'

Her heartbeat thudded and she could feel her airways closing. She had no choice, what could she do now he'd told her that if she didn't agree, he would hurt Steve and throw her to the wolves? She was glad Steve was back now, and he placed a drink on the bar. Danni picked it up and started to walk away. 'I'm going upstairs, Steve. I need to have a shower and calm down from the shock. It's an important match tonight and if we win, we only have two more games left to win the league.'

Danni shut the bedroom door behind her and leaned against it. She dragged the suitcase from under the bed – this time there was no chance for reminiscing. She went straight to the small, wrapped parcel, the one she'd hoped she'd never need. This small case contained everything that could make or break her. It not only had her few childhood mementoes in it, it was also all she had left from her years as Leigh – the stash of used banknotes and the pistol. Of course, the other memento was with her always.

But she'd have the last laugh, she thought, as she held the gun. Marco might have cut her so badly he thought she'd never play darts again. But not only had she proved that wrong, but also, she realised now, there was nothing wrong with her trigger finger.

Chapter Thirty-One

Danni didn't want to get up. She should have been feeling on top of the world. After all, the girls had won their match the night before, and were one step nearer reaching the final. She'd been looking forward to a decent lie-in, especially as she'd kept jolting awake, thinking about Si Farrow's threats. She'd finally got some shuteye just as it was getting light, but now Steve was up and searching for something – and making all the noise he could, it seemed.

'Bleeding hell, where did I put my phone? Have you seen it, Danni? You know what you are like for moving things!'

Danni was in no mood today to listen to this kind of dig. 'It's called tidying up, babe. You should try it some time.'

'Yeah, very funny. Now tell me straight – have you seen it? I need to get to the cash and carry and back here before opening time.' Steve huffed.

'I thought you went to the cash and carry yesterday?'

Steve was looking down the back of his bedside cabinet. 'I did but I've ran out of some other stuff, forgot to get extra bread and muffins. Brain dead I am.'

'You're always at that bloody cash and carry lately, are you sure you've not got another woman there,' she joked.

Steve didn't see the funny side and shot a look over at her. 'Not funny. Maybe if you helped out a bit more then I would get a bleeding break and wouldn't have to go out all the time rushing about.'

'That's out of order, Steve. I've done the lion's share all week while you've been swanning here there and everywhere. The cash and carry, then the bank, then you went over to Max for bloody ages. I've barely seen you. I've been serving with Alice most of this week and doing the kitchen. And to top it all, I was helping my mam out cleaning. Anyway, here's your ruddy phone, it was under your pillow.'

Steve grabbed it like it was a hand grenade, muttering something under his breath. Was he having a pop at her? But then he was gone, no kiss, no nothing. Danni sat thinking, her mind doing overtime. She'd been joking but maybe he really did have another woman. But Steve was always telling her how much he loved her and when the girls won the darts match last night he hadn't been able to keep his hands off her. She was just being silly, she decided. He'd told from the first time they got together that the life of a landlord was non-stop. She figured she had a couple of hours before he got back, and decided she'd best make herself get up to go and see Jamo's progress.

THE HUSTLE

Danni waited outside her mother's house and stared up at the bedroom window. The same window she'd peered out of for years waiting for her mother to come home, crying, praying, that she would be back soon. Danni banished the memory from her head and started to walk down the garden path only to be met by Jamo, looking agitated. 'Bloody hell, Danni, you could have warned me how bad this place was. I wouldn't let my dog stay here.'

Danni became defensive. 'It's my mam's house, Jamo, and she needs it decorating, not a bloody lecture about how bad it is. People get lost, Jamo, you know that more than anyone, don't you?'

Jamo backed off, realising he'd hit a nerve. 'Whatever, just saying it's a lot more work than I first thought.'

'So you want more money, just come out and say that then instead of beating around the bush.'

'No, bleeding hell, I only said it was a big job, don't bite my head off, woman, sorry I spoke.'

Danni had headed in, straight into the front room and looked about, nobody was there. She shouted behind her. 'Jamo, where is my mam?'

Jamo popped his head back inside, fag hanging from the corner of his mouth. 'She said she was going for a walk, the smell of the paint was getting on her chest. She's a good laugh is your mam, not a bad-looking woman too, I can see where you get your looks from.'

Danni ignored the last part. 'Great, she's probably gone to the park for a walk. It's a nice day, so the fresh air will do her good.'

Jamo was gone and Danni was alone again. She took her coat off and went upstairs. Once she was at the top, she looked at the bedroom door where she used to sleep, the paint yellow with years of neglect. Taking a deep breath, she gripped the grubby door handle and pressed it down. The door opened and she could see the bedroom fully, and her emotions took over. Danni walked in slowly and stood in the middle of the room. The bedroom was the same as she remembered it in essence, nothing had changed. But it felt smaller and sadder now she stood in it as an adult. This had been her only safe place, and everything in it had been precious to her. She walked over to the window and opened it quickly. Once the fresh air filtered inside, she inhaled deeply and closed her eyes. Slowly, she turned back around and looked over at the sagging single bed. Danni sat down on it. Her hand stroked the bare mattress and the tears flooded from her eyes. If this mattress could have spoken it would have told you what it had seen over the years, the neglect, the tears after the beatings, the fear. Danni's eyes went to a small brown box to the left of her. She reached over and picked it up. Wiping her tears away she started to look at the box of photographs, old snaps they were. Danni smiled as she held a photograph of her up in the air and studied it. She must only have been about six years old in it, she remembered the day. Her neighbour at the time had given her a bike, her daughter had got too big for it, and she handed it down to Julie for her daughter. Closing her eyes she had a flashback, the falls, the wobbling about, the crashes on the bike. Two days it took her to master how to ride that bike, covered in bruises, but so proud. She'd been delighted to finally have a bike of her own. These were happy memories, a time her mother wasn't drinking heavily, she'd actually cared about her then. She'd sometimes watch Danni and her friends wobbling up and down the pavement on their bikes. She flipped to the next snap. Josie and Mary flanked her on this photograph, they both looked so young. She smiled. They all had naff haircuts and the clothes they were wearing were probably bought from the charity shop or the flea market and made the photo look even older.

Danni jumped as Julie opened the bedroom door. She came and sat next to Danni and patted her leg with her cold hands. 'I told you that I never forgot about you. I often sat in here and cried my eyes out when I looked at all I had left of you. I just wish I could have sorted my shit out and got you back before it was too late. You know I never let anyone else stay in this room. It's your room – always was, always will be.'

Danni looked deep into her mother's eyes, and she could see there was genuine remorse there. 'I wished every day you would come back for me, Mam, but after the years passed, I learned to live without you. It was all I could do, it made me strong though, made me the woman who I am today.'

'And you're a lovely kind person. I won't take any credit for that because I know I let you down as a mother. It was the drink, you know that; it got a grip of me and it wasn't ever letting go. I lost myself as well as you, lost my self-respect.'

Danni just stared at the bare walls, faded patches and brighter parts where posters she'd once had tacked to the walls had fluttered down. There were questions she needed answering and now was the time. 'I know about the drink, Mum. But there are things I don't know – questions you'd never answer when I was here. You used to threaten me with a clip round the ear if I asked about my dad. Do you remember that time you said you'd chuck me out if I kept asking? You even locked me out one night when I'd not stop trying to find out. But you can't lock me out anymore. So, what happened to my dad, do you know who he is?' Danni could feel the air between them almost crackling with tension.

'Of course I bloody do. He was a lovely man; kind, caring, gave me anything that I wanted. Mikey. He'd have been a great dad.'

'So, what happened?' Even a first name was more information than Danni had ever had before. She had to tread carefully.

Julie hung her head low, shame, guilt, regret written on her face. 'I let myself down – I let you down – and slept with another man. It was a drunken mistake when your dad was working away from home. I was lonely.'

'So did he find out, did you tell him?'

'Yes, I regret it now. I should have just kept it to myself but the guilt ate away at me and I confessed all. I owed him the truth.' Julie swallowed hard and shook her head slowly, the hairs on her arms standing on end. 'He just packed his bags, not a word, and left me. I never knew where he went, and he never got in touch with me again.

You see your dad worked all across the country; he was a van driver and he never stayed in one place for long, he went where the work was. He wasn't from round here so there was no family I could ask, no colleagues, nothing. And can you imagine how many Michael Jones there are in Manchester alone?'

Danni's head was buzzing with all this information. But she had to carry on. 'What about me, did he never want to see me?'

Julie's voice was softer. 'No, love, he never even knew. When he went I didn't even know I had a bun in the oven. You.'

Danni was reeling. She'd never heard this story. Julie continued talking and rubbed her hands together to try and warm them up. 'I was devasted and my world had fallen apart right in front of my eyes. I lost the will to live if I'm being honest. I just about kept it together until you were born, but then I fell apart. I had no family to support me, on my own with a newborn, I thought I was going to top myself. It was only the sight of you, with your tiny hands and soft skin that stopped me. But from when you were tiny, I started drinking. The booze helped me get through each day, took the pain away, helped me cope. But I became dependent on it and that's all I could think about from waking up to going to sleep. As soon as you were old enough to be left with a neighbour, I started going out. The men down the pub bought me drinks, loved my company at first, but as the months passed, they all fizzled out, no one wanting more than a night's company. So I started settling for that. I welcomed them with open arms, craving love, someone who cared about me.'

Danni could see her mother was upset and she reached over and held her hand in hers. 'I never knew this, Mam.'

Julie lifted her head up and snivelled. 'I always mess everything up. Even being a mother, I messed that up big time too. I know I keep saying it, but I am sorry you know. From the bottom of my heart I'm sorry.'

Danni just nodded, her words stuck; she didn't really know what to say. 'It's our past, I can't really go back there either, Mam. It hurts too much; maybe we shouldn't speak about the past for now until we're both stronger. I just want to help you get back on your feet for now and then we can sit down properly and talk again.'

Julie could see Danni was fighting her feelings too and stood up. 'You can take those photographs with you if you want. I have you back in my life now and I'm never letting you go again.'

Josie's voice, shouting from downstairs, interrupted them.

'Up here, Josie,' Danni replied.

Josie burst into the bedroom and froze as she clocked the state of it. She was never one for holding back. 'Bleeding hell, it's like I've gone back in time, nothing's changed. Look, the dartboard is still there, Danni, do you remember the hours we spent playing on it?'

Julie ran to the chest of drawers and pulled out some darts. 'Look, I even kept your darts.'

Josie took them and stood facing the dartboard. 'Come on, Danni, a quick game or what?'

Josie passed her the darts and as she felt them in her hands Danni smiled. 'They feel so light. Look, the feathers are still all intact.' She stood facing the dartboard and took her pose. No hesitation. She hit one hundred and eighty, no messing about. Julie clapped her hands. 'Amazing. I remember taking you in the pubs with me and nobody could ever beat you even back then. You should have been a professional you should.'

Josie jumped about on the spot, excited to tell her news. 'Danni, when we have the league final, I have some guy coming to watch us. I found him on the internet and he's on the lookout for women darts players.'

Danni went bright red, her cheeks looked like they were on fire. 'What have you gone and done that for? I've told you before and I'll tell you again, I just play for fun now. I don't hustle anymore, and I don't want to be a bloody professional.'

Julie looked shocked, but could tell her chiming in wouldn't help. She changed the subject. 'Shall I make us a cuppa – that sorts everything.'

Danni wished all her problems in life could be solved so easily. Instead the mention of the match brought her back to Si Farrow's threats. Darts had once been her escape. Now the game had become a trap.

Chapter Thirty-Two

The Fox ladies' team were all dressed in their new personalised silk shirts. Since they'd won their last match, the community had heard that the girls were in the final and they were all out tonight in full force to support them. Ditching thoughts of paying any bills or affording shopping, the pub was heaving with folk blowing any cash they had on a decent night out. The place was noisier than ever, everybody trying to talk at the same time.

Josie, Alice, Frenchie, Betty, Jasmine and Danni all stood for a team photograph, wide smiles, arms around each other. Only Danni's smile faltered as soon as the picture was taken.

Steve stood watching his woman, proud as punch. Even Sef had come tonight to watch Josie in the final, and Jasmine had shyly introduced her girlfriend to the team earlier. There was an old man sat in the corner and Betty went to join him with a pint of bitter in her hands. 'I'm so glad you have come tonight. I thought you'd have my guts for garters when I told you I'd not been cleaning the church every Monday night but playing darts instead.'

Norris shook his head, and he reached over and squeezed her hand. 'I don't know why you didn't tell me the truth, love. God gets enough of your time – all day Sunday and all your prayers and rosaries. I love darts, Betty, and I think each week now instead of me taking my tablets early I'll come with you here and watch you play. It's nice to prove to the young ones that you don't stop having fun when you get your pension.'

Betty pecked him on the side of his cheek. 'I just hope I can hold it together with you watching. I've brought my good glasses with me tonight so say a little prayer that I win. I've done so many Hail Marys, Our Lady will be sick of the sound of me.'

Josie was on her second vodka and coke; her nerves were in tatters and she was constantly fidgeting. Sef could see she was on edge. 'Babes, you go out shoplifting every day and never flinch but you're letting a bit of sport get the better of you. Sort it out, babes, you're bigger than this. You've got nerves of steel.'

'I know, Sef, but come on, this is different. Everyone will be watching me. Say I'm the deciding game and I mess up, it's a big responsibility.'

'You'll be fine, you girls have got Danni. From what you say, she could beat the other team blindfolded. I'll tell you what, though. Maybe you just need a little incentive. Seeing you ready to do your thing, it's a proper turn-on, you know. If you win, when we get home tonight, I'll make you see stars. I'll do all your favourite things; you can just lie back and I'll ask for nothing in return. You'll be in seventh heaven, babe.' Sef waggled his eyebrows and Josie burst out laughing. He was insatiable.

'Keep your mouth shut; everybody can hear you, loon.'

Sef whispered something into her ear and she blushed. Josie winked as she walked away to see Alice, who'd brought a gang of mates with her, and Frenchie who had gone all out. She was dressed to the nines, hair done, make-up on point, her mam and two of her sisters were in the boozer with her too.

The away team were already here and everyone was waiting for the draw to see who was playing who. The local papers had even shown up; any excuse for a beer and a headline.

Danni saw Jamo walk in and even he looked like he'd made an effort: clean t-shirt, a fresh haircut and trainers that didn't look like they were about to fall apart. Danni had thought about inviting her mother, but remembered what she'd said; a pub was the last thing she needed when she was trying to stay on the wagon.

Steve was back now and he passed a glass over to Danni. 'Here, get a quick one in before you start, calm them nerves.'

Danni necked the drink. 'Just what the doctor ordered, Steve. I don't know why I'm more nervous tonight than when I knew thousands of quid were resting on each dart I threw. I guess I know it just means so much to everyone else, all the girls, and if we lose, I don't know what I will say to them. Look at them all over there.'

Steve shot a look over at the darts team and he nodded his head. 'I know, love, they have all put time and effort into this, haven't they? But it's you that's inspired them, led them. I hope you all smash it tonight.'

'Me too.' Danni jumped as a hand pressed onto her shoulder from behind her. She turned around quickly to meet the eyes of Si Farrow. She should have known he'd be here, with his brother right behind. Steve was already getting them a couple of beers on the house.

'You've got a good crowd in tonight, Stevie boy, that till is going to be full. Which will come in handy now your missus refuses to play for what you owe us.'

Before Danni could respond, the other team captain waved her over. It was game on.

From boozing and jabbering to pin-drop hush: the spectators were as quiet as mice when the players stood at the oche, only exploding into shouts and chants between legs. The girls had held up well as the evening had gone on, the matches level, but the next game was the decider: whoever won it would win the league. Of course it was Danni left to play last. The whole team gathered around as she picked up her darts. Alice stepped forward and spoke for the group.

'Danni, you've given us all hope again. I don't just mean playing darts, you've made us all believe in ourselves. Since you've coached us all we are all playing better, sure, but more than that, we take it home with us. In a shitty world, you've given us something to be proud of, something to do together. And, more than anything, you have been a great friend to us all. There is no pressure here tonight from us, win or lose, we all thank you from the bottom of our hearts. We're all winners for getting this far, no matter what.'

Betty was blubbing and Josie stood next to Danni. She slid an arm around her shoulder. 'Do this for you, D, it's what you deserve. Do it for every woman that thought they weren't good enough. Go and smash it, girl.'

Danni closed her eyes and inhaled deeply; she was in the zone now. Looking down at her old darts from when she was a child, she rolled them about in her hot palm. OK, they were old and far from the latest tech, but to her they meant so much more than any modern set she could have used. Danni took her pose at the oche and held the first dart in her hand. It was like she was alone, and she couldn't see anybody or hear anything around her. Her head was in the game; she couldn't hear the chatter in the room, didn't even see the man walking into the pub towards the bar.

The darts were played and it was a full house to start for Danni. But their competition was tougher than ever tonight. The opposition player stepped up and matched her dart for dart.

Si Farrow sat watching with his boys, and never took his eyes from Danni. This bitch would do what he said otherwise he'd show her what he was all about. He'd treated her with kid gloves for long enough now and if she said no again then the shit would hit the fan. Lucky for him, Steve had a loose gob and he had told him all about her background with her mam and how she'd come back into her life after all these years. He knew where Julie lived too, had already cased the house up, knew Julie's movements. It was obvious to Si that Steve might be Danni's fella, but if he wanted her to obey him, he had to go straight to where it would really hurt her. Julie was getting it if Danni didn't play nice.

Danni needed to hit double seven to win the league for the girls. Frenchie was grimacing and Alice covered her eyes with her hands, it was too much to watch. Betty held her hands over her chest, scared that this much excitement would give her a heart attack, while poor Jasmine – who was a woman of few words at the best of times – just sat watching the game in total silence, looking like her life depended on it. Danni twisted her dart around in her fingers and fanned the flight out. It was now or never, if she missed this shot then her opponent had three darts to get double twelve. Danni licked her lips and stood in her stance. A smile began to form on her face. Here it was, her last shot.

Double seven.

Shouting, screaming, clapping: The Fox was alive with noise. The locals were cheering and singing, beer spilling everywhere as they celebrated the win. They were stood on the chairs, punching their fists into the air, singing their heads off. Danni shook the hand of her opponent, then went to the girls for a group hug.

'We did it, ladies!' Danni couldn't remember a sweeter win than this. The girls screamed and hugged, swapped congratulations and shock. They had only gone and won the damn league; their names and photographs would be in the local newspapers, and everybody would be talking about this for months to come.

Steve ran over to Danni's side and picked her up in the air, spinning her around. 'I knew you could do it, bloody knew it!' he screamed.

Then, like a shadow falling across her, Si Farrow sidled over. He pulled her to a quiet spot and when he spoke, she knew he meant business. Something didn't sit right with her. 'The game is next week, and I want you there.'

'I've told you before I'm not doing it; you can threaten me and Steve all you like.'

'I get Steve mustn't mean that much to you so it won't be him who gets hurt if you don't play the fucking game, it will be somebody much closer, you get me?' His hot breath could be felt on her face.

Her face screwed up, the adrenaline from the win still flowing, leaving no room whatsoever for fear. 'Who the hell do you think you are treating people like this because you can't get your own way. Grow up, mate, and go and do your own thing. You don't need me to earn you money, do you?'

He let out a menacing laugh. 'You know my phone number so when you make your mind up, give me a bell, aye. The match is next Saturday. I'll give you all the details when you ring me.'

'I won't be ringing you anytime soon, so don't hold your breath.'

'We'll see about that. We'll speak soon, darling.' Si walked away and Josie was at her side. 'Is he still pecking your head about that darts match?'

'Yeah, he's threatening me now. At first he said he would do Steve in and now he said he has something else that'll make me agree. He's bleeding delusional. I'm not doing anything with that dodgy twat, I don't trust him as far as I can throw him. He doesn't know what's really at stake for me, doesn't know I've seen that world and only just got out alive.' She rubbed her thumb. 'If I step back in, Marco's cronies will find me before the first dart leaves my hand.'

Josie rubbed at her arms as a chill passed over her body. 'I don't want to spook you, but don't mess with Si Farrow; he's a head-the-ball, ruthless, will do anything to get what he wants. I've told you some of the stories about him and his boys and I for one wouldn't want to be in his bad books, so bear that in mind. Just watch your back, I don't trust him as far as you can throw him.'

Danni looked at her friend and kept her voice low. 'Let's see what he's got, because he'll get a big shock if he messes with me.'

The man from earlier walked over to Danni's side and smiled. He was tall and handsome, with a confidence it was hard to ignore. 'It's a long time since I've seen anybody throw darts like you, Ms Cox. My name is Andy Kane and I'm a scout. I think there are some interesting ways we could work together – big stuff, high profile, proper money. You're that good.'

'Do you really think that?' Danni was flattered.

Andy nodded as he pulled out a small white business card. 'Here's my details. Give me a ring and we can sit down and talk about some stuff. But trust me. You have a talent and with my help I can take you to the top of your game.'

She waited until he'd walked off before chucking the card in the junk drawer behind the bar. It was nice to dream, but there was not a cat in hell's chance she'd be calling him. High profile was the last thing she needed. Marco's men would find her in moments.

The celebrations went on until way past last orders. Steve let the girls stay after hours to have a few more. Most of the team were steaming, dancing and singing and not looking like they were going home anytime soon. Danni sat with her teammates and thought how long she'd waited for this – friends. They were the league winners and each of them would always have this memory. But, she noticed as she looked around the room, Steve didn't look happy, in fact he looked stressed to death.

Danni worried that Si had been on his case too – threatening all kinds of shit. She stood up and followed him as he left the bar through the door up to the flat. As she got to the top of the stairs she froze as she heard him on the phone to somebody. She pressed her body against the wall, her breath held. The conversation made no sense and her mind was already doing overtime. Slowly, she turned on her feet and crept back down the stairs and rejoined her friends. Tonight was definitely a night to remember – but maybe for all the wrong reasons.

Chapter Thirty-Three

It was the day after the win. Reality had hit. Alice had come round for her usual shift first thing, and the two women had spent the morning cleaning and getting the pub ready for opening time.

'Right, Steve, I'm going to my mam's. I've shoved the pies in the oven ready for the customers at dinner time and I've scrubbed the women's lavs too.'

'What time are you going to be back?'

'Don't get on my case, I'm just going to take my mam for a bit of shopping and I'm going to sit with her for an hour or so. Recovery can be a lonely business – she needs good people around her now. And come on, I've not seen her for years, she is still my mam after all you know, no matter what she's done.'

'I know, I didn't mean it to come over like I've got a problem with it. I've got a bit of stuff to do myself, that's all. Do you think Alice will manage the bar for a few hours while I nip out?'

'Ask her before she goes. She's just got the hoovering to do. I'm sure she will stay for a bar shift if you bung her a few quid.'

Steve walked to Danni's side and kissed her on the cheek. 'Go on then, the sooner you've gone the sooner you will be back.'

Danni grabbed her coat from the peg on the wall and swung her handbag over her shoulder. She was just going to say something to Steve, but he'd already left. Danni still hadn't found the right time to ask him about what she'd heard last night. She stood thinking for a few seconds and headed down the stairs.

'Hiya, Mam, how did you sleep?'

Julie rubbed her knuckles into the corner of her eye and shook her head. 'Not good, I was tossing and turning all bloody night long. Them idiots over the road must have had a party or something until well after midnight because they kept me awake singing and shouting all bleeding night long.'

'We need to get you moved from here, Mam. The house is too big for you, you need a flat or something, just one bedroom, plus it will save on rent and gas bills. I know we've got a lot of history here, but come on, it's not all happy memories. You deserve a fresh start.'

'I think you may be right. In all honesty I only ever stayed here so if you ever came back, you could find me.'

Danni smiled and looked over at her mother. 'I'll put the shopping away while you wake up. Do you want a coffee or a cup of tea?'

Julie pulled her cardigan around her tightly. 'Nothing for me yet. I need a fag before I do anything, that's been my breakfast for years and I can't function without it. Jamo said he could get me some cheap baccy, so hopefully I can start saving money not smoking fags anymore, they cost a bloody fortune.'

'It's hanging that, Mother, how can you smoke from the moment you open your eyes? If you're not ready to quit while you're getting sober, maybe you should get a vape. I can hear your chest rattling from here.'

'Always the goody two shoes, aren't you?' Julie swiped back.

Danni carried on into the kitchen and started to put the shopping away. The place was much better now it had been cleaned, and the fresh smell of lemons wafted up as she ran a cloth over the counters. Julie came and stood at the kitchen door, coughing. 'I'll have to book in and see the doctor later, these tablets he's given me are a nightmare, I'm still shaking like a leaf all the time. He said the tremors should get better, but nothing has changed.'

'Day by day, Mam, that's what they say.'

Julie stood scratching at her skin, bright-red blotches appearing on her arms. 'It's a bad day for me today, I need to keep myself busy because my head's all over the place and I can't think straight. I just need something as a pick-me-up.'

Danni turned and looked at her mother and her heart sank low. She'd heard this tone of voice before; it reminded her of all those times as a kid when her mam was ready to sink into a pit of despair, usually when she was craving the bottle. 'What about if we go for a walk, a nice bit of fresh air will do you good.'

Julie raised her eyebrows high. 'The effing park, are you having a laugh or what? I'm not a kid that needs taking to the swings. Anyway, I've not got the strength to walk down the garden path, never mind the bleeding park.'

'You need to keep busy, you said so. Tell me how can you do that sat here staring at four walls each day.'

'Oh, just leave me alone. I'm going back to bed to see if I can get some sleep, I'm always ratty when I'm tired.'

Danni grabbed her coat, she knew when she wasn't wanted. 'Right, I'll call back round later on. I will bring you a pie for your tea. Is there anything else you need before I go?'

Julie was already heading up the stairs back to bed, a bear with a sore head. 'No, I don't need anything.'

Danni had got into the habit of scanning the streets for the black car she was sure she kept seeing. She knew Steve thought she was paranoid, but she was convinced that last incident on the crossing was no accident. Suddenly, she saw it. A black BMW, engine idling, at the end of the road. It couldn't be a coincidence. She thought about ducking back inside to her mum's place, but she had to show them she wasn't spooked. And she was determined to get the numberplate. She'd prove to Steve someone was watching her, watching them most likely. She set off towards the car.

As she got nearer, she could see it had tinted windows – no chance of seeing who was inside unless she got properly close. But whoever was driving could likely see her in their rearview mirror by now, she realised. It was a top-of-the-range motor. She shivered. It had to be one of the

Royals. Who else had the cash for a car like this? She took out her phone to take a picture. Show them she wasn't scared.

It worked; the car moved off towards the junction. Danni put her phone back in her pocket, wondered if she should try to follow it. Suddenly, in a screech of acceleration, the BMW reversed at full speed towards her, swinging the back of the car round wildly, mounting the pavement. Danni was flung backwards, pitching over the tiny wooden fence of the front garden next to her. She heard a thud as the Beamer clipped a wheely bin, then spun its wheels and drove off.

Danni rolled over, she could feel small drops of blood rolling down the side of her head where she'd hit it on the flags. A man who was stood nearby climbed over the fence and ran to Danni's side. 'Hello, love, are you alright? Can you hear me? Are you hurt?'

Danni was shocked, and it took a few moments for her to reply. 'I'm fine, just give me a minute.'

The man held her hand and wore a concerned look as he tried to help her to sit up. 'Crazy they were. I saw it all. I bet it was a young kid with no licence in a nicked car. Do you want me to ring an ambulance or the police?'

Danni shook her head. 'No, I think I'm alright. You're right, it'll be kids in a stolen motor. I'm just shocked, that's all. The old bill won't come out for anything less than GBH these days – what could I tell them? I've bumped my head and had my life saved by a bin?' She laughed weakly, desperate to show the man she was fine and persuade him not to dial 999. She used the tree at the side of her to drag herself to her feet. The man tried to help but she waved him off. 'I'm fine, just a bit shook up, that's all. Once I get home, I'll be sorted. I'm not far. You get going. Thanks for helping me.'

The man gave her one last look and he got on his toes, relieved not to have been dragged into this any further. Danni staggered to the pavement, looking one way then the other. Somebody was out to get her for sure. Danni closed her eyes for a few seconds, pain surging through her head. She wobbled slightly and had to sit down for a few seconds in the bus stop a few steps away from her. She dropped her head between her legs and sucked in large mouthfuls of air. At least she had a picture of the car. She just had to stay alive long enough to work out who was behind the wheel.

Alice was clearly relieved to see Danni coming in through the door. She grabbed her coat from behind the bar and she was already leaving before Danni got to her. 'Bleeding hell, Steve said he'd be an hour, that was ages ago. Any other day would have been alright, but I've got a friend coming over tonight. I've cleaned this place from top to bottom but I've not even cleaned my own house yet; she'll think I'm a right scruffy cow if she gets there before me.'

Danni held the bar with a tight grip and Alice could see she was in pain. 'Are you alright, love, you look like you've seen a ghost.'

'No, Alice, a car nearly knocked me over and I went down like a sack of spuds trying to get out the way. I've smashed my head in on someone's garden paving.'

Alice peered at her. 'Oh, Christ, I can see the lump on the side of your head. Hold on, let me get the first-aid kit out and get you cleaned up.'

Alice was cleaning the cut on Danni's head when Steve finally reappeared. He stood at the side of them both. 'What's going on?'

'Some fucker trying to run Danni over.' Alice's shock had passed and she was furious now on her friend's behalf.

'For real?' Steve still sounded sceptical.

Danni was still feeling too dizzy to snap back. 'It was the same car, I know it. The one I've been seeing, the same one that almost hit me on the zebra crossing the other day.'

Steve rubbed her shoulder. 'Look, if you really think someone's got you in their sights, then we should tell Si. I know you don't like the guy, but what good's a bleeding protection racket if they don't protect you?' Steve caught Alice glaring at him and he turned and spoke to her.' Alice, sorry I took ages. I thought I'd be back much sooner.'

Alice growled over at him. 'An hour, you said. I won't be falling for that again.'

Danni stood up. 'Thank you so much for holding the fort, Alice. I'm going upstairs for a lie down, Steve. I'll take a couple of painkillers and hopefully this pain in my head will piss off.'

'Yeah, I'll be up soon to see you. If you need anything, just shout me.'

Jamo walked in to join them. 'A pint when you're ready, Steve.' Jamo plonked down on the bar stool, singing quietly to himself, chirpier than usual. Steve pulled him a pint and placed it on the bar next to him.

'Put some music on then, put that Ed Sheeran one on from the juke box.' Jamo was full of the joys of spring.

Steve pushed a few pound coins over at Jamo. 'Here, you put a couple on, not those shit ones you usually put on either.'

Jamo stood at the juke box, dancing about as the song started playing. As he ambled back to the bar Steve was intrigued. 'Come on then, spill the beans, what's made you so bloody happy, have you got a job or something?'

Jamo smiled from cheek to cheek. 'Better than that, Steve lad. I've got myself a woman. The first decent one in years, if I'm being honest. Well, that's if we're not counting that shag-bag, Donna Tarpul.'

Steve cringed. 'Don't tell me you slung one up her, she's had nearly every man who comes in here and I've only been here a few weeks.'

'I call it community service, Steve, she'd had everyone else so I didn't want to be left out. I thought, you know what, in for a penny, in for a pound.'

Steve burst out laughing. 'So come on then, who is it?'

Jamo tapped the side of his nose and smirked. 'None of your bloody business. It's early days yet and I don't want to jinx it. I like her, we just sit talking for hours. She's older than me but what does that matter when you have a connection with somebody.'

'Glad for you, pal, the tide must be turning for you. I hope it works out for you both.'

'Me too, pal, me too.'

Chapter Thirty-Four

Danni was determined not to let her fear show. She took a taxi to her mother's house, checking the road for any black cars as she hurried up the path and slid her key in the front door. She'd spent the time in between looking at CCTV footage from the pub and looking at the picture of the car she'd snapped, trying to track down details. But she'd drawn a blank. Danni pushed the door and realised she didn't even need her key. What was her mother thinking, not locking her front door in this area? She knew what the crime rate was like, she was dicing with death, inviting in burglars and worse. As soon as she saw her, she was going to give her a good bollocking, a grown woman behaving like a bloody idiot. She tried to push away the thought edging into her mind. What if she'd fallen off the wagon, left the front door unlocked because she was blind drunk? She'd only been gone a few hours, but that was long enough to neck a bottle of gin and pass out…

'Mam, it's only me,' Danni shouted about the house. She walked into the living room then went into the kitchen to bang the kettle on. She would have a brew with her mam and maybe she could tempt her with a few choccy biscuits, if she'd gone for a kip and not eaten. 'Mam,' she shouted again as she went into the hallway. Still no reply. Danni ran up the stairs and pushed the bedroom door open. The bed was still unmade and the TV was on. 'Bloody hell, Mam, where are you?' she mumbled under her breath, her heart rate rising.

Danni checked all the other rooms, panicking now as she ran back down the stairs. She'd searched everywhere, even the scrap of a garden and still, there was no sign of Julie. Finally she froze as she noticed the piece of paper with her name on stuck to the top of the television. It wasn't her mother's handwriting.

She held her breath as she read the note.

Don't worry, she's safe for now Danni. Ring me and let's get this darts game won and then I'm sure your mam will be back to you in one piece.

Danni dropped the note like it was poisoned. 'The evil sod,' she whispered under her breath. Her hands were shaking as she pulled her phone out of her pocket. She dialled the number with trembling hands and listened to the ringing tone. She didn't wait for him to speak before launching in.

'Get my mother back home now, she's not well, she needs her medication. I swear to you now, Si, you touch one hair on that woman's head and I'll make sure I hurt you more than you can ever imagine. You think you're some hard man, well, you've never seen a wronged woman. Trust me, I'll put you in an early grave. You don't know me and what I've been through and what I'm capable of.' She held the phone from her ear as he laughed out loud.

'Whatever, Danni. You've brought this on yourself. I might even tell your old girl that. I gave you plenty of chances to do it the easy way, but you chose this. It's no skin off my nose though. My offer still stands. Except of course it's not really an offer is it, more like instructions. I'll text where you should be and the time and date. You turn up and do your thing. Easy street. Like I said, play ball and your mam will be back nice and safe.'

'I want to talk to her. Put her on. If I don't speak to her then I'm doing nothing. Put my mam on the fucking phone now.' Danni pressed the mobile phone firmly against her ear and listened until she heard a faint whimper. 'Mam, are you alright? I swear to you now if they hurt you I will go to jail for the fucking lot of them.'

Julie's voice was low as she replied. 'Just hurry up and get me back home. I want to go home. Please, Danni, tell them to let me go home.' Julie was sobbing her heart out now and it was hard for Danni to hear. The next voice she heard was Si's. 'So, I take it you care about your mam, and you will do as we say?'

Danni sucked in a cold mouthful of air before she answered, the words almost sticking in her throat. 'I'll be there. Just let me know the details.'

'It's tomorrow night. We've got a warehouse in the Northern Quarter. And there's more money than you've seen in a lifetime riding on it, so you turn up, bring your A-game, play nice and everyone's happy. No funny business, OK? We'll text you the address, we'll send you passwords by a separate message. There's proper security, no riff-raff, no coppers – apart from the bent ones we know like a flutter – no one who's not prepared to spend big. You better be on your best behaviour. Everyone who's anyone in the Manchester gambling scene will show.'

'You have my word on it. Will you bring my mam there?'

The call ended without answer and Danni was still shouting down the phone line.

'Si!' she screamed at the top of her voice, but her words reached no one. Danni's legs buckled and she fell to her knees, sobbing.

Chapter Thirty-Five

Josie had lied to Sef, and said she was going to see her ill uncle at his house. She knew if she'd told him the truth he'd have stopped her from rushing to Danni's side, told her not to get involved. But Josie was involved – whatever she'd warned Danni about, it was happening. Josie gripped Danni by the top of her shoulder. 'I'm so glad you called me, babe. You need to be calm and all will be well. We're here now, you just need to get through tonight. One game of darts and your mam will be back home safe. The guy's a low-life twat. I did tell you, Danni, didn't I?'

'You did, but I never thought in a million years he would take my mam. The woman is ill, does he not realise that?'

'He's not arsed about anyone but himself, Danni. In fact, it probably made him keener to do it – she was a soft target. And look, we're in the big league now. Look at this place, it must have cost a mint.' Josie looked up at the vast warehouse. From the outside, no one else would have a clue what was going on inside. A couple of bouncers, all dressed in black, were the only clues. Josie and Danni took a breath, said what the Farrows had told them to tell security, and walked in through two heavy oak doors.

'I just want this over with. Josie, when we go in here, I want you to find him and tell him I want a quiet room for us to sit in before we play darts. I don't want to see anyone else, talk to anyone. I just want to steady my nerves, do the game, get out and get Mam. Tell him we want a couple of vodkas. Actually...' Danni looked around at the huge space they'd walked into: strobing lights, a DJ, hostesses carrying champagne bottles to groups of people that dripped money. 'Make that a bottle.'

The place was packed out. Josie and Danni threaded their way to the stairs. Another word with the bouncers and they were let up to the next floor. Josie wasted no time striking up chat with the guys on the door upstairs. Apparently there was a dog fight on tonight, a boxing match, and a few other money-spinners put on by the Farrows. Danni hung back as Josie tried to work out where the darts would be.

Josie finally found Si and coughed to get his attention. 'Danni's here. Though if it was up to me she'd have told you to sod off – kidnapping her mum, that's fucking low, Si. She wants a quiet room and a bottle of vodka.'

Si smirked. 'Oh, does she now? Cheeky cow, isn't she? Well she can wait, I've got a main head from Leeds who's not here yet, is he, Kes?' He turned to the guy next to him.

Josie blanked the other guy. 'Just sort it out, Si, and – just for the record – you're bang out of order. If she said no to you then you should have left it there. You can't buy everyone, you know.'

Si went nose to nose with Josie, eyes bulging. 'Keep the fuck out of my shit before I start on you. It's a fucking game of darts, it's not that deep. I've looked after that pub for fuck all, so she owes me. I let the fee slip after she won the first game of darts I set up and it's only right that she does me a favour in return. Come on, Josie, if that was anyone else, I would have still wanted fucking paying, so she got off lightly if you ask me.'

'She owes you nothing, she won fair and square, and that bet was that you drop the charges on the boozer. I didn't have you down as a man who went back on his word.'

'Aye, it is what it is, just show me a room for her to wait in and I'll be out of your hair.' Si shouted to a young lad and worded him up: 'Take this one and her mate to the green room, give them a bottle of what they want from behind the bar too.'

Danni sat in the small room and looked around her. She could hear all the shouting and whooping from outside. Danni covered her ears as she heard a dog yelping. How cruel these people were, inhuman bastards. Josie leaned back on the chair facing Danni. 'That Si is a proper wanker. On my life, he's got no morals, it's all about him and lining his pockets. I know I'm on the wrong side of the law but what happened to honour among thieves? At least I don't hurt a soul. Honestly, D, once tonight is done you need to tell Si and Tim to do one.'

'You're dead right. I just want to get this game over and get my mam back home safe. I wonder where he's banged her up?'

Josie jumped in. 'I've been asking around. I know he has a few lock-ups in Harpurhey, near Lankey's Pond. Our kid told me about it. Rumour is he once had a few kids who were trying to sell weed on his patch banged up in there for days to scare them.'

'Josie, she won't have had her medication and she'll be shaking like a leaf. She's not well, you know.'

'I know, love, just let's get this over with and get her back where she belongs.'

'I just want it done with. Did he say how long I would be sat in here?'

'No, but he's probably got you down as the main event and he said he was waiting for some bigshot from somewhere or other to show up, too.'

Danni poured herself a large vodka and ran her finger around the glass, thinking. She'd spent five years hiding from Marco's thugs. But this looked like so many of the events he'd put on in Leeds back in the day. What if someone saw her? She necked her vodka, relieved that, for once, Marco wasn't the person she really had to worry about. He could sit rotting in jail while she worried about the Farrows and her mam.

Si stood tall as he looked around the venue. This was a mint night – the biggest event he'd put on – and it looked the business. There were thousands of quid being spent on every floor. He just wanted Marco to arrive so he could see it. One look at this evening and he would see for himself now that he had the brains and the power to pull something like this off. It would mean a partnership that could change his future.

Instead of scrapping over bits of Manchester, him and Tim could use Marco's name and muscle to take on all-comers. And then, when the time was right, he'd take Marco down too. These old-timers had had their day. It was his moment. Sure he'd had to hurt a few people to get here – he thought how Danni's mother had screamed as they threw her into the lock-up – but you didn't get to the top by being nice.

He walked over towards the VIP area and said hello to a few of the punters. He was the main man here tonight, nobody else. He'd told his kid brother to go off and enjoy it. He loved the way people parted to let him pass. He felt like royalty, untouchable. And when Danni won it would get even better. He thought about how he'd celebrate. He'd half wondered about seeing if Danni would show him gratitude – the way he liked his women; on their knees. He looked at the glass of Krug in his hands and remembered he always kept a stash of Rohypnol in his office, just in case. It wouldn't hurt to have some in reserve. He went through a side door. The hallway was dark and there was one dimly lit light at the end of the corridor by the back office door. Si shoved his hands down the front of his pants and scratched his nuts. Rustling sounds, footsteps, made him look over his shoulder. A man dressed in black pointing his fingers to the other men who had now joined him on the corridor. A fire exit door opened, and Ben and Bert Royal stepped out of the shadows of the night and into the light of the one bulb.

Si didn't even have chance to let out a sound. A black sack was shoved over his head and he was dropped to the floor. He couldn't see when the claw hammer smashed into his head, not once, not twice, but three times. Ben and Bert joined the group as they dragged the comatose body back out of the fire exit. Ben slammed the door shut and they were gone. It had taken less than a minute. Si Farrow had been taken down.

Kes knocked on the green room door, and the woman he'd seen Si yelling at earlier answered. 'Have you seen Si Farrow?' he asked, trying to peer into the room, but the woman blocked his view. 'They're asking for him – the match is ready. If your pal is Si's supposed darts queen, she'd better shift her backside.' He walked off.

Josie shut the door. 'It's showtime, Danni! That guy said they're waiting for you and Si. Honestly, if that flash git is too busy showboating to come and watch the match, then sod him. Let's get in there, get it done.'

Danni nodded. It was time to go and do her thing. One game, that's all it was, she told herself, and then her mother would be back home safe, and she wouldn't have to deal with this tosser again.

Josie opened the door fully and stuck her neck outside. 'Come on then, let's get this over with.' Josie walked behind Danni, and they walked down the corridor to the main room. It was heaving, hot and loud with people cheering and boozing. She kept her head down low, shrugged when hands touched her body as she stepped through the crowds and onto the main stage.

She looked into the crowd but bright lights beaming into her eyes were blinding her. All she could see was the MC and her opponent. It was a washed-up old guy – she reckoned his heart had long gone out of it. She noticed he already had a few empty pint glasses at his side. The master of ceremonies took over and everything else was silenced. She'd always had this ability to shut out the noise. Had never realised that all those times she'd had to pretend to not hear what was happening to her mum downstairs when she was just a child, she'd taken that pain and made something stronger than steel out of it. Danni stepped up to the oche. Her mother's life was at risk, and these were the most important darts she would ever throw in her life, everything riding on this win. Danni rolled the darts around in her fingers and she began.

Kes moved closer to the stage, squinting, still not sure if he was seeing right. Surely not. He licked slowly at his lips and a cunning smirk filled his face. It was her, he was sure of it.

'Well, well. This is a turn up for the books,' he muttered under his breath. He started to back away from the stage and searched his jacket pocket for his mobile phone. It rang and rang. Why wasn't Marco answering? Kes left a voice message. 'Mate, I've found Leigh. It's her – it's actually her on the bill tonight. Although she's calling herself Danni. But I'd bet my life on it, it's her. Give me a ring as soon as you get my message.' The call ended and Kes walked back towards the main stage, eyes never leaving Danni. There was a price on her head and the money was his for sure now. He grinned as he watched her demolish the competition in the first leg.

But Marco Reece had other things to watch. He looked on, unflinching, as Ben Royal and his boys dragged Si Farrow out of the boot of the car. He could hear slight moans and groans. His body was flung on the floor near Marco's feet. 'Pull that off his head, let this rat see where this is coming from.' The sack was pulled from Si's head, and you could see his face was covered in blood, eyes swollen. Si rolled on his side and his voice was faint as Ben Royal bent down towards him and dragged him up by the crooks of his armpits, so he was nose to nose with him.

'I told you, you were a fucking pretender, look at you now, the game's up.' Ben swung his head back and head-butted him. Si's head went west, and he was out for the count. Marco stepped forward and sucked hard on his cigarette. He looked down at Si. 'Get rid of him, bell me when it's done. I've got places to go and people to meet.'

Ben knew the score and gave the heads up to his boys. 'Tie him up and fling him in the canal, tie a few fucking bricks around him too.' Ben followed Marco to his car and stood beside him. 'A good result for all of us, Marco. I told you I mean business. I'm your right-hand man now and anything you need sorting, just shout me. I'll have most of Manchester in my pocket soon enough and a few chancers who thought they could sell me out to Si fucking Farrow will be getting a visit.' Ben stood tall and pulled his shoulders back, sucking in large mouthfuls of the night air, his eyes wide with whatever he'd taken before he downed his enemy.

Marco flicked the engine over and nodded his head over at Ben. 'I'll be in touch.'

Marco could hear all the cheering as he walked into the main room. Si had talked a good game but the game was over now. It looked like the same could be said for the darts, although from the look on Kes and the boys' faces, it had gone their way. They were clearly celebrating victory. A shame he'd missed it – he always liked watching a good match – but he'd needed to check Ben Royal was a man of his word. And to top it off, they would have made serious money tonight. The other darts player looked gutted, and he could see a few people sat around him consoling him. Kes had mentioned something about how much this old fella had riding on the match. It was the kind of sob story he'd heard a thousand times when he was arranging nights like this. He imagined he'd bet his life savings on this game, money that should have never been touched. It was a tale as old as time – a man in debt, a make or break money match. And then heartbreak – his wife would divorce him, the loan sharks would be circling before he finished the pint he swigged now.

Marco found Kes and nodded his head at him. Kes immediately dragged Marco to the side of the room. 'Fuck me, mate, where the hell have you been? I've been belling your phone out for hours.'

Marco was puzzled – Kes should be on cloud nine after a big win. 'Why, what's gone on?'

'Gone on, are you having a laugh or what? The darts player Si brought with him was only fucking Leigh Cox. I never knew it was her until she stepped onto the stage – she's been calling herself Danni someone said – but once I was sure I got on the blower to you.'

Marco's nostrils flared and his hands rolled into fists at his side. 'Where the fuck is she now?'

'She left with her mate. Pretty weird, if you ask me – you'd have thought she'd be celebrating. She was gone the moment they called her name as the winner.'

Marco was wild. 'What the fuck did you let her go for? Five fucking years looking, she finally shows up in front of your bloody nose and you don't do a thing!'

'Look, boss,' Kes stuttered. 'I didn't see the point in causing a scene. I had to stay out of sight – if I could recognise her, then she sure as shit would have remembered me. I was waiting for you or Si to show to make sure we could stop her. But Si's not answering his phone either.

But before you have a coronary, don't worry. Old Kes wasn't born yesterday. I might not have been able to find you two, but I saw Tim Farrow and he told me where she was living now so I thought we could prepare properly for it and go and pay a little visit. Come on, mate, only fools go rushing in.'

Marco paced one way then the other. 'I knew that bitch would turn up one day, where has she been hiding?'

Kes nodded his head slowly and kept his voice low. 'Right here, apparently. She's been managing a pub near here: The Fox.'

Marco rubbed his hands together. 'Come to Daddy, my little beauty,' he growled. He sat down and got one of his boys to get him a drink from the bar. Tonight would be a celebration like no other. He'd got rid of a snake without doing any of the messy work, made a mint and now his target was back on the radar.

Kes sat down next to Marco and smiled. 'I don't know where Si has pissed off to, but I've got his cut here from Tim. He was here one minute and gone the next.'

Marco took the large brown envelope from Kes and shoved it in his coat pocket. 'He had to get off, told me to get his share and drop it off when I'm down his ends.'

Kes studied Marco. 'You hanging around then?'

'You bet. I'm going to get a hotel and, first thing tomorrow, Leigh is getting a social call. That bitch won't know what's fucking hit her when I land on her doorstep. Do you know how many sleepless nights that thieving slag has given me, Kes?'

'I can only imagine.'

'Every night, when I was in jail, she kept me tossing and turning. I knew this day would come, prayed she would be found.'

'Just make sure you don't get lifted. Manchester is on top, mate, and you can't just walk into her own boozer and take her down. This needs planning. She probably doesn't even know you've been let out of the slammer early. Play your advantage: you've got surprise on your side.' Kes knew Leigh was his boss's weak spot – he didn't want Marco destroying them both by rushing in.

'Surprise is right, Kes.' Marco smiled. 'That woman won't know what hit her.'

Chapter Thirty-Six

Josie scrambled up the steel roof, hanging on for dear life. 'Christ, Danni. When I got the address of this place, I thought you'd be sending Steve and some lads in, not me and you like a pair of cat burglars. Follow me up and bring that bleeding torch, I can't see fuck all up here.'

Danni clambered up some bins and climbed up onto the roof. She'd gone straight back to the green room after winning her match, hoping Si might be there with her mum. She'd kept her side of the deal – but there was no trace of Si. She'd called and called but she'd decided by now he must have shafted her. Then Josie had come to the rescue – a client had come good and texted the address of the Farrow lock-up.

There was no way Danni was sitting about waiting for anyone else to get over there. Julie was in danger, and she needed her found sooner rather than later. But there had been no answer when they'd banged on the door, and then thrown their weight against it. The corrugated metal hadn't moved an inch. Then Josie had suggested they try the roof. She took the torch from Danni and shone it down through the gaps in the roof, pressing her face down and calling out. 'Julie, Julie, are you there? It's Josie.'

Danni was by her side now, looking for a way in.

'Look, over there, Danni.' Josie swung the beam of light towards one corner. 'The sheets are loose, we can pull them back and get inside.' This wasn't the first lock-up Josie had found her way into – she'd told Danni about some of the different places her special 'discount stock' came from. Josie yanked back the metal sheet with both hands but it barely budged. Danni looked despairing until Josie opened her jacket and pulled out a small metal tool; it looked like a cross between a crowbar and a chisel.

Danni's eyes sparkled. 'Where the hell did you get that?'

'Ask no questions and I'll tell no lies, love. Did you think I was coming here tonight without being tooled up? I wasn't walking into Si Farrow's gambling den without a bit of insurance. If anyone had come for you, I'd have belted them.'

Danni rubbed at her cold arms and swallowed hard. 'I'm glad you did, if Farrow is inside here with any of his boys, I want you to whack every last one of them over their fucking heads with it. I brought something along too, a little present for any of them who get in my way.'

Josie wasn't listening, too busy forcing the bar under the edge of the roof and yanking it back with all her might. 'That should be enough, see if you can fit down there, Danni.'

Danni slid her body down the gap with the torch cord hanging in her mouth.

'What can you see, can you see anything or what?' Josie whispered.

'Nothing, it's pitch black. I'm just going to climb on this ledge and see what's what. Hurry up and get inside with me.' Josie slid her body inside now and squeezed past the sharp edges of the metal sheets. Danni had found her way down to the floor and waited until Josie joined her before she moved. The beam from the torch sprayed around the lock-up. No sign of life. Maybe Josie had got this wrong and her mother wasn't here after all.

'Mam, are you in here?' Danni held her breath and listened for any reply: nothing.

Josie started to look around by the light of her phone torch and she was rooting through things that she'd found on the floor. 'Danni, get over here and have a look at this.'

Danni shone the light fully on the corner. Boxes of vapes and baccy.

Josie moved on to the next pile and her mouth opened wide. She unzipped a holdall and pulled out rolls and rolls of notes. 'Sweet mother of god. There must be over a hundred grand here for sure.' Josie licked her lips and shot a look over at Danni. 'I don't care what you are saying but we're taking this money. Fuck Si and his boys, there is enough here to set us both up for life.' Josie was already hooking the bag over her shoulder as Danni walked over to two small doors at the far side of the room. She tried the first. The door handle was stiff and she had to shove it hard, but it was stuck. Danni screamed at the top of her voice as a big brown rat ran over her feet. 'Fuck, fuck, fuck,' she whimpered as she watched it run by. She looked behind her and waited until Josie was by her side. Josie was buzzing with the money she'd found and it looked like she'd forgotten why they were here in the first place. 'For crying out loud, Josie, put that bleeding bag down and let's see what's behind this door.'

Josie dropped the bag at her feet, but never took her eyes from it. Then the friends froze as they heard a noise from behind the door. Danni reached inside her pocket and pulled out the small pistol. She passed the torch to Josie before she whispered. 'Right, it's do or die time. If anybody but Mum is in here, I'm going to blow their fucking brains out.' Danni crept towards the first door; the sound of water dripping filled the air.

Josie whispered behind her. 'I'm shitting myself, Danni. If there is anyone there, they already know we're here. Can you even fire that thing?'

Danni gripped the gun tighter in her hand. Then, using her full force, she booted the door. It burst open, swinging on its hinges. While Danni waved the pistol around, Josie swept the space with the torch beam. The coast was clear, just a small empty room with a few car tyres in and some boxes. Danni let out a sigh and walked back out of the room. 'One door left; she's got to be in there. Or someone is, anyway – you heard that noise before? That wasn't another rat.'

Josie's adrenaline was pumping now. She sprinted to the last door and thumped it open with an almighty kick. Her eyes shot to the corner of the room where she could see something huddled up in the corner. 'Julie, is that you?'

Danni ran straight over to her mother and cradled her in her arms. 'Mam, are you alright? Have they hurt you?'

Julie was shaking uncontrollably, muttering incoherently. Danni knew they couldn't hang around. She helped Julie to her feet with the help of Josie and started to head to the door. 'Look, Josie. That bastard Si left Mam with three bottles of vodka and, by the looks of things, she's necked them all. He could have killed her.' She turned back to her mother. 'Everything is going to be fine, Mam, just you watch, you will be home before you know it.'

Josie led the way out, stopping to recover the bag with the money, yanking it over her shoulder. 'There is no way we are leaving that, Danni, not a chance in the world.'

If she'd been thinking clearly, Danni would have told her friend the world of pain that had followed the last time she'd made an escape with cash that wasn't hers. But right now, she could only think about her mother. There was no chance they'd get Julie out the way they'd come in. She looked towards the metal door ready to give up hope, when she saw keys hanging on a hook next to it. Bingo, she thought. Only someone with a lethal mix of arrogance and stupidity would leave spare keys on a hook. But even before she started trying them, she knew her prayers had been answered.

Danni looked around anxiously as she walked into her mother's house, guiding Julie into the front room. As the put the light on they could see the state she was in. Her face red and swollen, as if she'd been backhanded, her arms covered in deep red scratches. Danni didn't know whether they'd been done to her – or if they were self-inflicted over the hours she'd been locked up in the dark. Josie dropped the black sports bag at the side of her feet. 'We're not safe here, D.'

Danni nodded. 'Damn right. I need to get my mam's stuff – but we'll have to be quick. Si will be back here the moment he knows she's not there and now you've taken that money there will be a price on both our heads.'

Josie winced. 'We will deny it, how can he prove that we've got the money? He kidnapped your mam so let him bring it on if he wants. I'll tell the pissing police everything and what will he do then? Let's face it, he's not going to tell the dibble anything about that money, is he, because he can't prove where he got it from without admitting to what he's been up to. Why don't you take your mam back to the pub and let her stay there with you for a few days until Si comes knocking. Julie can say she climbed out of there herself. Come on, she's as thin as a rake and that gap on the roof was quite big. We stick to our guns and play this by ear, but one thing for sure is that this is our money, life-changing money, and I'll do what I have to to keep it. My kids need this money. I need it to sort my life out. He's getting fuck all back from me.'

Danni looked over at Julie, who had immediately curled up on the sofa in the foetal position. She tucked a grey blanket over her. 'You're right that she's not safe here, but she won't be safe at the pub either. The second Si knows his money has gone he'll be hot on our trail. He'll torch the place while we sleep – burn us alive. No, I need to get us out of here. Josie, will you stay here with mam while I go back to the pub and get my stuff together?'

'Where will you go? You're not leaving Manchester, leaving me?'

'I can't stay around here, Josie. It's like trouble follows me around. It's not fair to anyone for me to hang around – to you, Steve or my mam. I'm going to take her somewhere she can be safe, and for now that means far, far away from Manchester. I should never have come back here.'

Josie gulped, the realisation that her friend was deadly serious setting in. 'But what about us? We've only just found each other again. What about the girls, the darts team?'

'I'm no good to you all if I'm dead! And I will be if Si and Tim find me. I don't think they had any intention of telling me where they'd taken Mam – if they had they'd have brought her to the venue tonight. No, they were happy to let her die. That shows me all that 'one last hustle and then we're quits' speech Si gave me was bollocks. He wanted a payday, and if I'm not going to play for him, he won't stop till I'm six feet under. I have to think about me for once. And anyway, Josie, you'll be fine, you've always been fine, you're a survivor. And I'll be watching out. One day I'll come back. That's a promise.'

Josie snivelled and wiped the single tear that had fallen onto her cheek away. 'Do what you have to, Danni, but I'll always be your friend no matter where you land. Go on, piss off and do what you have to. I'll ring Sef and tell him to hold the fort until I get back home. Now go get your stuff, and be quick about it. I'll pack a bag of Julie's stuff while you're gone.'

Danni looked at her mother and her friend, for a minute imagining the life she might have lived, in a better world. Then she opened the door into the dark night and she was gone.

Chapter Thirty-Seven

It was the dead of night as Danni sneaked into the side door of the pub and stood with her back against the wall, trying to settle her breathing. This was going to be hard, there was no way she could get her case without waking Steve, and she owed him the truth. She'd have to say she was leaving him, setting up somewhere else, when in all fairness her man had looked out for her for so long. She licked at her dry, cracked lips and stepped towards the stairs. She heard a sound. It was well past closing but she wasn't sure if Steve was still having a drink in the bar because she could hear voices from where she stood. What if it was Si? Maybe he'd come here to celebrate, or gloat or try and persuade her to play again? Perhaps he might not have realised Julie and his cash were gone yet. She listened. Maybe she could pack her things and just leave Steve a letter explaining why she couldn't stay.

Danni was at the top of the stairs now and she made her way straight to the bedroom to start packing her belongings. She didn't need much; she could buy what she needed when they found somewhere to hole up. But she couldn't leave the things in her case under the bed. Flat on the floor, reaching under the mattress, she didn't see Steve step into the bedroom.

His tone was chilling, slow. 'And what are you doing?'

Danni jumped up from the floor. 'Steve, I need to leave here. Si took my mam and I had to play his damn game to get her back, but after I'd done what he'd asked, he blanked me. I had to go to his lock-up and find my mam. Steve, he gave her booze, left her on her own in the pitch black, she could have died, nearly did by the look of her.'

Steve just stared at her. Danni had expected anger, shock maybe, but not silence. 'Why are you just staring at me? I have to do what I have to do. I've lost my mother once before from my life and I'm not willing to do it again. If Si can abduct her, he'd do the same to me. It's not safe for you, me hanging around either.'

Steve was blocking the door, his hand resting on the frame. 'Your mother never gave a flying fuck about you. She left you, Danni, she was getting boned by anyone who would have her. You said as much. No, you're not running just because of your old wino of a mum. You're running because that's what you do. Fuck things up then scarper.'

Danni froze and digested what he'd just said. 'You sick bastard, why would you even say something like that when you know what I've been through.'

Steve walked into the bedroom and looked behind him quickly. He was stood in front of her now. 'You see the thing with you, Danni, is that it's always been about you.

From the moment I met you it was always about you and your problems, have you ever really thought about why I listened to your moaning? Why I put up with your endless victim stories about what Marco did to you?'

Danni was gobsmacked, speechless. 'I know you're upset, but speaking to me like this is not going to change my mind. I thank you from the bottom of my heart for everything you've done for me, but I have to leave here. I can't tell you where I'm going to go, but I'll let you know I'm safe when I can.'

'Secrets, secrets, that's all you've ever had isn't it, Danni. Well, you're not the only one.'

She spoke through clenched teeth. 'Oh, piss off, Steve, I'm leaving, end of, and I think it's for the better now I've heard what you really think about me.'

Steve let out a hollow laugh. 'I took you in, darling, kept you safe, a roof over your head. Did you think I did it all for love? I knew who you were and what you had done. Come on, give me a break, news travels fast in the world I live in.'

Danni felt like she was spinning. 'The world you live in, what do you mean by that?'

Steve walked to the window and looked through the curtains, checking the street for something. His voice was low. 'I told you I had a past. I told you about being a football hooligan and the cars I used to nick but there was more to it. I worked with Marco Reece a long time ago and knew him more than I let on. Enough to realise the guy was bad news and only cared about himself. The night you came into the pub I knew exactly who you were and what had happened, and I knew there'd be a price on your head, but I had to act daft and keep it zipped.'

'You sly bastard!' Danni yelled. 'Was none of it true? And why did you not sell me out to Marco's boys if you knew I was his missing Leigh?'

'Look, it wasn't all bad, was it? We're adults – we were both getting something out of the arrangement. All I had to do was wait to see who wanted you the most. Once Marco was sent down, I put a few feelers out.' Steve shrugged. 'Turns out another old friend of mine was very keen to find out where you'd gone. And so it started. It was a great little gig. I had to keep you safe for somebody, make sure they knew where you were every minute of every day. And plus, I got a shag out of it too, so it was all fair in love and war.'

Danni ran at Steve, her nails scratching his face. 'Bastard, who the hell do you think you are, who were you working for?'

Steve restrained her and threw her across the room with little effort. The door opened and Monica Reece stepped inside. She smirked at Danni and held her head to the side as she spoke. 'Did you think all this time that I never knew about you? I've always known about Marco's affairs, but I thought you would fizzle out when Marco had enough of you. I'll give you that though, he stayed with you longer than any of the others.'

Danni sat with her legs tucked up to her chest. This was the first time she'd ever seen the woman she'd heard so much about. 'I didn't know he was married at first, he told me it was over, and you were getting a divorce.'

Monica let out a sarcastic laugh and flicked her hair over her shoulder. 'And you believed him, did you?'

'Not really, if I'm being honest. But he controlled my whole life by then. When I finally told him I was leaving, and that I was done with him, Marco wouldn't let me go. Marco kept me a prisoner, stopped me seeing all my friends. He loved me, Monica, that's what he told me. But it was a twisted kind of love.'

'Oh, poor little Leigh. Or is it Danni you go by now? Did you get your heart broken? That's what you get when you mess around with married men. I've sat about for years while he's been in prison, and you think some little tart like you can take my man and get away with it? I wouldn't touch him now with a barge-pole, love. Despite what he wants, that ship sailed a long time ago. Steve is the only man that I will ever need.'

Danni couldn't control her shock, not knowing what to say. She looked at Steve then back at Monica. 'I can see you are confused so I will explain, not that I owe you an explanation.'

Steve went and stood next to Monica and placed his hand around her waist and kissed the side of her cheek. 'You see, Steve worked with Marco once or twice way back when, and when I put the word out I wanted to find you, he came to me. I wasn't looking for anything else at that stage, but over the years I came to enjoy Steve's little reports back to me and I started to feel like there was some kind of poetic justice. My husband had been sticking one up you, and now Steve was by my side, wiping my tears away. He's a good lover, wouldn't you say?' She grinned, feeding off Danni's shock. 'Come on, you don't take me for one of those women who stay at home pretending everything is rosy in the garden do you? I've had to make my own fun. You should have seen your face when I almost ran you down. I was enjoying that.'

Danni finally stood up. 'You're a psycho bitch, but you want Steve? Fine, be happy with each other. If you're looking for me to weep and wail, you've got the wrong woman. This whole thing is a sorry mess and I want shot of it all. But forget about you two doing the dirty. What you said earlier – about Marco. He's not out yet, is he? He's got years left on his sentence.'

It was Steve's turn to shake his head. 'Yeah, sorry, babes. I know you hate to be the last to know. He got early release around about the time we took on this place. If I let on I knew, I thought you might do another runner. And there's something Mon and I need before we can let you do that.'

Danni felt like all the blood had drained from her. She'd thought Si Farrow was the worst problem she faced, but compared to Marco, he was small fry. She'd heard Marco talk about how he'd had people tortured, watched them fight for life. She had no idea what Marco wanted from her but – she held her maimed hand instinctively – she knew he'd take what he wanted. She had to go – and go now. 'Fine, tell me what you want. An apology? Sure. I'll be gone soon and you two can live happily ever after.' She grabbed her suitcase from under the bed and started to throw her clothes inside it.

Monica shook her head. 'And you think you can just walk away from me? No, it doesn't work like that. I want the money back that you stole from my husband. I might call it part of our divorce settlement. So hand it over. It's my money, my daughter's money.'

Danni gulped. She hated the memories Marco's money held – but paying him some of it back might be her only chance of staying alive. 'Steve must have told you, I've spent most of it, I've got fuck all left.'

Steve rolled his eyes. 'You're a rubbish liar, D. It's in the suitcase, Monica, or at least twenty Gs of it is, it's been there for years.'

Danni gritted her teeth together, rammed her hand in her jacket pocket and pulled out the silver pistol. She pointed it at them both and she meant every word that she said. 'I'm leaving here tonight and if I have to take you two down to do it, so be it.'

Monica smiled. 'Nice you've got balls, Danni. In another life we might have been friends. You might be a great shot when it comes to darts, but I can tell you've never fired a gun, sweetheart. So you might as well hand over the cash. Do it now and we'll give you a nice head start before we tell Marco where you are.'

Danni knew this might be the best offer she got. She picked up the cloth bag of notes and offered it to Steve. But she had one last bargain to strike. 'Car keys,' she sneered. 'Throw them over to me.'

Steve placed his hand in his pocket and pulled out a bunch of keys. He took the car key off the silver ring and held it out to her. She took it, throwing the cash at his feet, and turned and ran, dragging the now nearly empty case, just a few old mementoes rattling around in it.

Danni jumped into the car after flinging the case into the boot. Her heart was racing like a speeding train. She opened the car window and let the cold night air in. Even though she knew in her heart that she'd never loved Steve like she was meant to, it still hurt, the betrayal. Taking a few moments to try to breathe, she flicked the engine over and stared at the road facing her. She didn't even really know who she was running from – Si, Monica, Marco? Tonight had been an eye-opener, but she told herself, it had only confirmed her instincts were right. She needed to get her mum away from this vipers' nest. She gripped the steering wheel and pulled out onto the main road. The sooner she was gone, the better.

Pulling up at her mother's house she saw Josie had turned the lights back off. Or what if it was Si? She got her phone out to call Josie, but stopped as the rear door opened. She must have been watching out for her.

But it wasn't Josie, or her mother. Big strong hands reached over, restraining her instantly. She couldn't breathe, thick fingers strangling her.

'Hello, baby,' Marco whispered into her ear. His hot breath was teasing the side of her neck. 'I knew I would find you one day, my princess.'

Danni struggled to move but she was going nowhere. Marco had a death grip on her.

'Now drive, bitch. There's an alleyway on the left. Go down there.'

Danni was dizzy with lack of oxygen but managed to steer the car down the deserted side road. Marco opened the car door and dragged her through the passenger side, head smashing against the car doorframe. Marco had always been strong, but she could tell he was prison fit now, and there was no way she was breaking free. It was D day and finally everything she had been hiding from for all these years was right in front of her now, waiting for what? Answers, money, revenge?

Marco dragged Danni to a patch of wasteground bounded by tall concrete fencing. It was pitch black and not a living soul was about, nobody to hear her scream even if she could get the air into her lungs, no one to stop this man from hurting her. Danni could see him now her eyes had adjusted to the dark, the whites of his eyes brighter than ever. He pushed her up against the fence, and as he squeezed her throat she wondered if this was how she died. But then she felt his lips on hers.

'I've missed you, Leigh, every day that you've been gone I've not stopped wanting you. I've thought about this day for a long time and what I will say to you, but now that it's here I can't find any words at all. I loved you – and you ruined it.'

Danni was dumbfounded. She'd been ready to die, not hear his declaration of love. Should she play along? Pretend she wanted him too? He shoved his knee between her legs, ran a hand up her thigh and something in her snapped. She couldn't do it. Couldn't play dumb for a man ever again. She was going to tell the truth – even if it got her killed.

'I ruined it?! Marco, you made thousands off me for years and yet you made me a prisoner, never allowed me to have friends, belted me for no reason. You promised me love, but you were already married. You never loved me, you just wanted to control me. And then you did this?' She waved her hand in his face. 'What do you expect me to do?'

He roared at the top of his voice like a caged lion. 'I expect respect. I pulled you out of the gutter when you were younger and gave you a life you could have only dreamed of.'

'You abused me, Marco, physically and mentally. I thought you loved me at the start but all you ever cared about was power. What we had? It was a sham.'

'The power is what you were attracted to, Leigh, you loved the life it gave you; the look people give you when you were on my arm.'

She knew there was some truth in his words. And she wasn't going to be afraid of it anymore. 'Maybe at first, but then the smile on my face turned to sadness. How could a man who said he loved me, hurt me so bad? Are you forgetting all the bad times, Marco? The slaps, the black eyes, ripping my clothes up, locking me in the house for days? Do you remember when you made me kneel and beg for food? That's not love. You got off on the control, Marco, the power you held over me like you owned me.'

'I do own you. Nobody else will ever have you now.'

'Do your worst, Marco. I've had enough of running. Death would be a better choice than living in a world with you again.' She'd feared this conversation for years. And yet each truth she spoke she realised it was tipping the power away from him and towards her. She could see a flicker of uncertainty in Marco's eyes. What had he imagined? That they would have a fight and then kiss and make up and she would be back by his side?

He sank his head low. 'I still love you, Leigh. I've had a lot of time to think, being locked away from the world, and I'm willing to take you back and start again. My marriage has been over for years. *You're* my future, Leigh.'

His words made her feel sick. 'I'm Danni now. Even hearing my middle name makes me shiver. I stopped being Danni when I thought Manchester was the worst place I could be. But being here, I've found myself again. Found people who believe in me in a way that you – or Steve – or any man, never really has. I'm going to walk away now and I don't want you coming after me. So, decide. What are you going to do about it? If you kill me then you kill me, but I'm not begging you for anything.'

For the first time ever, Marco Reece realised he couldn't get what he wanted. He couldn't buy her heart. 'I'll change, Leigh, I mean Danni. We can move away, live in the sun together like we talked about all those years ago. Don't leave me like this, I need you. Monica means nothing to me. She's a bitter cow I should have carted years ago. I only stayed because of the kid. Stupid I was. I regret that all. No one has ever meant anything to me like you have.'

Danni had already started to walk away when she heard the gunshot. She turned quickly and saw a woman's silhouette next to Marco. Danni turned away once more and kept on walking and never looked back.

Trisha Reece covered her mouth with her hands as she looked down at the gun lying on the floor in front of her. Her father was a bad man, she'd known that for years, but to know he'd never really cared about her or her mother? That was the final straw. His empire would belong to her now, and she had already planned what kind of leader she would be. If people thought her father was ruthless then they were in for a surprise. No, she'd decided Trisha Reece would be the name everybody would be talking about for years to come. It was a woman's world and one she would rule with a firm fist. She had listened to every word her father had spoken around her for years, listened while he joked about how he used women, listened while he overlooked her and laughed at her ideas. He wasn't laughing now.

Chapter Thirty-Eight

The Fox was quieter than normal. The deaths had sent shockwaves through the community and, as always, a code of silence reigned whenever the police were around. Si Farrow's body had been found in the River Irk and detectives were hitting a brick wall when they were looking for suspects. It was clear he wasn't a popular man – but no one was coming forward with a single lead. Coppers had watched Tim Farrow lead a funeral procession through the streets of Harpurhey, but although the streets were lined with people watching, no tears were shed.

The investigation into Marco Reece's murder was just as much of a closed book. West Yorkshire Police were drafted in; Marco had been on their radar since his release. Between them and the Greater Manchester Police there was no shortage of evidence to show Marco had upset plenty of people. But no one was talking.

Monica and Steve had left the pub months ago and nobody had a clue where they'd gone to. One of the regulars swore blind they'd spotted Steve in the back of a shot on some daytime TV series called *Escape to the Costas*, but no one could prove it. Instead, there was a new name over the front door, and the landlady stood behind the bar pouring a pint as her mother walked about the pub collecting glasses.

Danni Cox smiled as the doors opened. She didn't flinch in fear wondering if Tim Farrow was going to walk in. Trisha had sorted that out. After all, Danni knew she was the one who had ended her own father's life, so it was only right that her silence was rewarded. Ben Royal and his boys had been warned off, too, and none of them had been seen knocking about the area for months. The rumour was that they were in hiding after a few main heads from Liverpool were hot on their trail. Danni was enjoying answering to no one but herself. Although as she looked towards the door, she knew there would always be some customers getting free drinks.

Julie swung her arms around Jamo as he walked over. She kissed his cheek and told Danni to get her fella a drink on the house. Apparently Julie had told her while she was staying with her, recovering from her ordeal in Si's lock-up, that when Jamo was decorating her house they had just clicked. The chemistry was unreal, Julie had told Danni, who'd winced. There was such a thing as too much information. Though Danni had to admit they looked cute together.

Josie bounced into the boozer with Sef by her side. She was a business owner now, alongside Danni, and anyone could see she was taking her role seriously. No one had questioned where the cash had come from to renovate the pub. But it was gleaming now – with the games room the envy of all the other bars locally.

Alice, Betty, Jasmine and Josie all stood around Danni in front of one of the darts boards as she signed a contract with Andy Kane, the darts scout. The girls teased her that he wanted her for more than the darts. His charm had slowly won her over. He'd kept calling, even when she'd told him her days of dreaming of world titles were over – but he'd come back at her with all sorts of other offers. Invitational matches, YouTube promotions and now this sponsorship deal she was signing today. She turned round so the social media person Andy had brought with him could get some pictures of her new shirt. 'Danni "The Fox" Cox' was embroidered across it. Danni held up the brand of darts sponsoring her – they wanted her to be the new face of the women's game, and Danni had already planned on how she was going to spend the money, already working with the local youth club to get more kids into the sport. She was building the kind of club she would have wanted when she was a kid, lost and alone. A chunk of Si's money had already gone into setting the place up, and now this sponsorship deal would kit it out.

She smiled for the camera again, waving the contract. Was this it? Could she really give up the hustle? She thought she had once before, but she knew how life liked to keep a surprise in store. But she couldn't imagine leaving this place. Being back in this city that saved her. She owed Manchester her life and she was never leaving again. These people were her family, a community that would always have her back, and she knew now more than ever: home is where the heart is.

'One last picture,' Andy said, and Danni stepped up to the oche.

Old habits die hard and she ran her scarred thumb over the barrel of the dart, focused her eyes on the sharp point and then at her target. It was just a dart. Just a game. But a game that had seen riches won and gambled, reputations made and lives lost. But she wasn't living in fear anymore. Let anyone watch her. Let anyone challenge her. She was ready. In one smooth arc, she let the dart fly from her hand.

'Bullseye!' Josie shouted, as Danni turned and hugged the girls.

THE END

Acknowledgements

Thank you to all my family who has supported me, my husband James, my children Ashley, Blake, Declan and Darcy. Thank you to all my grandchildren. Big thanks to all my readers and followers on Instagram and Facebook and TikTok.

Massive thanks to Gen, Megan and Alice and all the team at HarperNorth for all their hard work and continuous support.

Harper North

Book Credits

HarperNorth would like to thank the following staff and contributors for their involvement in making this book a reality:

Fionnuala Barrett
Laura Braggs
Sarah Burke
Rhys Callaghan
Alan Cracknell
Jonathan de Peyer
Anna Derkacz
Morgan Dun-Campbell
Tom Dunstan
Kate Elton
Sarah Emsley
Simon Gerratt
Imogen Gordon Clark
Lydia Grainge
Monica Green
Natassa Hadjinicolaou
Jess Haycox
Megan Jones
Jean-Marie Kelly
Taslima Khatun
Holly Kyte
Nicky Lovick
Rachel McCarron
Millie Morton
Alice Murphy-Pyle
Adam Murray
Genevieve Pegg
Amanda Percival
Dean Russell
Colleen Simpson
Eleanor Slater
Hilary Stein
Emma Sullivan
Katrina Troy
Claire Ward